One SMALL RIPPLE

One SMALL RIPPLE

Amy Baldwin

One Small Ripple

Written by Amy Baldwin ©2020

Print ISBN: 978-1-7348-287-1-9
eBook ISBN: 978-1-7348-287-0-2

Manufactured in the United States of America

First Edition April 2020

10 9 8 7 6 5 4 3 2 1

Dedicated to my dear friend, Dawn Bowker.

I don't think you ever knew it, but you were very special.
You were like my very own, personal angel
sent to earth just for me.
I have never met anyone quite like you,
and I miss you terribly.

Also dedicated to my dear friend, Irene:

I'm not surprised Dawn was the person she was,
for she had a beautiful mother with a kind soul.

And dedicated to Dawn's brothers, Josh and Mark
and to their wives and families:

I know her passing left a big hole in your lives.
I pray that every sunrise you see reminds you
not only of Dawn, but of the day you will be reunited,
and I hope it fills your hearts with
JOY!

"Just as ripples spread out when a single pebble is dropped into water, the actions of individuals can have far reaching effects."

~ Dalai Lama

*"Life is a long experience of suffering, disappointment, and chaos.
But the moment you stop squirming against the catastrophe of being alive
Music flies out of the dark doom."*

*~ Uncle Cullen,
from the movie* Uncorked

Chapter One: Pain

"Sometimes, only one person is missing, and the whole world seems depopulated." ~*Alphonse de Lamartine, Méditations Poétiques*

At first, it was a simple awareness of light. Light — suddenly, insistently — burrowing its way into her mind, a mind that had been dark for some time, although she had no idea how long. She struggled to open her eyes and focus, fighting back panic because she had no idea where she was or what was going on. Fragments of the dream lingered. She dreamt she was drowning or suffocating. She was simultaneously afraid of the dream and of waking up. Voices floated around her like she was under water. Garbled, nonsensical voices. Had she heard her name just now? She couldn't be sure. Her head hurt and she couldn't make sense of what was happening. Adrenaline rushed through her blood and she tried to open her eyes, though the small task was inexplicably more daunting than it should have been.

"Hey, look!" a voice exclaimed. "She's coming around!" She didn't recognize the voice, even though Jodi had been one of her constant caregivers for the last four days. "I'll go find her mom and let her know. I think she said she was going down to the vending machines to grab a drink."

As the plump nurse squeaked off in her stark, white shoes and colorful scrubs, her patient's vision cleared a little more. Blinking hard, she realized she most definitely was *not* at home in her own room, and her heart jumped into her throat. *What's going on? Where am I?* Her panic level rose. Suddenly, another voice spoke right next to her. Her heart pounded in surprise.

"Don't worry, Angela, you're safe," a gentle male voice soothed. "You've been in an accident, and you're in the hospital. Your mom should be here shortly. Just relax."

Full blown panic seized her. Angie scrambled to sit up and quickly realized she couldn't. She didn't know if she were tied down or if her body simply was not obeying her will. The room came into focus and she surveyed it quickly for information. It was small, with mauve walls, tiled floor, and a bedside table on which sat a phone and a vase of flowers. The blinds on the window were open and she could see that it was nighttime. The nearby window ledge was covered with flowers and cards. A soft light over the bed shone down on her, and an inset ceiling lamp in one corner glowed. Directly across from the bed, a large, flat screen television was mounted on the wall, but it was turned off. Just to the right of the TV, a closed door set in an angular wall...a closet? Bathroom?

The words began to sink in. This was the hospital, no doubt about it. Angie had only been to the hospital a few times in her whole life, visiting friends who were recovering from surgery or relatives who had had babies. She couldn't remember ever being inside this one. She hated hospitals. They smelled funny, like iodine and rubbing alcohol, with people constantly coming in and out taking your temperature or blood pressure or asking questions. She had resolved some time ago that she would never be in one, not if she could help it. And yet despite all her resolve, here she was.

Angie's eyes welled with tears. She couldn't remember anything and that scared her almost as much as waking up here. The doctor, sensing her fear and confusion, spoke soothingly while he checked her chart notes, IV, and the monitor. He offered platitudes, telling her everything would be alright, not to be afraid, and that her mom would be with her shortly. Irritated, she turned her head away from him, not wanting to hear him, not wanting to believe any of this was real.

Just then, the door swung open.

"Angie? Oh, my baby girl! Are you awake? It's Mom!" Angie turned as her mother came barreling in, relief written on her face.

"Mom!" Angie's voice caught in her throat as she choked on the tears that were coming fast. "What's happening? Why am I in the hospital?" Her own voice seemed alien to her, scratchy and hoarse, and she tried to reach for her mom, but her arms wouldn't work. A new horror washed over her as she realized only her head and neck would obey her command to sit up. A tendril of the drowning dream coiled itself around her midsection, attempting to squeeze the very breath from her.

"Why can't I move?" her voice modulated up in pitch with her panic.

Her mother ran to her bedside, leaned in clumsily, and began stroking her daughter's face and hair. She pressed Angie's face to her own chest and rocked her as gently as she had been warned to do, while a steady stream of hushed comfort poured from her mouth.

"Okay! Okay, okay, okay! Shhh, baby, calm down! It's alright! Everything is going to be fine!" She crooned, rocking her daughter gently. Angie quieted somewhat and her mother leaned back, meeting her frightened gaze. Angie couldn't remember ever seeing that look in her mother's eyes before. She knew that whatever had happened, it was bad — so bad her mother didn't know how to tell her. She tried to inhale but her breath was shaky. The whole thing was surreal, like some kind of nightmare. She implored her mother with her eyes, and after taking another quick, shaky breath, tried to use a calmer voice, but failed.

"Mom, you're scaring me! What is going on?"

Angie's mother sat down on the bed and leaned in again to give her daughter an awkward, sideways hug, emotion strangling her ability to answer. They were both crying now, Angie from fear of the unknown and her mother from exhaustion combined with joyous relief. Four days had passed since the horrible car accident and Angie had been drifting in and out of consciousness ever since. She had been pinned in the car; the firemen had to use the Jaws of Life to get her out and she had arrived here in serious condition. Despite all that, almost since her arrival, the doctors expressed their belief that she would recover. She stabilized relatively quickly and had already come through several surgeries better than initially expected. Her vitals remained good, and given her young age, there was every indication that she would heal quickly. It wasn't until this moment when Angie finally came to, though, that her mother allowed herself to believe that maybe everything *would* be alright.

"Don't worry, honey, you'll be fine," her mother

murmured. She rocked her daughter's head gently for a moment, and then eased it back onto the pillow. "Lay back, sweetheart. It's very important that you don't get overexcited right now. I'm here, honey, I'm here." She accepted a tissue from Jodi, dabbed her eyes with it, then simply gazed in wonder at her miraculous little girl who had already beaten so many odds. The tears flowed freely as she contemplated all that they had been through in recent days. *Thank God! Thank you, God!* She thought about how easily her child could have been taken, too, like…

That thought was immediately dissolved by another of her daughter's many questions.

"Mom, the doctor said I was in an accident. What accident? I don't remember anything!" Angie's heart rate jumped visibly on the monitor screen and her voice betrayed how close she was to hysterics. *Why can't I remember?*

"I think it's probably a good idea if Angie just tries to rest right now," the doctor interjected, noting the monitor. Angie and her mother continued staring at each other and crying while he checked her chart again. "Let's see… you've pretty much only had antibiotics. I'd really like you to continue to rest quietly right now. Your body's been through a tremendous amount of trauma." He swiped through the top couple pages of her electronic file on the computer notepad he carried, mumbled something under his breath, and scrawled a few notes on the screen with a stylus. Glancing up at an almost empty bag of clear liquid hanging near the bed, he said, "Jodi, her saline needs replaced, and I'm ordering her some pain medicine."

Angie struggled to level her breathing. Everything was happening so fast, she couldn't think straight. Her mind struggled to absorb what was happening to her and the effort quickly exhausted her small energy reserves. Suddenly, she felt too drained even to cry anymore. She just wanted to close her eyes and escape back into the black nothingness she had enjoyed just half an hour earlier. Despite her pain and confusion, however, her teenage brain noticed that the doctor was very good-looking. His were the bluest eyes she had ever seen.

"Here, would you like a drink of water?" he asked. He picked up a mug of ice water from her TV tray, adjusted the bed so she was more upright, then held the straw to her parched lips. She drew in a shaky breath, took a few swallows, and blushed just a little when he smiled kindly down at her. Angie noticed that his neck was like a pro wrestler's, thick and firm. His chin boasted a slight five-o'clock shadow.

"Thank you," she said, blushing a little as the doctor lowered the bed. Her arms and shoulders ached from the small movement, and the room spun. She squeezed her eyes shut and blinked a few times, and the dizziness abated.

"Jodi, go ahead and change this bag out. When the medication arrives from the pharmacy, see that you administer it immediately." Turning to Angie, he stated plainly, "We've had you hooked up to an IV to keep you from becoming dehydrated. It's a simple mixture that contains electrolytes. See this?" He indicated the point at which the IV was attached to her arm, and then drew her attention to a spot a few inches above that where a portion of the tube branched off, its end plugged with a small rubber cap. "Thanks to this, we won't have to give you a pain shot. Instead, we'll shoot it straight into your IV here at this point. You won't even feel it going in.

The medicine will likely make you very drowsy, but don't fight it. The more you rest, the sooner you'll recover." He turned his attention back to the chart and scribbled a few more notes. Glancing up, he realized Jodi stood waiting for further instructions. "That's all for now, Jodi, thank you," he said, with a smile and a dismissive nod.

"Yes, Dr. Halverson," Jodi replied. She left to get another bag of saline. Angie noticed that Jodi also blushed under the handsome doctor's gaze. She smiled at how easily distracted she was. She'd just found out that she'd been in a bad accident and all she could think about was how cute her doctor was. She could already hear her best friend, Shawna, scolding her playfully for being so shallow and empty-headed.

As Jodi left the room to get another bag of saline, the doctor added notes to her virtual chart. Turning back to Angie, he surveyed her face quickly, worried that all the emotional upset was too much for her. He did his best to hide his concern as he did a cursory exam of the teenager.

"How is your pain level, Angie? Does it hurt when I do this?" He gently lifted her left arm, and she winced as a sharp stabbing sensation pulsed through her shoulder. Her stomach lurched and she fought a strong wave of nausea. It felt like someone was taking a hot curling iron to her shoulder and upper arm.

"Ow!" she yelped. "My arm is mostly numb, but when you lift it like that, it kills my shoulder – *ouch!*" she yelped, as he tugged on it again lightly. She instinctively tried to pull her arm away, but once again was unable to move the way she wanted. Her eyes burned with new tears, and she blinked quickly, trying to hold them back.

"Okay, good," he murmured, more to himself than to

her. He released her arm, lowering it gently back to the bed, but he wasn't finished with his examination. As he moved to the other side, Angie found herself stunned by his particular choice of words. She wondered to herself what could possibly be *good* about having such pain. *Is he a sadist?* Cute or not, she was annoyed. The doctor waited patiently for Angie's mother to move out of the way, then reached for her other arm. "Now, what about when I lift this arm?" He picked up her right arm even more carefully, supporting the wrist and elbow as he did so. "Do you have pain in this shoulder, too?"

"Not as much," she began, but then she winced and gasped as a sudden throbbing ache flooded down her arm. Noting her reaction, Dr. Halverson delicately lowered it back to her side. Her mother flew to her side again, stroking her cheek and crooning to her like she had when Angie was a little girl and would get sick or hurt.

"I'm sorry, Angie, I know that must hurt a lot. I wouldn't move your arms at all if I didn't have to," Dr. Halverson apologized. Both adults watched her carefully as she squeezed her eyes shut again and held her breath.

"I'm okay, I'm okay," she finally whispered once she could breathe again. She took a deep breath, then asked shakily, "Are both of my arms broken?" The strange fogginess she had awakened with had dissipated, her awareness sharpened by the pain, and she finally noticed both arms were in casts. The left one wrapped around her fingers and went almost all the way to her shoulders. The right one wasn't nearly as big. It, too, was wrapped around her fingers, but it only went to about halfway between her elbow and shoulder.

Dr. Halverson and Angie's mother exchanged a quick

glance, neither one completely sure of what to tell her. Dr. Halverson took the lead. He knew that it would be nearly impossible to keep all of the truth from the girl right now, so he focused his mind on the few things he felt she could handle at the moment.

"Ah…yes, they are. It seems that you thought you could stop the other car from hitting you. It's a fairly common reaction. People usually either put their arms out like you did, or they instinctively wrap them around their heads," Dr. Halverson explained. He decided that was as good a place to begin as any. He looked Angie directly in the eyes, hoping she would see that his answers were earnest without detecting that he was holding back.

"*Car* accident? I was in a car accident? When? I don't remember anything about it." She searched her memory for something, anything, any tiny clue as to how she had landed here, and came up empty. She turned her attention back to her mom. Theresa Gianelli, also hesitant to say anything that might agitate her daughter further, answered her tentatively.

"Yes, honey, you were in a car accident, and you broke both your arms." She and Dr. Halverson exchanged a loaded look. She, too, wanted to reveal as little as possible while still remaining honest. If Angie pressed her for exact details, she didn't know what she would do. She had never lied to her daughter. So, she kept her answers as brief and veiled as she could.

"I'm just glad you're awake," she replied. "Let's concentrate on getting you well. You'll have plenty of time to hear all the details about the wreck. In fact," she added with false cheerfulness, "you'll probably get sick of talking about it before everything is back to normal…"

Her voice trailed off and her stomach lurched at the thought. *Normal? Would things* ever *get back to normal?*

"I agree with your mom," the doctor chimed in. "It's really important that you don't worry about it right now. Again, the most important thing for you to do right now, at this moment, my young friend, is to get as much rest as possible." He smiled down at her and winked, mesmerizing her with his sparkling blue eyes.

"How long will I have to stay here? I *hate* hospitals!" If she could have moved her arms, she would have crossed them over her chest in an act of defiance. She knew it was childish, but she had this weird feeling that her mom and the doctor were lying to her – or at least not telling her everything – and to top it all off, she was worn out, nauseous and in a tremendous amount of pain.

The doctor smiled at her. He was youngish – late twenties or early thirties at most, by her estimation – and was movie-star handsome. He was tall, maybe six foot or six-one, with thick black hair that curled around his neck below his ears, and he had rugged, chiseled features, out from which shone those incredible blue eyes. They were the color of her mother's cobalt vases, the ones that were everywhere in their small apartment. She smiled back reflexively.

"Well," he replied with a glint in his eyes, "you'll probably be here for a *little* while longer." He winked at her again. Her smile instantly faded into a frown, and she turned her face away from him and her eyes filled with tears again. She wished everyone would just go away if they couldn't be straight with her. Why was everybody being so evasive? She wasn't a baby – why couldn't they just tell her what was going on?

"May I have a word with you in private, Mrs. Gianelli?" Dr. Halverson nodded in the direction of the doorway, and Angie's mother got up hesitantly to follow him out into the corridor. "Meanwhile, Angie, try to rest. You should begin to feel the effects of that medication almost immediately." While he had been examining her, Jodi returned with the saline bag and what appeared to be a small vial and a hypodermic needle. Now, as the doctor turned to leave, she quickly detached the old bag of fluid and attached the new one, setting the drip flow gauge. Then, she deftly measured the liquid medication into the syringe, and just as adeptly, attached it to the protrusion the doctor had just shown Angie. She pressed on the syringe, pushing the medication into the IV. Angie started to protest about her mom leaving the room. Were they going to talk about her? What could he possibly say to her mom that she shouldn't hear? But the little time she'd been awake had left her completely drained, and true to Dr. Halverson's word, the medication started working immediately. She decided maybe she'd just close her eyes for a few minutes and grill her mom for information later.

. . .

"What is it, Doctor? What did you want to tell me?" Angie's mother asked. She hoped this would be a short conversation, because she didn't want to leave Angie alone for very long now that she had regained consciousness. They were still in the doorway, so he took her gently by the arm and led her out the door and down the hall, away from Angie's room.

"Let's talk in the conference room, shall we?" he replied politely. "You must be tired, and we can sit down there. Would you like a cup of coffee or juice or anything?"

Theresa shook her head and walked alongside the doctor in silence until they reached the large, smartly decorated conference room. As they stepped inside, automatic lights blinked on one by one, and he closed the heavy door firmly but quietly behind her. He motioned to a stuffed gray office chair near the huge mahogany conference table and took an identical seat next to her as he tapped the notebook and opened Angie's chart. He perused the file and after a few uncomfortable minutes of silence, he spoke.

"Mrs. Gianelli…"

"Miz," she interrupted bluntly, sweeping her shiny, black hair away from her face and tucking it deftly behind her ears. She was a pretty woman, he noted. Petite – he guessed she was all of five-foot-four. She was physically fit and tone for a woman of thirty-six. Her large, sea green eyes, youthful and unlined, were fringed in long, black lashes. Obviously, she took good care of herself, he thought.

Lately, however, with the crazy schedule she was keeping, she found little time to think about hygiene. She realized that she wasn't even sure if she had brushed her hair that morning. Like her daughter, she had noticed on more than one occasion that Dr. Halverson was handsome. She blushed, embarrassed to find herself thinking about that. She forced herself to focus. All that really mattered right now was Angie.

"Excuse me?" He glanced up at her retort in mild surprise, as if he wasn't sure he'd heard her correctly.

She cleared her throat briefly, then repeated, "It's 'Ms.' I'm a 'miz.' Angie's father and I are divorced. I've just never gone back to my maiden name." Her eyes bore into his. "Please just call me Theresa."

Dr. Halverson shifted uncomfortably in his seat. In the four days since Angie became his patient, he also found himself somewhat distracted. Theresa Gianelli was a beautiful, youthful looking woman, and he had had fleeting thoughts (unprofessional thoughts, he reminded himself) of asking her out at a later date, but he'd thought she was married. This new information rendered him momentarily unable to remember what they were talking about.

"Oh, um…okay," he answered, with a shy, embarrassed smile. Immediately, he shifted in his chair and adopted a more professional expression, one that better fit the news he was about to give her. "Anyway, *Theresa*, what I need to share with you may be hard to digest. I can't think of any way to put this gently, so please just allow me to be blunt: Angie's left arm was severely injured in the accident. Both the bones in the forearm were broken. She broke almost every bone in her left wrist and hand." He shifted again in his chair, searching for the right words.

"What I'm trying to say, Ms. Gian…uh, sorry, Theresa, is that Angie might not be able to use her left hand fully anymore. With physical therapy, she should regain some movement, but there is a very real possibility that she won't have much fine motor control. This means she may not be able to grasp a fork or a pen; she probably won't be able to use that hand to eat or to write. Is she left-handed?"

"No, she's right-handed," Theresa responded, dazed. She was trying to listen but was finding it difficult to fully comprehend what the doctor was saying and it was no longer because she was swooning over his good looks. Angie was only seventeen – she was young and strong. Don't young, strong kids heal up pretty fast and fairly completely?

"Well…you say there's a *possibility*…" she faltered. "Doesn't that mean you're not really sure?"

"Well, yes, that's true. It's really hard to tell at this early stage and much of your daughter's recovery will depend on her level of determination. However, whether or not she makes a full recovery, she is facing months of painful rehabilitation." The doctor paused, watching Theresa's face to make sure she understood everything he was telling her. Her shocked expression made it abundantly clear that she did.

"Of course, she could surprise us all and make a full recovery," he added gently, moved to compassion by Theresa's stricken look. "It's been known to happen. However, I think I'd be remiss if I gave you false hope. When she put out her arms, presumably to stop herself from going through the windshield, her radius almost completely shattered. Her ulna snapped and was shoved up into the musculature around the humerus, past the elbow." He moved closer to her until their shoulders almost touched, and opened the file with Angie's x-rays. She blushed at the nearness of him, but the radiographs captured her full attention.

"When we did her surgery," he continued, pointing to different places on the x-rays, "we were able to pull the bones back into position and we put in a lot of pins and screws in an attempt to restructure her radius. The bones look fairly good. I guess what I'm saying is we won't know the extent of the damage to her muscles and nerves until she starts trying to use them. And she won't even be able to try, really, for at least another four to six weeks, when we remove some of the pins and replace her casts." He stopped speaking and gave her a moment to process everything.

As the bleak prediction sank in, Theresa began to cry quietly. She was glad her daughter was still alive, of course, but she knew that not regaining full use of her arm and hand were going to be very difficult for Angie to accept. Over the last few years, she'd been learning to play the guitar. She was a natural and was already pretty good at it. She'd always loved to sing. As far back as Theresa could remember, Angie had always sung to herself, no matter where they were. Now that she was learning the guitar, she'd even started writing her own songs. Theresa knew she was biased, but she really thought Angie's songs showed promise and that she was very good. More than once, she'd commented to Theresa that she just might like to make a career out of singing and playing, and until this moment, Theresa had pictured her accomplishing that goal. If she didn't fully recover, she could kiss those dreams goodbye. How do you tell a teenager that her biggest dream may not come true? She covered her face with both hands and breathed deeply a few times in an attempt to regain control.

Dr. Halverson cleared his throat quietly, then he reached across the table and grabbed a box of Kleenex that was placed there for just such occasions. This sort of news was always so difficult to break to families, and he felt he had never learned how to do it quite right. He put a hand on her shoulder and spoke gentle encouragement as he handed her a tissue.

"Look, Theresa, your daughter is really going to need you to be strong right now, okay? I recommend not telling her too much for the time being. She's still pretty fragile. As for you, force yourself to think of all that she still *can* do. At least she's still alive. Be glad you still have her." As she dabbed her eyes, he further admonished, "I would wait awhile to tell her about her friend, too. For now, let's try to keep her focused on getting stronger."

Her tears subsided and she nodded quietly. She dabbed her eyes and then looked up at the doctor, trying to put on a brave face.

"So, what's next for Angie? How long will she have to stay here? When can she come home?"

Her expression was so pitiful, he fought back a sudden urge to reach out and stroke her cheek. *Wow, she's really pretty.* He forced himself to sit up taller. He tried to sound more professional, too – more like her daughter's doctor than a silly, love-struck schoolboy.

"That's really going to depend on *her*," he replied. Tapping to close Angie's file, he pushed back from the table and stood up, indicating that their meeting was finished. "So much of a patient's recovery depends on his or her own attitude, on the belief that recovery is possible. Since she's just regained consciousness, we'll watch her for the next few days – let her try some solid food and see if her digestive system is functioning normally. Then we'll concentrate on getting some physical therapy started. The therapist will come by early next week to assess her. If she thinks Angie is ready, she'll begin working her arms through non-intensive, gentle exercises." He sighed. He needed to forewarn her about the difficult weeks ahead.

He waited until she stood and her eyes met his again, and issued his warning kindly.

"I'll be honest with you, Theresa — you're looking at months of recovery. There isn't much we can do in the way of therapy until the bones heal. As soon as she's strong enough, she can go home, but she'll have to come in for daily therapy for the first few weeks, then several times a week, and so on. It's going to be a long haul. I wish I could tell you differently, but you need to know the truth so you can gear yourself up emotionally."

· · ·

*T*heresa peeked into Angie's room and made sure that she was sleeping peacefully, then headed down to the parking lot. It was very late, and she had to go back to work the next day. She'd already missed four days. She had stayed by Angie's side day and night since the accident. Jodi had brought in a cushy recliner the first night, but Theresa hadn't gotten any decent sleep. Any tiny moan from her daughter and she'd immediately wake up. Tonight, though, she was exhausted and knew she needed to get a good night's sleep before work tomorrow. She knew, too, that it wouldn't do either of them any good if she didn't get proper rest. She only lived about twenty minutes away, so she could return quickly if an emergency arose.

As she waited for her car to warm up, she mulled over the doctor's words. Tears threatened to overtake her again, but she pushed them back, resolving firmly that she had to keep it together for Angie's sake. She wondered briefly how Shawna's parents were doing. In the last few days since the accident, she had been too busy with Angie to even call them. Not surprising, given that she'd always been too busy to really get to know the Howsers, either. Shawna and Angie had become best friends five years ago, in sixth grade, when Theresa and Angie had first moved to Somers, Montana, after the divorce. From the moment they met, Angie had spent practically every waking minute of the last five years at Shawna's house. Shawna hadn't been over to their place nearly as much because Theresa worked such long and erratic hours, and neither she nor Shawna's parents thought it was a good idea for the girls to be at her house alone, without any supervision.

Not that the girls were inclined to get into trouble. In what little time she had managed to interact with Shawna, she observed that she was a very sweet, level-headed girl. Angie, however, had a bit of a mischievous streak. No, it was better if the two teenagers were somewhere where an adult was handy, just in case. Or it *had been* better, she reminded herself. It was so hard to think of Shawna in the past tense.

Theresa swung into her oil-stained space in the apartment complex parking lot and pulled on the emergency brake. After climbing out of the car and hitting the button on the fob, locking the doors, she walked over to the mailboxes and retrieved the few bills her box contained, then headed up the stairs. The minute she unlocked and opened the door, Angie's cat, Tater, starting weaving around her legs, mewing pitifully. Shoot! She'd forgotten to feed her this morning. *Poor kitty! I love you, but you're just not a priority these days.* She forced herself to pour some cat food into the cracked, lime green ceramic dish and splashed some fresh water into the mismatched, steel water bowl before she forgot again. In the kitchen, she dropped wearily onto a barstool and pulled out her phone to check her messages. Then she stood back up and put the phone on speaker so she could listen while she fixed a piece of toast and poured herself a glass of merlot. She set the phone on the counter while she dug out the toaster.

"Hi, honey, it's Mom," the first message began. Her mother's buttery-soft voice filled the empty kitchen. "I was just checking in on you, you know, to see how you and our girl are holding up. Call me when you can, I know you're busy. Love you." *Love you, too, Mom.* She sighed as she reached over and erased the message. The "voicemail lady," as Angie called the disembodied voice, announced the next message.

"Um…yes," a semi-familiar female voice began hesitantly. "Hello? Ms. Gianelli? This is Eileen Howser, Shawna's mother. I'm sorry to bother you. I was just, uh… well, *we*, that is, Grant and I, were just wondering how Angie is doing. Is she allowed to have visitors yet? I also wanted to let you know that we're having the memorial service for Shawna on Monday at Eastside Christian Center. It'll be at eleven o'clock. We realize that you have a lot on your own plate right now, so if you can't make it, we understand, but I thought you'd want to know. Anyway, I hope you know that you can call us anytime, and I also want you to know that we are praying for you and for Angie's healing. God bless you both." The message ended with Eileen Howser rattling off her phone number quickly and then hanging up.

Theresa nearly choked on the piece of toast in her mouth and she swallowed a big gulp of wine to get it down. Then she set the wineglass down and picked up her phone. She started to erase the message but decided to wait and listen to it again tomorrow so she could jot down the details of the service, which she'd forgotten already. She wondered vaguely what she would say to them when she called. The doctor was right – at least Theresa still had Angie. She couldn't imagine what it would be like to know she'd never see her again, never hear her silly snorting laughter or see her struggling over her homework or crying over some boy that she liked. *Shawna's parents must be in agony.* She sat down heavily on the stool again and put her head in her hands. A thousand thoughts filled her mind.

The accident had been so stupid and completely avoidable. The girls had been on their way to school on Monday morning. It was Red Ribbon Week, when schools focus on teaching about and emphasizing the dangers of drugs, tobacco, and alcohol abuse. The girls were heading in to the high school early so that they could decorate the gym for a spirit assembly later that day. Impossible as it was to believe, they were hit head-on by a young woman who, ironically, had been up drinking and doing drugs most of the night before. As so often happens in these kinds of tragic accidents, the girl who caused the wreck walked away from it relatively unscathed – only a broken ankle and a few bruises. *She only had to spend one night in the hospital!* The thought made her angry.

The girl would later testify in court that she had been driving home to get ready to go to work and woke up hours later in the hospital, but that was all she could remember of the accident. She had tested positive for methamphetamines and alcohol, but so far had not admitted to using either. The one witness, a truck driver out on a delivery, would later state in court that she had crossed over the center lane into the oncoming traffic and did not appear to be conscious as she did so. Investigators believed she had fallen asleep for a moment and her pick-up truck crossed the center line, right when the girls were traveling in the opposite direction in Shawna's little compact car. She literally drove right over them. *One moment of carelessness caused all this heartache*, Theresa reflected morosely.

As she thought about the phone messages, she marveled at Eileen Howser's strength and grace. Had she really said that they had been praying for *her*? How could she sound so together, so composed, considering what they were dealing with right now? Well, she had to call them back. *Tomorrow*. Too much time had gone by already and Theresa was ashamed of herself. She knew she'd been running away, not wanting to accept reality. If they could call her to see how *she* was doing, the least she could do was to return the favor. She didn't relish the thought of calling, though – what was she going to say to them? She was happy, of course, that her own daughter had survived the accident, but she was afraid of that emotion transferring through her voice to the Howsers, who were suffering the loss of theirs. Theresa sighed and stood up, pushing the stool against the counter. It was going to be a difficult call to make. There were just no two ways about it.

She opened a few bills, threw away the envelopes, and set the bills in the basket she kept on the kitchen counter. Then she dumped the last of her glass of wine down the sink, threw away the bit of uneaten toast, swiped the counter just enough to remove the crumbs, turned off the kitchen light, and went to bed. It would be several hours before anything resembling sleep would visit her. When she finally did nod off, her sleep was fitful, full of dreams about Angie, Shawna, and the impending conversation with the Howsers.

Chapter Two: Heartbreak

"The heart was made to be broken."
~ Oscar Wilde

When Angie's eyes opened several hours later, the sun was just beginning to rise. She watched intently as the sky outside her window turned from crimson to hot pink to a bright sherbet orange to lemon yellow. She loved the black silhouettes of the trees against the fire-like backdrop. It was a beautiful sunrise and Angie stared at it until it finally melted away into daylight, absorbing it like a sponge, like she'd never seen the sun rise before. The clouds were full of shapes, looking for all the world, Angie thought, like fairies, swooping back and forth in slow motion across the sky. The thought cheered her. She had always liked stories that had fairies in them, because they so often came to help human beings in times of trouble, like Tinkerbell assisted Peter Pan. Maybe this was a sign that she would get better.

Just as she was entertaining the thought, the door opened, and in plowed the duty nurse carrying a plastic tray upon which sat a single dish covered with a plain, brown plastic dome. The nurse was not the same one Angie remembered from last night. This woman was thinner and looked older, but wore similar colored scrubs and the same type of squeaky white shoes. Her gray hair was cropped on top, like an overgrown crew cut, but long in the back, with a medium sized braid that fell just below her shoulder blades. Seeing that Angie was awake, she smiled at her and introduced herself pleasantly.

"Ah, she's awake again. Wonderful! Hello, sweetheart, I'm Carel. I heard you woke up last night. Your mother must be so happy! The doctor ordered you some breakfast. Nothing fancy just yet, mind you. We have to be sure you can stomach food before we give you anything too rich. And so, voila! I give you…gelatin!" With the flourish of a tuxedoed waiter in a fancy French restaurant, she lifted the cover from the plate theatrically, revealing, indeed, a tiny square of green gelatin underneath. That was all. It wasn't much, but Angie was hungry and it looked good to her. She tried to sit up but couldn't, and as the memories of last night returned, she was overcome with frustration again. She couldn't stem the flow of tears. When was anyone going to tell her the truth about what was happening?

"Look here, sweetheart, we can move the bed." Carel noticed Angie's frustration at her inability to sit up, and she quickly moved to her side. She spoke rapidly in an attempt to dispel Angie's fear. "See this button right here? If you push it, you'll sit up. Push the other one and you'll lay back down again. You can adjust it as much as you'd like." She placed the bed's control in Angie's right hand. Angie attempted to push the buttons, but pain shot up her arm and she cried out.

Carel lost no time retrieving the remote. Soon, she had Angie sitting up with her pillows adjusted and her meal positioned on the small, moveable table right in front of her. As she did so, she continued to speak soothingly.

"Don't you worry, little lady, I've seen this sort of thing before, once, a long time ago. A friend of mine was in a car accident and had a similar injury to her arm and hand. It took several months of intensive therapy, but she did finally regain the use of her hand. So, don't you fret. Here, I'll feed you this gelatin so you can start getting stronger." At Angie's obvious embarrassment, Carel said, "Hey, there's nobody here but us chickens. Nobody's going to see you being fed like a baby, so don't you worry. But you've got to start eating if you want to speed up your recovery." Carel smiled encouragingly, and Angie shyly opened her mouth. It was such a small portion of food that Angie finished it all in within a minute or two. Carel went to the sink in the corner next to the TV. She dampened a small white washcloth, then brought it back and gently wiped Angie's face.

The small effort of eating the gelatin left Angie completely exhausted. Carel lowered the bed, leaving Angie's head raised just a little. Then she rinsed the cloth under some fresh warm water and bathed Angie's neck and shoulders with it. When she was finished, she took a small, soft hand towel and gently dried where she had washed. She lifted Angie's head a little and fluffed her pillow around it. Then she straightened the sheet and blanket over Angie and pulled them up almost to her chin, tucking them around her lovingly. Finally, she put another shot of sedative into the IV. Angie watched sleepily. She found all of Carel's fussing about endearing and strangely comforting. It made her feel like maybe everything would be alright.

"The doctor's ordered a sedative. He wants you to keep resting for now. The sedative will wear off around lunchtime and I'll be back to help you then." Distress clouded Angie's face, so she added, "In fact, I'll be in and out while you sleep, so don't you worry, okay?" Angie relaxed as Carel finished tucking the sheets in around her. She closed her eyes as Carel moved to pull the blinds closed. Then Carel lowered the bed until Angie was almost prone, and within five minutes, she had drifted off into a deep, dreamless sleep.

. . .

When she awoke several hours later, the blinds were reopened and the room was bright with the midday sunlight streaming in through her window. The trees outside her window glowed brilliant orange and the nearly cloudless sky was a silvery powder blue. She had scarcely taken in the beauty of the day, when the door opened and in came Carel, carrying a dark brown plastic tray upon which sat another dish covered with a plastic dome identical to the one she had brought that morning. "More gelatin?" Angie asked, dispassionately. "What flavor this time?"

"Oh, no, my sweet, I have a surprise for you!" Carel smiled down at her. "The doctor was by a few hours ago, while you slept. He said since you were such a good girl and ate all your breakfast, you could have a *real* lunch. Ta-da!" She removed the dome, revealing a mug of a steaming, unknown liquid that smelled vaguely of chicken, and another plate of gelatin, this time red.

"What's so special about that?" Angie grumbled. "I still see gelatin – oh, what, did I get soup, too?" she added, sarcastically. Her left shoulder ached and she was getting tired of not being able to move the way she usually did. In addition, she was aggravated about not remembering the accident.

"Now, now, don't be a crabby apple," Carel chuckled, setting the tray down on the moveable bedside table. "Actually, it's not soup, it's *bouillon*. Not too thrilling, I know, but hopefully by this evening, you'll be able to start trying some solid food. We need proof that your digestive system is working first, though." She raised one eyebrow conspiratorially at Angie, and as her meaning became clear, Angie flushed with embarrassment.

"O…kay. I'll see what I can do," she said, dropping her eyes and focusing her attention on the food.

"Well, it'll happen when it happens, so don't try to force anything!" Carel smiled cheerfully as she used the remote to raise Angie back to a sitting position. "Now, let's get this feast into you. It's not much, but you'll be amazed at how rejuvenated you'll feel, even though it's just liquids. If all goes well, later on I'll be able to take that out, too." She nodded at the IV in Angie's wrist which was still attached to a fluid bag hanging next to the bed.

Just then, the intercom squawked on, and an unfamiliar voice crackled, "Carel?"

"Yes?"

"Can you please come to the nurses' station for a minute?"

"Be right there," Carel replied. She looked quickly at Angie. "I'll be right back, so get your taste buds ready!" She winked at her, then breezed out of the room.

When she returned, it only took a few minutes for Angie to finish the chicken broth and cherry gelatin.

Carel was right, it did make her feel better to have a little something in her stomach. Her shoulder throbbed, though, and Carel administered another dose of medication. She offered her a drink from a new, blue water bottle with a bendable straw sticking out of the top, and placed it on the side table when Angie was finished. Then she fluffed up Angie's pillow and straightened the blankets as she'd done before.

"Would you like to watch something on TV, or do you just want to sleep?" Carel asked.

"I don't know. I'm not really sleepy but I don't think I want to watch TV." She scrutinized Carel closely as she contemplated asking her what nobody else seemed willing to tell her. She decided she might as well give it a try.

"Carel, what happened to me? How did I get here?" Tears of self-pity flooded her eyes. Ever since she'd awakened last night, without a clue to what was going on, she'd been plagued with a feeling of impending doom. Something was nagging at her, in the back of her mind, but she couldn't bring it to the forefront. Not remembering what had happened in her very own life was extremely unnerving. She'd heard of people getting amnesia, but somehow she'd never thought it could happen to her.

Carel, who had moved to the other side of the bed and was reaching for the power button on the TV remote, stopped and turned slowly. She gazed down at Angie with sympathy. *It must be torture to not remember, and that's not even the worst of it – you poor girl.* She had to choose her words carefully. Dr. Halverson had made it clear that nothing should be done or said to upset his patient, not for a few days at least, until she was stronger.

"Well, sweetheart," she began hesitantly, "you were in

a really bad car accident. Don't you remember anything about it? You were brought into the emergency room early Monday morning. Today is Friday. You've been pretty much unconscious until last night. You're a very lucky girl to…to even be alive." She stopped; she was afraid her stammering had given away too much. She knew that Angie had no idea that her best friend in the world was dead. Imagining how she would feel in Angie's place, she changed her tone, putting false brightness in it.

"You know, you're going to just keep getting stronger and stronger, and hopefully, you'll start to remember things and you won't feel so disoriented. That's how it went with that other person I told you about, my friend who was in a similar accident. I know it's really hard to be patient in a situation like this, but truly, the best thing you can do right now is to rest as much as possible. All of your questions will be answered soon, I promise. Okay?" She could tell by Angie's expression that she wasn't buying it, but she was determined not to say more. Resting really was the most important thing for her right now. "Don't worry, hon. Trust me. All questions will be answered in time."

She walked over and adjusted the blinds to divert the bright sunlight off of Angie's face. "Better?" she asked. Angie just nodded glumly. The medication was taking effect and she was getting groggy. She watched sleepily as Carel pushed the button and lowered her bed. She decided to close her eyes, just for a minute, and then she'd press Carel a little harder for some real answers. Something about Carel's expression indicated that she knew something important. As she began to doze, she didn't even hear Carel leave the room, closing the door softly behind her.

...

The next few days were a flurry of activity, relatively speaking. Her mom continued to visit, and she, the nurses, and the doctor continued to brush away Angie's questions, always telling her that she'd know more in time, to be patient, and so on. Theresa had gone to Shawna's funeral on Monday and then straight to the hospital to sit with Angie. She'd talked her boss into giving her a few more days off, though heaven only knew how the lost income was going to be made up.

Angie was oblivious to anyone's problems but her own. She would have been really annoyed with all of them if it weren't for the fact that she had started some mild physical therapy, which caused her so much pain that she usually slept for hours afterward. She was eating solid foods again to her relief, and her digestive system seemed to be working just fine.

Two days prior, as promised, Carel had removed the IV, and afterwards, she had helped Angie into a lovely albeit too-short shower, during which time her bedding was changed. She had to be really careful with her arms, which still didn't move as she wanted them to. She wasn't able to wash her hair, so Carel did it for her. Normally, she would have been embarrassed to have someone else bathe her, especially a stranger, but Carel didn't seem to mind, and she was so sweet, anyway. She fussed over her like a mother hen. She wrapped Angie's casts carefully in plastic, then washed her. Afterwards, she dried her, unwrapped the casts, and helped her into a fresh gown. She'd been right; Angie felt almost human again as Carel helped her back into the clean bed. The sheets were soft and fresh-smelling.

Getting in and out of bed was no easy task. The lower half of Angie's body had not been badly injured in the accident, so she could still bend at the waist and sit from standing. However, without the use of her arms, she had to be lifted into a sitting position and helped to stand. When she got back in bed, she could turn and sit on the edge of it. However, the nurse would have to scoot her back, lift her legs onto the bed, and adjust her until she was centered.

The worst of it was having to be helped whenever she needed to go to the bathroom. Angie was always cranky during the process. She knew she should be more gracious; after all, the people assisting her were just doing their job and probably didn't like it any better than she did. It annoyed her so much to be unable to function on her own. It was so undignified and humiliating.

When she wasn't sleeping, she watched TV, which helped to pass the time, although she had to wait until someone came into the room so she could get the channel changed. Before she began therapy, she couldn't move her left arm or hand much at all, and her right hand still wasn't able to grasp the remote or push the buttons properly. As such, except for when her mother was there, she was frequently stuck watching some inane channel like the Home Shoppers network. Consequently, most of the time, she just slept.

The first time the therapist came in to work with her, Angie thought she must enjoy making people hurt. The woman just picked up her arms and moved them around doing different exercises with them. Even though she always explained very nicely what she was doing, she ignored Angie when she cried out in pain, telling her to "be brave," that she knew it was "uncomfortable." *Uncomfortable?! It feels like someone is holding a flaming torch to my shoulders the whole time you work!*

Still, she seemed pleased with the progress Angie was making. In the few short sessions they'd had since she started working with her, Angie had already gained back a tiny modicum of control – she was able to open and close her right hand, and could even push the remote control buttons on her bed. Everyone, including the doctor, was greatly encouraged. Dr. Halverson cautiously theorized that Angie might regain the full use of her arms after all, but only stated as much to Theresa. Angie still had no clue that she was even in danger of losing the use of them.

She was feeling better about having to stay in the hospital, though. Everyone, her mom included, seemed to think she was recovering well, better than could reasonably be expected.

. . .

On Monday night, one week after the accident, Angie woke up in a cold sweat, screaming at the top of her lungs. She had been having a terrible nightmare. She and her best friend, Shawna, had climbed into Shawna's car and headed to school. They were going in extra early to put up some posters and flyers and to decorate the gym in the school colors of orange and black, as well as some red, for a Red Ribbon assembly. The girls were laughing and joking as they always did when they were together, when suddenly, a truck swerved into their lane. There wasn't even time to think about what was happening, and Angie heard a deafening crash. Then, all was silent and black, and she had awakened from the dream screaming hysterically.

Jodi, the nighttime duty nurse, came flying through the door and over to Angie's bed. She placed her cool hand on Angie's forehead, and crooned, "Shhh! It's okay, honey, it's okay – what's the matter, did you have a bad dream? You need to stop screaming, honey, please. You'll scare the other patients." Angie hadn't even realized she *was* screaming and she stopped immediately, but she couldn't stem the deluge of tears streaming down her cheeks.

"Wh…where's my mom?" she stammered, the tears choking her voice. "I want my mom! I think I remember something and I need to ask my mom! Where is she? Can you please get her for me?" Angie sobbed. The dream left a terrible lingering realization that Angie couldn't push away. *Where was Shawna? Why hadn't she come to visit Angie? How could her best friend not have visited her by now?* She had been so doped up on pain medication most of the time that she hadn't even thought about the fact that Shawna hadn't come to visit.

"She's already come and gone, tonight, hon, you'll have to wait until…"

"Call her and tell her she needs to come over. Now! Do you hear me?" Angie's voice rose an octave, threatening to morph into hysteria again at any moment. She continued sobbing uncontrollably.

"Alright, honey, don't start screaming again, I'll call her." Jodi picked up the phone and dialed Theresa Gianelli's number. It was written on the room's white board, but at this point, Jodi and most of the staff knew the number by heart. "I'll see what I can do, okay? It'll be alright, sweetie, just calm down." The other end of the line began ringing. By the end of the third ring, Jodi was tempted to hang up – she knew from her conversations with Theresa how little sleep she was getting, and she'd only gone home a couple of hours prior. She didn't want to wake her up just because of a little nightmare. She was about to disconnect when Theresa answered.

"Hello? What's the matter? Is everything alright?" She could see the hospital's number on the caller ID, and she immediately panicked. *What now?*

"Ms. Gianelli, this is Jodi at the hospital. Angie just woke up screaming and crying, saying she remembers something about the…accident," Jodi murmured, glancing sideways at Angie. She was trying to choose her words carefully so as to not distress Angie further. "She's really upset. I know you've only been home a few hours, but do you think you could…"

"I'll be right there." Theresa hung up the phone, flicked on her nightstand lamp, jumped out of bed, and began running around her bedroom, frantically pulling on her jeans, her black turtleneck, and her socks. Tater, who had been snoozing lazily next to Theresa on the bed, lay staring at her through yellow eyes, purring loudly, oblivious to Theresa's frantic movements. Theresa pushed her foot impatiently into one shoe and had a moment's panic searching for her other shoe, which turned up under the bed. Then she ran to the living room, grabbed her coat and car keys, and flew out the door to her car, her shoelaces still untied.

· · ·

*F*ifteen minutes later, after speeding the whole way to the hospital, Theresa opened the door to Angie's room tentatively, half hoping that Angie might have calmed down or maybe even gone back to sleep. She wasn't sure she was ready to face this moment. She knew it would come eventually but was secretly glad when it was naturally postponed. However, as she peeked through the doorway, she saw Angie was wide awake. Her eyes locked onto Theresa's with laser focus as her mother stepped softly across the floor and sat down next to her on the edge of the bed. The look on Angie's face nearly broke Theresa's heart.

Before she could speak, Angie blurted, "Mama, where's Shawna? She was in the accident, too, wasn't she? Is that why she hasn't visited me? Is she here at the hospital, too? How bad is she? Can I see her? I think I should see her, Mom! Will you please take me to her! She must be so scared – I know *I* have been!" The torrent of words broke off as quickly as it started, and she waited tensely for her mother to answer her.

Theresa just stared, struggling for words to begin. She felt like a traitor, not having told Angie before now, but Angie had only been awake for a few days, after all. It seemed ironic that only that morning, Theresa had been to Shawna's memorial service. Both Eileen and Grant Howser had hugged Theresa tearfully and had asked about Angie. Theresa was awestruck at their ability to graciously meet and greet the people who had come to help them say goodbye to their daughter.

"Mom?" Angie watched her mother's face intently and her own paled as realization swept over her. It hadn't been just a dream. It was a memory. "Mama?" she continued in a weak voice. "Where's Shawna? Is she okay? What's going on?" Her breathing became ragged and shallow as she careened towards hysteria again, and Theresa knew she had to figure out what she was going to say, and quick. Obviously, there was no avoiding the truth now. *Is there a good way to tell your child her best friend is dead?* She reached up and stroked Angie's face gently, her eyes locked on her daughter's. Incredibly, she was able to speak, though she was sure her voice would fail her.

"Angie, you and Shawna were in a head-on collision on Highway 93 as you were heading into school last Monday morning. Shawna…" she swallowed, tears choking her voice, "Shawna died at the scene. I'm sorry, baby. I'm so sorry." She continued to caress Angie's face, as her own tears made their way steadily down her cheeks. Angie's expression was confused, and she began slowly shaking her head. Theresa realized just how hard this news would be for her daughter to hear. She braced herself for the inevitable onslaught of whatever came next. She honestly didn't know what to expect, because she had no idea how *she* would react if the tables were turned.

Angie held her breath and her face turned ashen. Her whole body began to tremble uncontrollably. *There is no way I'm hearing this. This is not happening to me.*

"No," she breathed bluntly. She raised her head to look her mom in the face and blurted in a slightly stronger voice, "*No.* No way. You're lying. *You're lying!*" Her eyes blazed at her mother, but Theresa just continued to hold her gaze and nodded her head. Angie's thoughts swirled together.

Suddenly, everything came rushing back, like somebody opened up the floodgates of a dam, and she was hit with the full force of her memory. Her head dropped heavily back onto the pillow and she closed her eyes, her tears rolling down the sides of her face and into her hair.

She remembered getting up extra early for school that day. She and Shawna were in charge of decorating the gym for the Red Ribbon Week opening spirit assembly. They were going to meet five or six other kids who had volunteered to help out. Shawna had pulled up to Angie's apartment at around seven a.m., and Angie had gone into Theresa's bedroom to tell her they were leaving and to kiss her goodbye. Then, she'd grabbed a chocolate muffin from the plate on the counter, swung her backpack over her shoulder, and had run out to meet Shawna.

The roads were clear. It was early October in Montana and while snowfall at that time of year isn't unheard of, the residents were graced this season with a few extra weeks of sunshine and fairly warm midday temperatures. The high for that Monday was anticipated to be around 68 degrees. There had been increasing frost in the early mornings, though, and the trees were afire with autumn's showy leaves. The early morning air hung heavy with the scent of woodstoves bringing warmth and comfort into chilly kitchens and living rooms. It was the time of year when everybody gets ready to hunker down for the winter, like a mass hibernation was about to take place.

The sun peeked over the Flathead Range as the girls turned left onto Highway 93 off of Boon Road. White frost sparkled on the tips of the grasses on the roadside, but the girls weren't worried about black ice, not this early in the season. Traffic at this time of day was pretty light, too, and as they accelerated to the speed limit of 65 miles per hour, neither girl had a care in the world. They chatted and joked, talking about what decorations they were going to use and who might show up to help. They had just passed the Glacier Tree Company sign, a short distance from where the divided highway joins back together and the two directions of traffic are not shielded from each other by a land barrier. As the road curved to the right, they noticed headlights coming toward them.

At first, it just looked like an optical illusion. The curve in the road made it appear that the truck was heading straight at them. It wasn't until the very last instant that they realized the truck actually *was* coming right toward them. With both vehicles traveling at 65 to 70 miles per hour, the whole thing occurred in seconds. They collided almost completely head-on, but the driver's side of both vehicles took the full force of the crash. Angie had screamed and put her hands up as if she could somehow stop the inevitable. Shawna hadn't made a sound. The truck came right on up over the front of the small compact car. Metal crunched loudly, glass flew, and tires screeched – a horrible, deafening, slamming noise upon impact. Then everything went black.

As Angie's thoughts returned to the present, she looked into her mother's eyes again, and knew it was true: Shawna was dead. There was no way she could have survived such a devastating crash. "Mama…?" she faltered. Waves of shock and disbelief crashed over her. How was she going to go on without Shawna? She couldn't even process the idea. It wasn't real, it couldn't be. Her chest heaved with building emotion and tears spilled down her face. "Mommy…" she cried. Sorrow and frustration overwhelmed her as she tried again – and failed –to reach out her arms for comfort. Her breathing became ragged as hysterics overtook her, and then she wailed– desolate, heart-wrenching sobs interrupted only by necessary, choked breaths.

"I know, baby, I know," her mother cradled her and rocked her, just as she had done the night Angie first woke up. There were no words. What can you tell someone who has just lost the most important person in her life? What can you say that will make any difference, that will make it somehow easier to accept? Nothing.

Theresa reflected on the words that well-meaning people had spoken at Shawna's funeral service. *She's in a better place now. There's a reason for everything that happens. We just have to accept it as God's will and go on. Trust God.* Personally, Theresa felt the words were trite, and they irritated her. Theresa had been raised in the Catholic church, and had a concept of God. She believed God had created everything, but that was about the extent of her beliefs. In her view, God wasn't much more than a puppeteer who didn't really care about the puppets. He was a kid with an ant farm. Still, she knew those people were struggling to do the impossible: To make sense out of something that made absolutely no sense whatsoever. To fill the void, breach the great chasm that had been created by the senseless death of a beautiful young girl.

No. Theresa knew, from the vantage point of age and life experience, that only time would make things easier. It had begun.

Chapter Three: Birth of a Friendship

"A sorrow's crown of sorrow is remembering happier times."
~ Alfred Lord Tennyson

heresa stayed with Angie for the rest of that night, stroking her face and wiping away her tears, not speaking. What could she say? Angie sobbed continuously for the first couple of hours. She refused all offers – water, juice, a warmed blanket. That was the hardest part for Theresa – watching her daughter suffer the worst pain imaginable and having absolutely nothing to offer her in the way of comfort save holding her. When the time came, Jodi administered more intravenous medicine. Once the sedative began to take effect, she quieted down, staring sullenly into space. After twenty minutes or so, she closed her eyes, but even under the influence of the powerful drugs she didn't really sleep. She continued to moan and shake her head in disbelief. The moment Theresa shifted her position on the bed or ceased caressing her face, her eyes popped open in alarm. Once she ascertained that Theresa was still there, she'd close her eyes again and her erratic breathing would slow somewhat. Jodi had an orderly bring in a recliner again, in case Theresa wanted to sleep, but she remained on the bed, glued to her daughter's side.

As she watched Angie struggle to rest, Theresa reflected on the last few years. She thought about when she and Angie had first left Greg, her husband and Angie's father. That had been such a hard time on both of them. Of course, *she* knew why she was leaving, but it was harder for Angie. Although Angie hated the constant fighting and yelling, and even though she was grateful for a change that would bring more peace into their everyday lives, she was tremendously upset to leave behind her own security net of friends.

The first few months had been the worst, when they had arrived in Somers and didn't know anybody. Ironically, she and Angie were the ones who were always fighting then. The littlest things would set Angie off, and then she'd scream accusations at Theresa about how all of it was her fault. The tension in their tiny apartment had been so thick it could almost literally have been cut with a knife.

Angie stirred fitfully in her sleep. She wasn't really sleeping – she, too, was thinking. She thought about how Shawna had been the first person to really bring any normalcy into her life. Angie's life had always been tough. From the time she was a small child, she had known emotional upheaval. As if her parents' constant bickering hadn't been bad enough, they always seemed to want to put her in the middle of their disputes, like they thought she, a child, had some wisdom to impart that they could not locate on their own. As a result, Angie spent a lot of time in her room alone, avoiding them. She filled her time writing dry, sarcastic poetry about families in which the members were at odds with one another. Her favorite childhood poet was Shel Silverstein, and she tried to imitate his humorous style of writing. Somehow, though, her poems came out much more caustic and unfriendly.

> *Parents are strange and foreign creatures*
> *Their few and un-redeeming features*
> *Include a knack for spitting while yelling*
> *And spending precious time in telling*
> *Each other exactly where it is that they can go.*
>
> *At night, alone, they unzip their skins*
> *And right in the place where their hearts should have been*
> *Sits a pot of poison brewing*
> *Anger, hatred, slowly stewing*
> *Watch out; don't get splattered when they blow!*

When she wasn't writing poetry, she was singing. Her uncle, Theresa's brother, Mike, had given her an old, hand-me-down Panasonic stereo. The "Thing" (as she lovingly called it) had a working 8-track player, and her uncle had given her some old tapes to play in it, including artists like Eric Clapton, the Rolling Stones, and Led Zeppelin. Except for the Grassroots tape, which she liked a lot, she rarely listened to the old 8-tracks. The stereo had a working turntable, though, and whenever she could, Angie would get one parent or the other to take her to stores like Rockin' Rudy's, places that carried old LPs (long-playing, vinyl records). Most of that music was dated, too, but Angie found some she really liked to sing to. She loved Joni Mitchell, Carole King, and Olivia Newton-John the best. She would hide in her room and pretend to be a famous singer, using a hairbrush as a microphone and posing in front of her mirror. In the midst of those flights of fancy, she was famous and far removed from her real life; people all adored her and wanted to spend time with her. Nothing painful could touch her.

At the end of her fifth grade school year, her parents announced that they were getting a divorce. It was just as well, she had thought at the time. She was sick of their fighting, anyway. Most of her friends' parents were separated or divorced, so it didn't seem completely unnatural that her own would do so. In fact, she hoped that maybe it would make things more bearable for her at home – less fighting would mean a more peaceful household, right?

She and her mom moved from the family home in Missoula, Montana, and found a dinky apartment in the vicinity of rural Somers, about two hours away from her dad and her old life. At first, it was like an adventure. She and her mom took some furniture from the house, but they had to go out and buy a dinette, as well as a couch and chairs for the living room. At the Salvation Army, she and her mom had chuckled at some of the weird and wonderful styles of furniture that were available. Most of it was pretty dated, going all the way back to the early nineteen-seventies, and some of it looked like it would fit better in the lobby of a low-class motel than in someone's living room. All of it was decrepit, but it was affordable.

After the initial excitement of moving wore off, though, Angie realized quickly that divorce does not mean that people stop communicating. Her parents argued daily on the phone, trying to settle who would get what, and bickering over how much child support her dad had to pay. Her mom would threaten to take her dad to court and sometimes Angie could actually hear her dad's angry shouts coming through the receiver, even if she was standing clear across the room. The calls usually ended with her mom shutting herself in her bedroom, crying. Angie was still mostly alone. In fact, she was lonelier than ever. At least in Missoula, she had had a few friends that she could visit to escape her unhappy home. Now, she was in a totally new area. By her estimation, it wasn't even a real town. During the first weeks, she hadn't seen any kids at the apartment complex. Then one day she saw a girl about her age while she was taking the garbage out to the dumpster, a tall, pretty blonde, but the girl only glared at her when Angie waved, and asked her what she was looking at in a rude voice. Angie had glared right back, and then had turned quickly and stomped back inside without saying a word.

She seemed destined to live her life like a turtle – always alone and inside her protective shell, which was growing thicker by the day. In the fall, she had started sixth grade at Somers Middle School, and that had been the gateway to her first experiences with true happiness.

. . .

*T*he bed creaked and shifted as Theresa got up. She was stiff and needed to move. Angie's eyes popped opened and the panicked expression on her face was heartbreaking.

"I'm not going anywhere, sweetheart," her mother whispered. "I just need to stretch. Go back to sleep, baby." Angie's eyes drooped shut again, and as her breathing slowed, Theresa sighed in relief. She yawned widely and tried to clear her bleary vision. There was no way she was going to be able to go back to work today as she had told her boss. Oh, well, this was a family emergency, for heaven's sake. They could just deal with it. She'd already missed all of last week and knew that her paycheck was going to be practically nonexistent. She tiptoed across the room, grateful that the door didn't squeak as she snuck out. She needed coffee, stat.

As she passed the nurses' station, she noted the time. It was four-fifteen in the morning. Worried that Angie might wake up while she was gone, she hurried to the vending machines in the lobby. Bad coffee was better than nothing, she decided, and she put a dollar in the machine. A cup dropped into its slot and a liquid resembling lightly steeped tea began to squirt down into it. When it was filled, Theresa extracted it from the machine, then turned to a small, side table upon which sat napkins, stirrers, and packets of sugar, sugar substitute, and powdered creamer. She shook two sugars and three creamers into the drink, stuck a stirrer in the cup, and stirred while she headed back to Angie's room. *It doesn't even smell like coffee*, she noted disdainfully. *Oh, well, at least it's hot.*

She couldn't rush back to the room without risking spilling the coffee and burning herself, so she took advantage of her necessarily slowed pace and looked at some of the art on the walls. The hospital had been remodeled a few years back and the walls were decorated with artworks by local artists. Some of them were really nice. The abstract works were bizarre and she smiled quietly, wondering who would actually paint such strange stuff. Or better yet, who would decorate their home with it? Angie would love these – she'd have to remember to show them to her someday.

The opposite wall of the hallway down which she strode was banked with floor-to-ceiling windows that looked out on a tiny, well-kept courtyard with border gardens, a tiny, winding sidewalk, and a few benches placed here and there. The night was pitch black. A few raindrops had splashed on the windshield as she had raced back to be with Angie, and the temperature had dropped significantly from what it was just a few hours earlier when she'd first gone home. Theresa meandered over to the window and tried to peer out. She could feel the cold radiating through the glass and her breath left a foggy spot. In the dim glow of the meager lighting, she couldn't really see much, but there were puddles on the sidewalk and judging by the splashing on their surfaces, she surmised that it was raining harder now. She hoped it wouldn't get much colder and that the rain wouldn't turn to snow.

The hospital felt completely deserted. It was so quiet down here where the gift shop and snack shack were tightly closed up for the night. She sipped at the coffee, knowing she should get back to the room before Angie woke up, and flinched at the awful flavor. Suddenly, she felt absolutely drained. She leaned her head against the cold window and nursed a brief moment of self-pity, even allowing a few tears to escape down her cheeks. This all felt much too hard. It was too much. She couldn't deal with it. She wanted to scream. What had people said earlier that day? *God knows what's going on. He has a reason for everything.* A reason? What reason could there be to explain all this heartbreak? Who was God to put her little girl through such a horrible experience, just because he had his own "reasons?" Exhaustion melted into anger. There was *no* good reason that *she* could see for what was happening! Did God delight in putting people through these types of excruciating circumstances? To what possible end?

And where on earth is Greg? She had called and called him, but he hadn't gotten back to her yet. She knew that on his long hauls as a trucker, he went through lots of places where he didn't get any cell service, but she thought he would have at least looked at his phone by now, just to check for messages. He didn't even know what was happening to his own daughter.

She started at the thought of Angie, and realized that in her tired, contemplative state, she had been gone much longer than she meant to be. She dumped the coffee into the nearest drinking fountain, then crinkled up the Styrofoam cup and tossed it toward the trash receptacle, bending over to pick it up when it missed. *It was lousy coffee, anyway.* She hurried now to get back to Angie's room, feeling guilty. What if Angie had awakened while she was wasting time?

She needn't have worried. When she snuck quietly back into the room, Angie didn't even stir. Theresa tiptoed to the vinyl recliner the hospital personnel had placed by Angie's bed. She sat down on it and reclined back as quietly as she could and gazed lovingly at her beautiful daughter. Her eyelids grew heavier by the minute, and before she knew it she drifted off to sleep.

Although she hadn't been aware of her absence, Angie did hear when her mother returned. She didn't bother to open her eyes, though, heavy as they were with the sedative she'd been given. Even though she was extremely groggy, she couldn't sleep. Time passed excruciatingly slowly. Every second that passed was filled with inescapable grief.

As she tried to wrap her mind around the idea that she would never see Shawna again, she thought she might go crazy. Her brain flat-out refused to accept the truth and her heart…well, she finally understood what people meant by "heartbroken." Hers felt like it was torn into two pieces that couldn't possibly be put back together again, broken as irreparably as Humpty Dumpty. Desperate thoughts crowded her mind. *Shawna. How could you leave me? What am I gonna do now? Who will care about my problems? Who on earth will ever understand me the way you did?*

Shawna smiling. Shawna's infectious laughter. Shawna's kind heart. She had been like a real, live angel, sent to earth just for Angie.

Angie's thoughts drifted to the day they'd met. It was on the first day at her new school, and she had really missed her old one in Missoula and all of her old friends. Summer had been filled up with moving and furnishing the new place, as well as exploring the Flathead Valley's many hiking trails. She hadn't really thought about school until suddenly, it was time to go. Porter Middle School in Missoula had been a normal-sized school, at least. She and her closest friend, Kaitlyn, had looked forward to going there. They had heard that there were lots of good-looking seventh and eighth grade boys there, and that the nearby high school, Big Sky, often sent students over to help as teacher's assistants. Occasionally, they had heard, some of those students were really attractive guys, too. Older cute guys – what could be better?

This new school was dinky and the nearest high school was seven miles away in Kalispell. So much for handsome high school guys dropping in. Although it was rural, it wasn't horrible. The classrooms were large and the population small, so none of Angie's classes felt overcrowded, as they often had in Missoula. A newer building, it was situated in the middle of farmland and had beautiful views of the nearby Flathead Range. Flathead Lake, the "largest body of fresh water west of the Mississippi" (as she had already heard a dozen times that first day), was relatively close and there was even a peekaboo glimpse of it from Angie's homeroom class. The building was u-shaped, with the sixth-grade wing down one long hallway, the seventh and eighth grade wing down the other, and office space and Title 1 classrooms down the perpendicular hallway that connected them.

Everybody already seemed to know everybody else, and as she observed people's interactions and overheard conversations that first day, she gleaned that most of the students had been going to school together since kindergarten. Nobody even looked at her during her first few classes, which was fine. She hated trying to make small talk. The teachers were friendly and helpful, so that gave her a little hope, and she was too busy just trying to figure out where to go next and listening to all the first-day spiels (expectations, rules, the usual) to really pay attention to anyone else, either.

When the bell rang signaling the end of fourth hour, Angie stood up to leave and accidentally bumped into someone. Before she could even open her mouth to say, "Excuse me," the other girl shoved her roughly.

"Hey! Watch what you're doing, moron!" the rude girl growled.

Angie picked up her notebook and pencil which had slid off the desk onto the floor when the girl pushed her into it. She stood back up, her temper rising, and looked the other girl directly in the eyes, her mouth locked firmly shut. The rude girl glared back. She was tall for a sixth grader, maybe five-foot-eight, Angie estimated. Her blonde hair fell in shiny ringlets over her shoulders and she had very pretty features. She had a small upturned nose and large brown eyes fringed with the longest lashes Angie had even seen. Her well-developed figure was accentuated by her tight-fitting clothes, a small bejeweled tank top with a cute, black mini-skirt. Her clothes didn't look expensive, but with that figure they looked really good, Angie thought. Too bad she was such a…

"Are you planning on moving anytime in the next century?" the pretty girl snapped. "Why don't you take a picture? It lasts longer." She grinned at her own joke and the two girls standing with her snickered. She looked familiar. Where had Angie seen her before?

Suddenly, she remembered – this was the same girl who had been so rude to her in the parking lot of her apartment complex that one day. "What's your problem?" Angie asked angrily. "Why do you have to be so nasty? It's the first day of school."

Recognition swept the girl's face, too. "O.M.G! You're that *ugly* chick who lives at my apartments! Ugh! Now I have to deal with seeing you at *school*, too? Great." She pantomimed gagging herself with her finger, and the other two girls laughed again.

Just then, the teacher approached the group. "You ladies need to hurry or you won't get any free time. Recess only lasts twenty minutes, and then the duties will call you in for lunch." The girl and her friends turned and began to make their way towards the door. The blonde's eyes never left Angie's. The teacher noted the tension between the them. "Is everything alright, girls?"

Miss Colton was a young teacher, with pretty golden-brown hair and hazel eyes. She enjoyed being outdoors, as evidenced by her deep tan. She had on a simple floral dress and sandals and wore no make-up.

"Everything is just *fine*, Miss Colton," Blondie replied in an overly sweet voice. She threw Angie a threatening look, then turned and started walking towards the door.

"Just a moment. Callie, isn't it?" Miss Colton asked her.

"Yes," Callie answered haughtily. She turned and looked the teacher up and down quickly, then wrinkled her nose in disapproval. Angie couldn't believe a student was being so blatantly rude to a teacher and stared as the scene played out.

"Could you please put both of your arms down at your sides?" the teacher asked politely, but firmly. Callie sighed in exasperation. She put her books down on the nearest desk and complied with the teacher's request. Her fingertips fell a good two inches below her skirt line. "I'm so sorry, Callie, and I don't mean to embarrass you on the first day of school, but we have a dress code here. Your shorts or skirts must extend to your fingertips or below, even if you wear tights underneath them. It's all in the handbook you received in homeroom. Didn't your homeroom teacher say anything to you? You'll need to go to the office and call home to see if someone can bring you something more suitable to wear."

Callie reached up with both hands and tucked her hair behind her ears. She smiled a saccharine smile, looked Miss Colton directly in the eyes, and intoned with false sweetness, "My parents are both at work. There's nobody who *can* bring me any other clothes."

Miss Colton smiled back but her expression was all business. "Well, then I guess you'll spend the rest of the day in the office. At any rate, please go there now and find out what you should do. The principal will be happy to help you with that."

Callie glared at Miss Colton, then threw a dirty look at Angie. "I guess I'll see *you* at recess and we can finish the conversation we started," she remarked coldly. Then she turned on her heel and briskly left the room, her gaggle of cronies following closely behind. The other two girls shot her dirty looks, too, and one of them sneered at her as they exited. "Later!" she said, giving a mock salute and smirking sarcastically. She was a pudgy girl with bad acne and her red, shoulder length hair hung in greasy tendrils around her face. Angie felt sorry for her. She seemed like a really unhappy person.

"Goodbye, ladies," Miss Colton said in a no-nonsense tone.

She turned her attention back to Angie. "How are things going for you, Angela?" she asked kindly. She had been impressed with the girl's responses during the introductions at the beginning of class. Besides being a really cute girl, she had an intelligent sense of humor. Angie had long, wavy hair the color of espresso, with big, dark green, intelligent eyes, and a smattering of brown freckles over high, ivory cheekbones a supermodel would kill for. She had an almost perfectly heart-shaped face and dark, pink bowtie lips. When Miss Colton had asked her how she liked Somers compared to Missoula, her reply of, "Oh, about as well as can be expected, given they're as different as diamonds and dollar store glass," caused the teacher to choke on a giggle before she asked her to elaborate.

"Oh, you know, I'm totally fine, Miss Colton, really." Angie answered. She liked Miss Colton. She put on a brave smile so her new teacher wouldn't worry unnecessarily.

"Really? Because it looked to me like Callie Simmons and her associates have it in for you. They have something of a reputation that followed them here from the elementary school in Lakeside. If they give you any trouble, even if it's just name calling, you'll be sure to let me know, won't you? We have zero-tolerance for bullying at this school."

"Oh, sure, Miss Colton. I wouldn't worry about me, though. I'd be more worried that they might all trip over their broomsticks and hurt themselves." Angie smiled conspiratorially at Miss Colton, and the teacher laughed in spite of herself.

"That's not very nice, Angela," she scolded playfully. "True, maybe, but not very nice." They exchanged knowing grins. "Alright." She turned Angie and started scooting her towards the door. "Let me know, okay? You're going to be late for lunch recess. Have a good rest of the day."

"Thanks, you too," Angie answered.

. . .

The throbbing in her arms invaded her thoughts now, urgently taking precedence over her memories and forcing her back into the present. Angie moaned. She wanted to stretch so badly, and not being able to move made her want to scream. "Ow…." she murmured softly. Her left arm, especially, ached with persistent pain. In the recliner next to her, her mother stirred.

"What's the matter, baby?" She sat up quickly, stretched, and yawned widely. "Are you hurting again?"

As she woke more fully, the awful truth drifted back onto Angie like a shroud. "Shawna!" Angie whispered, and then she started crying again, her shoulders shaking.

"I know, honey, I know," Theresa crooned. She put her arms carefully around her daughter's head and neck and hugged her gently.

Just then, the door opened and Jodi entered briskly holding a blood pressure cuff. "Oh, good, I didn't want to have to wake you up to take your vitals…oh." She stopped short as she noted the scene in front of her. She looked at Theresa and understanding flooded her as Theresa shook her head slightly. *"Oh!* I can come back and get your stats in a little while. Do you need something for your pain, honey?"

"Angie?" her mom inquired softly. "It's time. How about Jodi gives you some more pain medication, babe?" Theresa asked. Angie only looked back at her blankly. Tears streamed silently down her cheeks and her body shook with noiseless sobs. When she didn't respond, her mother answered for her. "Yeah, I think she'll have some now, Jodi. Can you please bring her some cranberry juice?" She knew Angie really liked cranberry juice and sought to comfort her in any way possible.

"Sure, of course, I'll be right back," Jodi answered. She turned and left the room as swiftly as she'd arrived.

Angie's tears slowed to a trickle again, and her exhausted sobs quieted. Theresa stroked her face tenderly. As quickly as she had left, Jodi returned with two pills and a cup of cranberry juice. She pushed the button to raise

Angie's head enough that she could sip at the juice.

"I've got her," Theresa said. She took the juice from Jodi and she held the cup so her daughter could drink, cradling her head gently with her other arm. Angie swallowed the pills obediently, and Theresa laid her back against the pillow and lowered the bed again. "You might as well go ahead and take her vitals now, Jodi. Then she can go back to sleep. Okay, baby?" Angie continued to stare absently. She didn't care what they did. It didn't matter. Nothing mattered.

Jodi was already swiping the digital thermometer across Angie's forehead. After she took her temperature, she checked her blood pressure, scribbled her findings on her computer notepad, and then straightened the sheets and blankets. "The medicine should take effect pretty soon, honey," she said softly. "Can I get *you* anything, Theresa?"

"No, thanks, I'm good," Theresa smiled wanly at her. She turned back to Angie, who was drowsing on the pillow. "She looks like she's going to go right back to sleep. I think I'll try to catch a few more zees, too."

"Good," Jodi said softly. "Get some rest." She turned quietly and exited, turning off the light over Angie's head and closing the door as she left.

Theresa continued to sit next to Angie for a few minutes, caressing her face the way she always had in times of trouble since the day she was born. Angie's breathing quieted. She stared absently at nothing through heavy eyelids. After a moment, she closed her eyes and Theresa knew she was out. She moved back to the chair and threw the small afghan Jodi had brought her over her legs. After one more quick glance at her daughter's face, she closed her eyes, too, and let sleep overtake her.

. . .

As she drifted in and out of consciousness, Angie's thoughts returned to that first day of school. After her conversation with Miss Colton, she had taken her notebook and supplies and placed them on the floor outside of the room where she had her next class, following the example of several other students. Then she had headed outside. It was such a beautiful day. It was a shame to have to spend it at school, she reflected. The temperature in early September was still hot – 79 degrees – and most of the kids were wearing shorts. The sky was a brilliant blue with only a few gauzy clouds floating here and there. The warm air hummed with the buzzing of bees and sounds of kids playing, and the smell of fresh cut grass made her suddenly homesick for Missoula. She wondered what her friends there were doing right now. Was it their first day of school, too? She'd have to text Kaitlyn as soon as she got home. She'd send her one right now, except the school had a rule that cell phones were to be turned off and left in backpacks during the school day. To avoid hers being stolen, she had asked her homeroom teacher to keep it for her until the end of the day.

Angie glanced around quickly, noting that most of the students were hanging out together in groups. Some squeaked back and forth noisily on the swings. A large group of boys was out in the field playing football. Basketballs thumped against the pavement on the nearby court. A few solitary students lounged here and there on the grass, reading or talking; others sat on the benches, just watching the activity. Near the opposite set of double doors, a rowdy four-square game was underway. Angie strolled over to a patch of cool, green grass and plunked down. If she had thought about it, she would have brought the book she was currently reading, *Twilight*, outside with her, but the incident with Callie had caused her to fall behind everyone else and in her haste to get outside, she hadn't even thought about what she would do once she was there.

It was just as well. Right when she landed on the grass, she heard a familiar voice.

"There's the little trouble-maker now!" Angie looked behind her and saw Callie and her sidekicks fast approaching. There was nowhere she could go; she was trapped. It didn't matter, though. She wasn't afraid of this girl, only mildly irritated with her.

"Thanks a lot for getting me in trouble," Callie spat at her. Angie continued to sit quietly and watch the boys playing football on the field.

"And just what exactly did I do to get *you* in trouble?" she asked. She didn't bother looking up at Callie. Clearly, there would be no reasoning with her.

"If you hadn't tripped me, Miss Coldfish might not have noticed my skirt," Callie complained. "I had to call my dad at work and now I'm gonna get it when I get home. And it's all your fault."

Angie glanced at her and noticed loose, long-legged, red basketball shorts had replaced the black miniskirt. "Wow, nice shorts! Where'd you get those?" she smirked. Callie's face clouded with fury.

"I had to put on my gym shorts! Mr. McGill wouldn't let me go back to class unless I changed." She kicked Angie's leg hard. The other girls snickered when Angie yelped in pain.

"You're dead meat!" Callie hissed. "I'm not through with you, not by a long shot. Stay out of my way! This is a friendly warning."

Angie rose to her feet and the other two girls backed away slightly when they saw her black expression. Callie continued to stare coldly at Angie. Angie stared back. Even though she was a good three inches shorter than Callie, she wasn't afraid.

"Or what?" she asked menacingly.

Callie stepped in closer and lowered her face until it was level with Angie's. She opened her mouth to speak, but just then, the bell rang. The duties called out to the kids, directing them to the door they would use to go to the cafeteria. "You'll find out," Callie warned ominously. "You don't want to mess with me."

"Ooo! I'm *so* scared!" Angie put her hands to her face in mock horror.

Callie stared for another long moment. As she turned to go inside, she mumbled, "You will be." She and the other girls sneered at her, then turned and strode quickly to the door.

"Whatever," Angie said, mostly to herself. She waited until the group was a good fifteen paces away, then she also started for the door. As she began crossing the small, open courtyard, she felt someone's eyes on her. A few feet away, a sandy-haired girl with big, golden eyes was watching her, incredulous. She looked like a pixey with an open, friendly face. When their eyes met, she smiled tentatively at Angie. The smile was also friendly and Angie quickly smiled back.

"Hey," the new girl spoke first. "How are you? I've

never seen anyone stand up to Callie before. She's been a pest ever since we were in kindergarten. Still using the same old line, I see. *I'll get you, my pretty, and your little dog, too!*" She spoke the phrase in a high cackle and raised both hands like claws and waved them up and down, and then she laughed. The sound was like bells, all tinkly and light. "I'm Shawna."

Angie chuckled at the "Wizard of Oz" reference. So, this Shawna thought Callie was a witch, too. This girl had friendship potential. "I'm Angie," she said. She extended her hand in a gesture of welcome, and then worried that maybe she was being too formal for a kid, but before she could pull her hand back, Shawna grabbed it and shook it enthusiastically. They grinned at each other, and since the duties were calling at them to hurry, they headed together quickly towards the entryway of the building.

When they got inside, there was a line formed along the wall just outside the cafeteria. The principal, Mr. McGill, gave instructions on how to give their lunch numbers, how to go through the line, and the expectations for the lunchroom.

"Please give your number *slowly* to Mrs. Rumsey if you are having hot lunch. Your lunch number is the same as the student number on your schedule. If you are having cold lunch, you can go on in and find a seat. Remember – hands and feet to yourself!" Mr. McGill walked over to a small group of boys who were already pushing each other playfully. Angie couldn't see Callie or her loyal followers. She guessed they must already be in the lunchroom.

She turned to look at Shawna. "So," she began, "you've been in this district since kindergarten?"

"Yeah…well, basically," Shawna answered hesitantly.

She appraised Angie's face and decided she could trust her, even though they'd just met. "Our family lives in the YWAM camp just outside of Lakeside."

"Why-Wam? What's that," Angie asked, genuinely curious.

"Y-W-A-M. It stands for Youth With a Mission. It's a Christian organization."

"Oh," Angie responded noncommittally. She didn't want to hurt this girl's feelings, but she had never heard of such a thing, of living in a "camp." She surveyed her curiously. "So, you've always lived there?" Shawna had been the first person her age to speak civilly to her since her arrival that morning and she was anxious to show the right amount of inquisitiveness. She seemed nice enough, and Angie had lived in the area for three months already and hadn't made even one friend yet. As much as she hated small talk, she was more afraid of losing this opportunity.

"Yeah...well." Shawna seemed to be searching for the right words. "See, we do a lot of missions work around the world, so whenever we are in the States, we live in a house at the camp." Over the years, some kids had made fun of her and her family, so Shawna waited to see how Angie would respond. Sometimes it was hard being a missionary. They talked about it a lot at church. In this era of "political correctness," some people, even some Christians, felt it was intrusive and presumptuous to go to other countries and try to foist their beliefs off on others. The truth, Shawna knew, was that the missions trips involved a lot less preaching than people thought. It was more about living and working alongside people of other cultures to create understanding. It was about building new relationships. Of course, her family wanted to share their great hope with people, so if somehow that led to talking about God, well…

Angie had never met a real, live missionary before. Sometimes, when she channel-surfed on Sundays, she'd come across various ministry programs. Some seemed legitimate. Others came across as really phony and even pushy in the way they tried to cajole people into believing in God. They all seemed overly focused on donations. She decided to reserve judgment for the time being. Shawna had been nothing but friendly, so Angie didn't press her too much for details. She wasn't religious herself, but she was open to the idea.

"So, where all have you been?" she asked.

"Um…well, we've been to Thailand, Cambodia, Japan, India, Bangladesh. We're going to Costa Rica in a month! I'm really excited about that!"

"Wow! Costa Rica, huh? Sounds hot and buggy to me!"

"Yeah…well…have you ever seen pictures of it? It's really pretty."

"Nope." Angie stopped. They were at the front of the line. She tried to remember her student number but came up blank. Mrs. Rumsey kindly asked her for her name. She typed it in, then she scribbled the elusive number on a piece of paper and gave it to Angie.

"Probably be a good idea to memorize it," she said kindly, winking. "It also serves as your library number. Don't forget to take a milk!"

"Thanks," Angie replied, sheepishly. Everything was so new and different – would she ever figure out how to do everything? She grabbed a light blue container of skim milk from a nearby cooler, then got into another line leading to the serving counter that separated the lunchroom from the kitchen. She took a quick look around her at the students already seated and eating. Callie and her friends were hogging one half of a table and were clowning around noisily. A lunch duty walked up to them and quietly requested that they settle down. As soon as she turned her back on the girls, they started making faces at her and imitating her nice request in snide voices. Just then, Callie caught Angie looking at them. She took her index finger and slashed it menacingly across her throat, then she smiled a fake smile and went back to mocking people with the other girls. They had moved on from the duty and were harassing a skinny kid with glasses who had dared to try to sit at the opposite end of "their" table.

Angie ignored the gesture and turned back to Shawna. "So…no. I mean, I *have* seen pictures of Costa Rica. I did a report on it last year, so I know a little bit about it. But I've never been there. I've actually never been outside of the United States." It was a sobering thought. In reality, she'd never even been outside of Montana before. It was suddenly strange to think how differently she had lived her life compared to Shawna.

"Well, you should come over sometime. We have tons of pictures and brochures. Some of them were taken by other families we know who have been there before." Shawna looked hopefully at Angie. "In fact, you can come over today if you want to. Well, if my mom says it's okay. I'd have to call her first. And if your mom says it's okay, too, of course. Maybe you could ride the bus home with me, and then your mom could come get you or something."

"Sure, that sounds cool," Angie enthused. She didn't know why exactly, but she felt really close to Shawna already. Maybe she had just been without a friend to talk to for too long, Whatever the reason, she found herself excited at the prospect of hanging out with Shawna. She would have to call her mom at work to get permission, but she couldn't imagine her mom saying no to her. Theresa knew all too well how much Angie had struggled over the summer, having to go through everything without even having her friends to run to. She was relatively sure that her mom would be as glad as she was at the prospect.

"Sweet!" Shawna gushed. They made their way through the lunch line and found out that as long as the weather was nice, they would be allowed to eat outdoors.

"Just be sure to throw away all your garbage and bring the trays back in," Mr. McGill instructed them.

The girls strolled happily to the picnic tables. There weren't too many students eating at them because bees were plentiful in the late summer heat. Neither girl was particularly bothered by the bees, and they absentmindedly shooed them away as they ate and talked. When the bell rang a few minutes later, they couldn't believe how fast time had passed. They quickly returned the trays to the kitchen and headed down the hallway to the sixth-grade wing. As they walked, they chatted and made plans for the afternoon. They would both try to call their moms sometime during the next period. They figured out that they had a sixth-hour elective together – art – and agreed that they would finalize their plans then. As each headed in her own direction towards their fifth hour classes, they waved shyly at each other.

"See you in an hour!" Shawna bubbled.

"Later!" Angie called enthusiastically.

"Don't take any junk from anyone!" Shawna joked.

"No way! If she tries to get in my face, I'll...I'll..."

Angie realized she didn't have the slightest idea what she would do if she had any more run-ins with Callie today. "I'll…well, I don't know!" she giggled. "But I won't take her junk!" she insisted stubbornly, grinning. Just then, Shawna disappeared with a last, quick wave through the door of the health classroom, and Angie found herself at the door to her next class, math. She stopped and peeked in cautiously, surveying the room. Callie was nowhere in sight. One of the girls who constantly followed her around was there, but she glanced away quickly when Angie's eyes met hers. *Not so tough when you're by yourself, huh?* Still, she made a conscious effort to sit as far across the room as possible from the other girl.

The rest of the day passed without incident. As it turned out, Language Arts was the only class in which Angie would have to endure Callie.

Chapter Four: Healing

"It has been said, 'Time heals all wounds.' I do not agree. The wounds remain. In time, the mind, protecting its sanity, covers them with scar tissue and the pain lessens. But it is never gone."
~ Rose Kennedy

he soft notes of a pretty Chopin nocturne filled the room where Angie had physical therapy. Three months had passed since the horrible accident which had left her broken and shattered, both physically and emotionally. The casts had been replaced by removable splints, which were currently off and set to the side while the therapist, Chloe, gently pushed Angie to work a little harder.

"You're getting really strong, Angie," she encouraged. Angie winced as Chloe pulled her left arm straighter. The ever-present pain was at least bearable now. "You've come a long way and you're doing much better than anyone could have anticipated. That's good, but now I want you to start working a little harder. I feel like you're just going through the motions. Where are you today?" Only a few years older than Angie, Chloe had short, spiky black hair and wore three earrings in one ear and two in the other. Her fashion style was young and funky. They were more like sisters than patient and therapist.

Truthfully, Angie was thinking about a lot of things

besides her therapy. There were a million things going on at school, not even taking into account all of the work she needed to do if she were going to pass eleventh grade. Her mom had just started dating the dashing Dr. Halverson, who had finally mustered up the courage to ask her out after Angie was no longer officially his patient. Additionally, the Howsers were getting ready to travel to Ukraine and wouldn't be back for six weeks.

She shook her head and tried to focus. She pushed the giant lavender-colored rubber ball away from her a bit further this time, held the position for a count of ten, and then rolled the ball back towards herself. Late afternoon sunlight filtered through the vertical blinds on the large windows and a big ray shone directly on Angie, warming her slightly. The sunlight belied the sub-zero temperature outside and the warmth, though minimal, felt good. For months now, the snow and cold had kept her feeling constantly chilly.

She smiled when Chloe commended her for her efforts, and switched to the next exercise, one in which she lay on the large exercise table and worked her shoulders using light barbells. Lifting the weights over her head while keeping her back against the table brought those muscles into play as well, and Angie was pleased at the strength she knew she had developed during her sessions. Although she only officially had therapy twice a week now, her mom made sure that she did her exercises every day after school. Bravely, she soldiered on, pushing herself through the short set of exercises while biting her lip whenever pain shot up through her arms and shoulders. Although she had regained most of the use of both arms, she still dealt with numbness and tingling in her hands, particularly her left.

For the first few months, she hadn't even really missed playing her guitar, but now she tried to pick it up every day. Frustration always killed her joy, as the numbness in her left hand made very difficult to push the strings down on the fret board with enough strength to create an actual tone. Her right hand was only slightly better, and Angie realized quickly that she couldn't finger-pick as adeptly as she could before the accident. More often than not, she would only spend a few minutes attempting to play before she put the instrument aside in aggravation.

"Well, that's all for today. Good job!" Chloe patted Angie on the knee and took the free weights from her. She placed them back in their grooves on the weights rack. "You know, I think you should start swimming. You're strong enough now, and it would be a great way to work out your arms and shoulders without putting too much stress on them. Since you're a therapy patient here, you can use either one of the pools without having to pay dues." Angie took her therapy sessions at the local gymnasium, which was affiliated with the hospital. The pool was in the same complex.

"That would be cool! I've always like to swim," Angie enthused. "I looked into joining once, specifically so I could use the pool, but the monthly dues were way more than my mom or I could afford."

"Here," Chloe said, holding out a small piece of gray paper. "This is a referral from me. If you go down the long hallway to the right, you can get signed up and they'll give you a temporary membership card. It's right down that way," she pointed. She physically turned Angie, who had automatically headed towards her car out of habit, in the right direction and gave her a light, playful push. "Do it now, tonight, before you head home," she ordered with mock sternness. "The main pool is open from five in the morning until ten at night, so you should be able to fit some swimming into your schedule, eh? I'll see you next week."

Angie laughed. Chloe could be so bossy sometimes, but Angie hardly minded. She thought about the shape she'd been in when she started therapy. Thanks to Chloe and her constant nagging, Angie was healing far faster than anyone originally hoped. The rest of her body was getting tone and fit, too, a goal she had set for herself at the beginning of the school year, so that was good. A nice side-effect of the therapy.

"Okay, okay! I'll see you next week! Thanks, Chloe," Angie laughed. She walked quickly down the hall to the registration office.

On her way home, she thought about Shawna. She always thought about Shawna. Although it was true that now that she was back in school, she was forced to concentrate on other things, her best friend was never far from her mind. In fact, nothing she did or encountered every day was free of thoughts of Shawna – what would Shawna have said in this situation or that, what would Shawna do if she were here. Tonight, Angie thought about how much she and Shawna had always loved swimming together in the summertime. They lived relatively close to Somers Bay, where there is a public beach, and they had spent most of their waking hours there together during the summer months. Angie knew that Shawna would have been so jealous that she could swim at the gym.

As always, thoughts of Shawna made Angie's heart

ache. Only a few months had passed since the accident, and they had been the hardest of Angie's short life. She couldn't picture her whole life ahead of her without Shawna. To protect herself, she tended to keep her thoughts in the here and now, as much as she could. Even thinking about tomorrow was tough. The teachers had always teasingly referred to them as The Bobbsey Twins because they never went anywhere apart. If you found one of them, you would inevitably find the other. Living without Shawna was like trying to breathe without lungs.

Pulling into the apartment complex parking lot, she noticed a familiar shiny, black BMW parked in the visitor's spot next to her mother's car. So, the doctor was visiting. Again. Angie sighed. She was totally happy for her mom, but this was getting to be a daily occurrence. Was he planning on moving in?

Over the course of the previous few months, Theresa and Dr. Halverson had become good friends. Of course, they saw each other almost daily for the first month after Angie woke up. What started as an occasional cup of coffee together had turned into…what? *An actual relationship, that's what.* She didn't really mind, though. Truth be told, she really liked the doctor. She worried that maybe she liked him a little *too* much. Sometimes she felt little twinges of jealousy towards her mother over the burgeoning romance. Mostly, though, she was just really glad for her.

"Hey!" she called as she entered, dropping her pack on the chair by the front door and her keys onto the small, decorative table next to it. She quickly rifled through the mail on the table, tossing the pile back down after ascertaining it was all bills for her mom. David Gray's "This Year's Love" softly played on the stereo. A current favorite of both women, it wasn't unusual for Angie to come home and hear his music playing.

"Hey, you!" her mom called cheerfully.

The tangy aroma of her mom's homemade lasagna, along with the sweet scent of fresh-baked bread, filled the small apartment. Angie's stomach growled loudly as she strode into the kitchen. Her mom and Dr. Halverson (or Jack, as he now insisted she call him) were sitting relaxed at adjacent corners of the dining room table. They sipped fresh-brewed coffee. Angie noticed that Jack's hand covered her mom's on the table. He squeezed it gently, and then quickly let go, standing to acknowledge Angie's entrance like a gentleman from bygone days. Theresa smiled up adoringly at him. Both he and Theresa were aware that their new relationship made Angie slightly uncomfortable. He repositioned himself on the other side of the table, making a spot for Angie near her mother. He motioned to her, inviting her to join them.

"Oh, hi, Mom. Hi, Doc...um, I mean...Jack!" Angie smiled shyly at him. His answering smile made her blush and caused her heart to race. She *was* a little uncomfortable with her mom's new boyfriend, but it wasn't for the reasons her mom thought. Theresa believed that Angie wasn't ready to see her mother with anyone but her father. Because of that, she and Jack always downplayed their relationship when Angie was around. The truth was that Angie still had a bit of a crush on Jack herself, and being around him always made her self-conscious. She knew he liked her mom, not her, and obviously was way too old for her. She had figured him to be at least thirty when she first woke up from her coma. She now knew that he was actually thirty-five. *He's still hot.* A Mona Lisa smile played on her lips at the thought.

Theresa stood when Jack did and rushed to hug Angie.

"How was therapy, babe? What does Chloe think of your progress? Are you hungry? Do you want to eat right away, or do you have some homework you want to do first?"

Angie laughed at the barrage of questions. Her mother always talked too fast when she was nervous. She returned her mother's squeeze and started answering her questions as she fished a glass out of the dishwasher and pulled the milk carton from the fridge.

"Therapy was really good today," she began, as she poured herself half a glass. "Know what's great? Chloe got me access to the pool! Now I can swim whenever I want to!" She returned the milk to the refrigerator and went to join Jack and her mom at the table.

"Seriously?" her mother answered, incredulous. She knit her eyebrows together in sudden panic. "What's the catch? As in, what's this going to cost?" The week and a half of work she had missed right after the accident had made a huge dent in their budget, and although Theresa was exceedingly frugal with her money, she still wasn't completely caught up on the bills.

"That's the cool part, Mom!" Angie gushed. "Since I'm a therapy patient, I can use the pool for free!" She and her mom exchanged a gentle high-five as Theresa sighed in relief. "It opens at five in the morning and closes at ten at night, so I should be able to fit in a few mornings and a few evenings a week!"

"Perfect, Angie!" Jack enthused. "Swimming is a great way to exercise your arms and shoulders and is relatively low-impact!"

"That's exactly what Chloe said!" Angie smiled at him, then lowered her eyes quickly and focused on her glass of milk so he wouldn't see how much she liked looking at him.

"Well, that's wonderful, sweetheart," Theresa replied happily. Angie drained the last of the milk in her glass and stood up, while Theresa positioned herself back at the table, right next to Jack. He immediately took hold of her hand again. Angie took in the small decisive action and smiled, delighted for her mom. Ever since Jack and Theresa had started dating a few weeks back, Theresa's whole countenance had changed. She was constantly smiling and chipper and flitted around the apartment like a hummingbird. The positive effect of the pairing on both of them was unmistakable from day one. It was the happiest she had seen her mother in years – or ever, for that matter. As for Jack, he practically glowed around Theresa.

She grinned at the lovebirds. "Yeah," she offered, "Chloe thinks I'm healing really fast. She thinks I'll be ready to cut down to once a week, starting next Wednesday." As she headed to her room, she called over her shoulder, "As far as the other stuff you asked, yes, I'm hungry, but I do want to finish my homework really fast. I only have a few more math problems to figure out. Then we can eat and watch a movie or something!"

"Um…oh…" her mother stammered. Angie turned to see Theresa blushing and exchanging a loaded look with Jack.

"Unless you've got other plans?" Angie asked, raising one eyebrow knowingly. Her mother and Jack went out together almost every night since they'd started seeing each other.

"Well, uh…we *were* thinking of going to see a movie at the theater in town," Theresa began hesitantly. "But we can stick around and watch a movie here with you, if you want…" She glanced at Jack, and he nodded and shrugged.

"Sure! We could definitely stay and watch something here, together," he said, almost too earnestly. "You must feel like we abandon you quite a bit." Then he added, "In fact, I should just go home after we eat. I have a difficult surgery Monday morning that I need to mentally prepare for." He looked at Theresa, his disappointment obvious.

Angie tried to rescue the two flustered adults. "Aw, c'mon, I'm a big girl. It's Friday night! Go out! I need to brainstorm some ideas for my essay, anyway. We have to compare 'Romeo and Juliet' to a modern novel and talk about writing styles and stuff like that. Plus, I want to play my guitar. Or try to," she said, blushing. She hoped her admission wouldn't cause them to ask her to play for them again. She had tried a few nights ago and it became readily evident that she wasn't really able to yet. The whole thing had been horrendously embarrassing.

To her relief, they didn't ask.

"How about this?" her mother bargained. "Jack and I will go out tonight and let you get some of your stuff done. Then tomorrow, let's go rent some movies and order pizza and plan on spending the whole evening together, the three of us. Unless you have something else planned?" she asked, raising her eyebrows. She knew full well that Angie didn't have any plans. Since the accident, Angie hadn't been out at all except to go to school, therapy and doctor's appointments, or to do the grocery shopping. Theresa knew that Angie still cried almost every night over Shawna. It had been three months, but her daughter showed no signs of moving on. She never stayed after school or went in before classes to join other kids in their various activities. She lived her life like a nun and stayed sequestered in her room.

Angie's dejected expression almost gave her away. She smiled bravely and answered, "No. I don't have anything planned. That sounds good, Mom. You two go out. Have some fun, will you? I'll be just fine."

. . .

A few hours later, long after Jack and Theresa departed for the theater, Angie sat crying in her bedroom. She had spent the last forty-five minutes trying to play and sing a song that she and Shawna had written together. Her voice rang out strong as ever, but her playing was not what she'd hoped. She could only withstand a few moments' pressure while trying to hold down chords with her left hand, and her right hand kept going so numb; she couldn't even feel the strings beneath them. She'd finally just shoved the guitar a little too roughly into its stand, and then crumpled in a heap on the floor next to it. For a long moment, she just lay there, letting despair wash over her. And then she had let out an earsplitting, frustrated scream.

It was a good thing it was Friday. Not only were her mom and Jack out, but so were most of the residents of the complex, so nobody heard her scream or came suddenly banging on the door demanding to know what was going on, and nobody called the police. On one hand, she was glad she didn't have to answer for her behavior; on the other, she was flooded with self-pity at the realization that she was really alone. Not just because her mom was out. She was alone because Shawna was gone. Gone, gone, gone. Gone for good.

She curled up in the fetal position on the floor and let lonely and desolate thoughts ravage her mind while the tears flowed freely. It occurred to her that everyone was alone. They were alone inside their own minds. Even when someone was right beside you with their arms wrapped around you, still you were ultimately alone. Sadness overwhelmed her.

Like a freight train lumbering across a long and lonely prairie, the thoughts kept coming. She lay with her eyes closed and let them have her, not trying to control them or stop them. She thought about her dad and how he'd only been up once to see her. When they all lived together, she hadn't seen much of him because of his long hauls. At the time of the divorce, it hadn't occurred to her that living apart would mean spending even less time together. She knew he loved her and that he hadn't been to see her because he was down south running loads there and would be until spring. Still, she was wallowing, so she let every little thought meander through her mind, not evaluating them or analyzing too much. If a thought fed her self-pity, she let it stay and make a few circuits before other ones pushed it away.

Now, here she lay, depressed beyond all reason. The tears slowed as emotional exhaustion overtook her. She wondered about the medicine cupboard in the bathroom, wracking her brain to remember what drugs it contained. She was pretty sure nothing by itself would really harm her, but also thought that maybe if she took everything, that would do the trick. She wanted the pain to end. She just couldn't deal with life anymore.

No, that's not an answer, sweetheart. The words weren't audible. She felt them rather than physically heard them. Along with them came a powerful and inexplicable feeling of warmth, acceptance, and love – unlike anything she had ever experienced.

Instantly, she pictured the Howsers. Right after she was released from the hospital, she had hesitated to see them for fear of the pain seeing them would cause; however, after a few weeks she finally went to visit. For five years, they had been like surrogate parents to her. When she wasn't home, she had been at the Howser's. After she finally went to see them, she wondered how she could have stayed away. Even though it was certainly painful to be in their home, in the place where she and Shawna had spent so many wonderful times together, she was greatly comforted to see and hug them again. With that first painful trip behind her, Angie had made a point of going over now at least once a week. They always asked her about her mom and school, and always tried to feed her (Mrs. Howser had a thing about cooking for people). She'd thought it would be awkward to spend time with them, but it was as natural as breathing. She was constantly amazed at the grace with which they had handled everything.

The two families had attended the sentencing hearing of the girl who had killed their precious daughter and friend. Although they did not feel compelled to offer testimony that would garner the girl a lighter sentence, Eileen and Grant each had a chance to speak to her in court and both stated that they forgave her and would always keep her in their prayers. They told the girl's family members that they understood that the situation had to be horribly difficult for them, too, and that they would be praying for all of them as well. Of course, they also testified to how painful their loss continued to be and how big a hole Shawna's death had left in their lives.

Angie and Theresa had borne witness to the Howsers' public forgiveness of their daughter's killer in wide-eyed astonishment. Theresa had even commented to Angie on their way home that day that there was no way in creation *she* could ever have been so magnanimous. If anybody ever hurt *her* baby, she was sure she would want kill them with her bare hands.

Now, as Angie lay curled up on the floor, having just, however briefly, contemplated taking her own life, she thought of the Howsers, and then of her mom, and shame washed over her. How could she possibly even think of bringing that kind of pain upon all of them? Tears of shame replaced the tears of self-pity. She considered crying out to God, as the Howsers had suggested many times that she should do, and she did manage to whisper, "Please, God, help me." The sound of her own voice broke through her private reverie and brought her crashing back to the present. She suddenly felt emotionally stripped bare. She felt vulnerable and strange and a little embarrassed.

Her eyes opened and she realized she had been lying on the floor for a good while. What time was it? She glanced at the clock on her nightstand and realized it was eleven. She had been there on the floor for two solid hours. Slowly, she pulled herself up. She berated herself for being such a selfish baby, but then the same inexplicable warmth washed over her again. She felt like she was being spiritually hugged. Just as she had earlier, she felt as though someone or something was telling her that she was loved and needed to stop being so hard on herself.

She felt deeply comforted and she realized in amazement that she no longer felt alone or sad. She was at peace. She didn't know to what she should attribute these sudden feelings of well-being. She got up off the floor. Her mom and Jack had said they might go out and have a few drinks when the movie was over, so there was no telling when they would be home, but it didn't matter. She was completely at ease for the first time in months.

After taking a long, leisurely, hot bath, she put on some pajamas fresh out of the laundry. They were so soft and smelled so good. She felt as soothed as a swaddled baby. The peacefulness still surrounded her, and the bath had left her feeling very sleepy. She knew she didn't have to wait up for her mom, so she went out to double check that the front door and sliding glass door to the deck were locked. She put fresh food and water out for Tater. Then she turned out all the lights except the tiny one above the stove.

In her room, she switched on the small nightstand lamp and batted the overhead light off. As she got into bed, she grabbed her mp3 player and started to plug in her earphones. It was her habit to fall asleep listening to some soothing rock songs that she liked. She had put together a "sleep" list, with the softer and more melodic tunes of Led Zeppelin and Pink Floyd and Radiohead and Muse. She usually listened to it every night until she fell asleep.

Tonight, though, she felt compelled to leave the music off. She worried that she might not be able to fall asleep without it, but she flicked off the little lamp, and no sooner had her head hit the pillow than she was out. Her dreams were lovely and peaceful. Shawna was in them, but they were together and happy. She dreamt of playing her guitar and singing without pain. She slept more deeply than she had in three months.

Chapter Five: Into the Unknown

*"The future is called 'perhaps,' which is the only thing
to call the future. And the only important thing is
not to allow that to scare you."*
~Tennessee *Williams,* Orpheus Descending

*N*ow that Angie was down to one day of therapy a week, she and Chloe had decided to meet on Wednesdays, since it's the natural midweek mark. Of course, Angie was supposed to keep doing her exercises every day at home. The second week of the new schedule, Angie brought her swimsuit with her to her session. She planned on trying out the pool right after she finished with Chloe. Nearly two weeks had passed since she'd been granted access to it and she still hadn't taken advantage of it. She chastised herself for not going sooner.

The pool was tied up for the first half hour after she finished therapy. The high school swim team used it for training, since they didn't have their own. Angie decided to use the time to give herself a small tour of the whole facility, which turned out to be very big and quite nice. There were several rooms dedicated to everything from yoga to spinning classes to martial arts, and there was even an indoor walking path and a climbing wall. What impressed her the most was all the space that was dedicated to kids twelve and under – they had their own gymnasium and fitness rooms. The whole place reverberated with the sounds of voices and the clanking and whirring of exercise equipment.

Once she finished exploring, Angie got a keycard for a locker and went to the women's locker room to change into her swimsuit. She took the requisite two-minute shower and even thought to run the water a little cold near the end so the pool would feel warmer. There were actually two pools – the large, Olympic-sized pool that the swim team used, and a smaller, warmer therapy pool. Although the water temperature in the therapy pool sounded the most inviting, the schedule on the door indicated that it was primarily designated for geriatric and preschool swim classes. At the moment, both categories of people were using it, and the tiny room echoed a little too loudly with the young ones' enthusiastic squeals. Angie decided to use the large pool; even though it was ten degrees colder, the room seemed quieter to her just then.

The large room had its share of noise but it didn't bother her as much. She was one of only ten or so people present, and the sounds of their bare feet slapping on the wet deck and of the water splashing against the edges of the pool bounced around her. The air was humid and reeked of chlorine. The other women there swam without swim caps, and Angie deduced that they must not be required to wear them. She thought that was odd, since most pool managers make a big deal about the filters getting clogged with long hair, but ultimately, she didn't mind. She found the rubber hats constrictive and uncomfortable, since she had a lot of hair. Besides that, they were just plain silly-looking. She had had hers since fifth grade and it still sported most of the giant rubber daisy attached to the crown. She had braided her hair tightly, so Angie tossed the cap quickly aside. She squatted down by the side of the pool.

She bent down and dipped her hand in the water, which was cool but didn't seem unreasonably cold. She adjusted her position until she was sitting on the pool's edge and tentatively stuck one toe in the water. It still didn't feel too cold, so she scooted closer and dropped both legs in. She let them dangle, allowing her skin to adjust to the slightly chilly water. Goosebumps rose on her arms and she rubbed them to warm herself. In the lane next to her, a woman dove in, yelping loudly from the cold when her head emerged a few seconds later. She turned, noticed Angie, and grinned.

"It's really not all that bad," she promised.

Angie didn't answer her; she only smiled back quickly and then looked down. She really wasn't in the mood to make small talk with strangers. She just wanted to swim. The friendly lady took the hint and began swimming a lap. The splashing echoed off the walls. Angie watched the water rolling back and forth against the side of the pool and marveled at its color. When she was a child, it always amazed her that the water could look so turquoise, and yet when she tried to pick some up in her hands, it was clear. It wasn't until years later that she found out it was because the walls of the pool were painted blue to create the illusion. It didn't matter. She still thought it looked pretty.

While she contemplated the color of the water, she heard footsteps slapping along, coming from the direction of the men's showers. She tried to see who it was using her peripheral vision, but couldn't tell. So, she turned her head and pretended to look for her towel, which she knew full well was on a nearby chair, and used the opportunity to take a peek at the new arrival. A shock of recognition jolted her. It was Mark Kennedy, a guy from school. No, Angie corrected herself, not just any guy – *it's Mark Kennedy!* She'd only had a huge crush on him since sixth grade. Angie had to remind herself to breathe normally and not hyperventilate. *For heaven's sake, just breathe!*

She needn't have let herself get so worked up, because Mark jumped right into the pool without even noticing her and started swimming in large, strong strokes down his lane. For the moment, she was exempt from actually having to talk to him. She could just enjoy the view. She admired his muscular arms, perfect, not too skinny but not overbuilt. His back was strong, too, and he fairly sailed through the water in a synchronized rhythm.

Suddenly, Angie became self-conscious. She hadn't thought of the possibility of running into anyone she knew. She glanced down at her left arm, which had some minor scars left over from the accident and the subsequent surgeries. In her mind, she was hideously deformed, even though the scars were minimal. What if he came over to talk to her?

She had met Mark once, though she doubted he would remember. She and Shawna had attended a birthday party a couple years back for Mark's sister, Halle. The party was held at the roller rink, which doubled as the Boys and Girls Club. At the time, Mark was working there after school as one of the club leaders, so he was able to rent the place at a discount for Halle's party. The girls were all freshmen and Mark was already a junior, but Angie remembered him being very cordial and sweet when he was introduced to the younger girls.

And she reminded herself about how the girls all swooned over him, too. Some threw themselves at him in a most embarrassing manner. Not that she had blamed them. Mark was an incredibly good-looking guy. His ash-blond hair was shaggy and he used hair treatment and made it stick out in all directions. Long, light lashes surrounded blue-green eyes that sometimes looked turquoise. His smile was framed in totally adorable dimples and was that of a genuinely happy person. Even back then, he had sported a decent build.

Angie remembered thinking she had never seen a cuter guy in all her life. If she'd nursed even a tiny idea of talking to him that night, though, it was quickly dispelled. He was never alone, not for one single minute all evening. Girls followed him everywhere. If they weren't bold enough to come right out and talk to him, they hung out as close to him as possible, talking too much, laughing too loudly, trying desperately to get his attention. From what she could remember, their efforts fell on deaf ears and blind eyes. Mark spent the majority of his time spinning songs for the kids to skate to and talking to a couple of his buddies who had shown up to help out with the party. If he was interested in all the attention he was garnering, nobody ever would have known it.

A loud splash brought Angie back to the present. Two more girls had entered the pool. They were roughly two years younger than Angie, she surmised. They swam a little, but mostly spent their time whispering and giggling after they caught site of Mark. The way they interacted reminded her of how she and Shawna used to be.

The observation transported her back again to the night of the party and to another memory of her early friendship with Shawna.

. . .

A few hours had passed since they had arrived at the rink and were introduced to Halle's hot brother. Shawna and Angie, who had just begun ninth grade, were having the time of their lives. Mark kept an excellent selection of popular songs playing all night and the girls had skated to almost every one. A couple of times, they took short breaks and went out to the lobby to get drinks or something to eat or to use the restroom. The music inside the rink blared. The overhead lights were dimmed, and strands of colored lights and mirrored disco balls hung from the ceiling, creating a party atmosphere. A couple of times, the girls went to the lobby just to escape the loud music. When the doors shut behind them, the lobby, although filled with kids, was markedly quieter – they could actually hear each other speak.

During one of these trips out, they ran smack into Callie Simmons. She reared back like she'd been tazed and looked like she was about to start something, but her friends called to her from inside the rink. Instead of saying anything, she made a face like she smelled something rotten, and then turned and went inside to skate. Shawna and Angie were relieved; they weren't scared of Callie, but they were having a great time and didn't want it spoiled by an altercation with her. They counted themselves lucky that she had seemed preoccupied.

A half hour or so later, they were just getting ready to go skate some more when Halle approached them. She held her cell phone in her hand and she looked upset. She motioned the girls to follow her and they sat together at a nearby booth.

"Have you seen this?" Halle asked them, holding out her phone. Displayed on the screen was a message poking fun at Shawna and Angie and implying that they were gay because they spent so much time together. "Check your phones – from the way people are acting, I'm betting she sent it to everyone in her contact list!"

Shawna dug her phone out and scrolled to the message inbox.

"Well, she didn't send it to me," she stated. "Of course, I would have been surprised if I was even in her contacts. Oh, well. Sticks and stones. I'd rather people thought I was gay than unkind, so that's her cross to bear!" Shawna shrugged and grinned.

Angie also checked her messages. She hadn't received the nasty note directly from Callie, but another one of their friends had forwarded it to her to make her aware of it. Instantly, her blood boiled. It always amazed her that Shawna never seemed bothered by stuff like this – it usually made Angie so mad, she couldn't see straight.

"Who does that hag think she is?" Angie fumed. Looking around, she noticed some of the kids staring, laughing, and pointing at them. "The way she thinks she can do or say anything she wants to just frosts my cookies!"

Shawna laughed her tinkly laugh. "Aw, c'mon, Ang! Don't let it get to you so much. Who cares what she thinks, anyway?"

Just then, she spotted Callie heading their way carrying

a drink cup in one hand and a bag of popcorn in the other. As she approached the table, she adopted a contrite expression.

"Hey, girls!" she called out in a saccharine voice when she was a few feet away from their table. "I thought I should come apologize for sending out that message. That was totally uncalled for, and I shouldn't have…oops!"

Suddenly, she pretended to trip and the cup of pop she was carrying splashed all over the front of Angie's shirt. Angie flinched, sucking her breath in as the icy drink cascaded down her favorite tie-dyed t-shirt. Kids at nearby tables started laughing.

"Oh, no!" Callie exclaimed with false alarm. "Oh, Angie, I'm SO sorry! I didn't mean to, honestly!" But even as the words came from her mouth, some of her nasty little followers started to laugh and snicker, pointing at Angie. Callie immediately lost her fake concern and giggled.

"Aw, that's really too bad, Angie! I guess you'll have to go home now!"

Shawna's mouth hung open in utter surprise that anyone, even Callie Simmons, could be so mean. Then her eyebrows furrowed together and her expression became more menacing than Angie had ever seen it. Shawna stood up and got nose-to-nose with Callie. To everyone's surprise, especially Angie's, she uncharacteristically looked like she was about to punch Callie in the face. Shawna was no Bible-thumper, but she usually did subscribe to the "turn the other cheek" manner of dealing with this sort of situation. She rarely got angry.

Before she could say a word, though, suddenly there he was. Mark Kennedy, seeing the "accident," had grabbed a bar towel and rushed over to Angie's aid. He handed her the towel, and Angie mumbled her thanks and began mopping up the sticky pop, which had soaked her shirt front and was dripping off the table onto her jeans, too.

"Wow, are you alright?" Mark asked Angie. His big, turquoise-green eyes reflected genuine concern. "I have a shirt in my car that you can borrow if you want." He smiled kindly down at Angie, who could only blink back at him in surprise. He had a lovely voice, deep, soft and velvety, and Angie blushed and smiled. Then Mark turned to where Shawna and Callie were standing nose-to-nose. Seeing that Shawna was about to lose her temper, he stepped in between them, gently moving Shawna to the side so that now he was the one in Callie's face. She smiled sweetly and began to thank him, but he cut her off before she could even begin.

"Stow it!" he barked. "You know, I can't say for certain, but from where I was standing, it totally looked like you dumped that drink on this girl on purpose!" Callie adopted her trademark "innocent" expression and tried to look chagrined. Even Callie wasn't immune to Mark's good looks, and in spite of the circumstances, she was flattered that he was speaking to her. She attempted to use the charm that usually served her well.

"Wh…what?" she stammered, looking baffled and smiling sweetly. "I don't know what you mean, Mark. It was totally an accident! I would never…"

"I said stow it!" Mark commanded. "You know, you may have been blessed with nice looks, but that's all you have. If you aren't careful, someday you won't be in school anymore and you'll find you have a shortage of real friends. As time passes, so will your looks, and then maybe you'll wake up unattractive and alone, and you'll understand how nasty you were as a kid. Maybe you'll want to apologize or something, but it will be too late. Nobody will care about you or what you think anymore. Actions have consequences, you know?"

Then he turned away from Callie as if she didn't exist and focused on Angie and Shawna. Callie just stood there mutely, reeling from the sharp words.

"Come with me, ladies, and we'll get you all fixed up," he stated kindly.

All of the kids in the snack area started clapping and hooting their appreciation. It was hard to tell which they appreciated more – Mark's chivalry towards Angie or his having put Callie in her place. Either way, as he, Angie, and Shawna walked towards the club entrance, Callie could only watch them go, bewilderment and astonishment reddening her face. Then, she turned her wrath on the cheering crowd.

"Shut up, morons!" she screamed. They only laughed at her and clapped louder. She took a few threatening strides toward the nearest table, looking like she was gearing up for battle. The table's occupants shrank away from her obvious fury. At that precise moment, one of Mark's friends, Ben Shafer, who was helping to chaperone the party, approached her and moved in between her and the table of cowering students.

"I think it's probably best that you leave now," he stated firmly. He brushed his long, brown bangs away from his forehead. His well-muscled biceps flexed beneath his tight-fitting t-shirt as he crossed his arms over his chest and adopted a no-nonsense stance, looking Callie straight in the eye.

"What?" she shrieked angrily. "YOU can't make me leave!"

"No, but if you don't, I will call the police and have them remove you. I'm pretty sure THEY can make you leave," Ben challenged. "Now, get going, or I'll talk to the head of the club and have you eighty-sixed from it permanently." He stood his ground and stared at Callie without a hint of emotion. It was obvious from all who witnessed the scene that Ben had no intention of backing down.

"Fine," Callie retorted crisply, "but you'll be sorry! My dad is a lawyer. I'll sue you!"

Ben only laughed at the wimpy threat. "Really? From what I've heard, you don't even have a dad! Besides, I have a dozen witnesses. Give it your best shot! You won't win, and you'll just end up never coming in here again. Now, please leave," he added, the smile on his face replaced by seriousness.

The whole room watched silently as Callie, fuming and cussing, sat down and took off her skates. She threw them to the side of the room instead of returning them properly, nearly hitting two kids who were at the other end of the bench putting their skates on. Then, she yanked her coat out of the locker she had stashed it in, and stomped toward the front door, passing Mark, Shawna, and Angie, who had already retrieved the shirt from his car and were heading back inside. By now, most of the skaters had left the rink and come to the snack area to watch as word of the confrontation spread.

"And YOU!" she spat angrily, pointing a finger at Angie as she backed out the door. "You'd better have eyes in the back of your head, because when you least expect it,

I'm coming after you!"

Angie started to reply, but Shawna grabbed her arm and pulled her towards the restroom, saying, "Come on, Angie, you can't argue with her, you know that. She's been making the same threat for years. She's full of hot air and we all know it. Let's go change your shirt." Angie let Shawna tow her away, but her eyes remained locked on Callie's.

Before anyone could say anything else, Ben stepped up once more and placed himself between Callie and the other girls. He pulled his cell phone from his pocket and pointed at the door.

"Go now, or I'm calling the police," he promised in a steady voice. Mark smiled appreciatively at his bold friend. He crossed his arms and took a stance of solidarity next to Ben.

Callie balled up her fists and made a screechy, angry noise at the boys. Then, she turned, put her nose in the air, and sauntered slowly out like she was royalty and nothing could touch her.

The whole room exploded with applause. Ben gave a small bow and walked back to man the snack bar, which had a good-sized line of kids waiting to be served. Nobody complained, though, because they had all enjoyed the show. Angie and Shawna returned and decided to resume skating. Mark went to help Ben with the long line of customers, so he and Angie didn't get much of a chance to talk just then. With Callie gone, the charged atmosphere in the room dissipated as people went back to skating or eating or talking to their friends.

. . .

"Are you planning on swimming or just waiting to see if your legs really will shrivel up? It's an old wives tale, you know."

The question startled Angie back to the present. She looked up and saw Mark smiling down at her, same turquoise eyes, same beautiful face.

Glancing at the clock, she realized she had been deep in thought for about twenty minutes with her legs dangling in the water. She quickly clapped a hand over the worst scar on her left arm. He followed her self-conscious movement with his eyes but said nothing. Embarrassed, she smiled back at Mark awkwardly.

"Actually, I was just thinking…" her voice trailed off, as she didn't know what else to say. She had been thinking about his kind gesture and about how good his shirt had smelled when she put it on.

Mark sat down next to her and the two younger girls observed from across the pool in jealous silence. As Angie watched, they whispered to each other behind their hands and started giggling again. Angie quickly looked away.

"You're Angie, aren't you?" Mark asked. "I don't know if you remember me. I'm Mark. Mark Kennedy."

"Um…yes. I do, actually. I mean, I am. Angie, that is." She shook her head like she was trying to clear her thoughts and blushed at her own awkward response.

"I thought so," Mark replied, nodding. They both looked down at the water again. Mark searched for another way to get a conversation going. Finally, he faced Angie again.

"So, how are you? I see you at school from time to time, but we never seem to cross paths. I've been meaning to find you and tell you how sorry I am about the accident and Shawna and all. She was a really nice girl. She went to my church. You two were pretty close, weren't you?"

The question brought a stab of pain to Angie's heart. No one had really said anything to her about the accident in months. When she returned to school and people asked how she was doing, she usually brushed them off, pretending that she was fine. If pressed further, she would shut them down by saying she had to be somewhere and walking away. It was all just too painful to talk about. Talking about Shawna wasn't going to bring her back, after all. Eventually, people gave up trying to express condolences and just left her alone. She was grateful when people just stopped asking.

As usual, she hoped to avoid the topic all together, but when Angie moved to get up, she discovered that she had been sitting for so long that her rear end had gone to sleep. As soon as she moved, she got "pins and needles" that electrified her seat and the backs of her thighs. Her arms, while much improved, still didn't really provide much in the way of strength. In the end, she wasn't able to shimmy away like she'd hoped she could. So, she did the only thing she could do: She let go of her left arm, leaned forward, and let her body weight pull her over the edge and into the water. The movement was graceless and almost comical. She tried not to gasp as the cool water enveloped her. Feeling returned to her legs as she dog-paddled to keep from sinking. She felt like a completely uncoordinated idiot. Refusing to look Mark in the eyes, she turned her face slightly in his direction.

"I'm sorry," she mumbled, accidentally swallowing a gulp of pool water with the effort of speaking. She coughed a few times and sputtered, and said, "I really need to get a few laps in and get going. I didn't realize how late it was getting." She started swimming away from him.

"Angie," Mark called to her. "I'm sorry, I didn't mean to…"

"No, it's alright, really. We'll talk soon, okay? I just really need to get going right now," Angie called over her shoulder after swimming a few strokes away. It was the most she could say, because then she started crying. Despite the tears and the heaving of her chest, she managed to swim slowly and methodically to the other end of the lane, projecting the appearance of calm, and when she turned to swim back, Mark was gone. The giggling girls had moved from the pool to the nearby hot tub and were no longer paying her any attention.

Nice going, dork! He was just trying to be nice. For some reason, Mark's disappearance left her feeling lonelier than she had in many weeks. She swam to the nearest ladder and managed to climb out, although her arms throbbed with the effort. Blinded by tears, she stumbled her way back to the locker room, snatching her towel up from the chair as she passed. By the time she reached the showers, she was sobbing uncontrollably. The shower room was empty, and she was grateful, because she was able to give herself over completely to her grief. For the next ten minutes, she stood under a spray of hot water and cried until she was cried out and the water started to run cold.

Her emotions spent, she dragged herself from the showers to the locker room, changed into her clothes, then rolled her wet swimsuit up in her towel and threw it in her gym bag. Her despair from a few moments earlier was replaced by an inexplicable peace, just like a week or so ago, on the Friday evening she had spent alone.

She dropped the key card in a little box on the wall and headed up the stairs. As she crossed the empty lobby towards the exit, she thought about her reaction to Mark's simple inquiry into her well-being and flushed red with embarrassment again. *What's wrong with me? He was only trying to be nice. He probably thinks I'm a freak now.*

Deep in thought and walking fast, she slammed into the exit door and was surprised when it barely moved. Usually, it swung right out; now, it resisted against a strong wind. Some snowflakes flew through the small opening on icy air and swirled around her feet. Amazed, she looked through the glass door and saw that a full-force winter storm had blown in while she was swimming. The cars in the parking lot, the nearest only twenty feet or so from the door, were almost invisible in the swirling white of the blizzard. The wind came in powerful gusts, seemingly from every direction, and brought with it a cold that cut like a knife. Angie stopped to take her ski hat and gloves out of her bag and after throwing them on, pushed harder against the door until it gave way. The icy wind immediately chilled her to the bone. She turned her back to it and zipped up her coat as far as it would go. There was still space between the top of her coat and the bottom of her hat, allowing the biting wind access to her face and neck, but it would have to do. Bravely, she turned and began navigating the snowy, icy parking lot in search of her car.

Almost immediately, she slipped on a patch of ice and fell, her feet sliding out from under her. She landed on her backside. Her first instinct as a teenager was to look around quickly and see if anyone had noticed her fall. Through the blinding snow, she thought she saw a figure approaching her. Not wanting to seem like an invalid, she rolled to her side and attempted to stand up, but her feet had trouble finding purchase on the slippery, snow-covered asphalt. It almost would have been funny if she hadn't been so cold. She felt like she was in a scene from a silly comedy.

Suddenly, from behind her, a pair of strong hands gripped her by the shoulders and started pulling her up.

"I've got you, Angie," Mark shouted above the howling wind. When he almost had her standing up again, he lost his own footing and fell backwards, pulling Angie down on top of him.

"Oops!" he hollered, grinning. "Let's try that again!" Angie rolled sideways off of him and got on her hands and knees, while Mark attempted to right himself. He managed to stand back up, then he held his gloved hand out to Angie who was still on all fours.

"Here!" he yelled.

"Like I should trust you?" Angie yelled back, smiling. She grasped his hand as Mark anchored his foot firmly against the curb and leaned back. This time, he was successful at getting her back on her feet. The pulling hurt her arms, but she wasn't about to complain.

"Where's your car?" he shouted. She pointed towards where she had parked, and putting his arm around her firmly, he began towing her in the direction she indicated. For the moment, she was too cold and dazed to even think about the fact that Mark Kennedy had his arm around her, other than it felt strong and solid. Angie was amazed at how much snow had accumulated in spite of the wind. She knew her mom was going to be worried about her driving in these conditions. They both knew she wasn't that great at winter driving, so whenever possible, she avoided it all together. Oh, well. There was no avoiding it now – she had to get home. She planned to call her mom as soon as she made it to the car.

When they reached the little compact, Mark started shaking his head. He yelled something but Angie couldn't hear him above the wind. She unlocked her door and motioned for him to get in the other side. She climbed in and tossed her gym bag into the back seat as Mark opened the passenger side door. He got in quickly and hastily yanked the door closed again.

"Phew! Dang!" Angie commented, as soon as they were both inside the car with the doors shut. She rubbed her gloved hands together to create some friction. "Holy cow, it's cold! I thought the weather report said there *might* be a winter storm, and I thought it was supposed to hit tomorrow, or I wouldn't have even come out." Her breath escaped in frosty clouds as she spoke.

"Yeah, well, you know, weather prediction isn't an exact science…not yet, anyway," Mark huffed, out of breath from the cold. The way he said, "Yeah, well…" reminded her of Shawna and she bristled as another bolt of pain shot through her heart. She tried very hard not to show it, and it worked – he didn't notice a change in her at all. He took off his gloves and blew on his hands, and then slapped them against his pants legs to try to summon feeling to his fingers.

"What were you yelling a minute ago?" Angie asked, putting the key in the ignition and starting the car. She put the heater on full blast to try to get the windshield, now covered in ice, to start defrosting. Arctic air assaulted both of them in the face, so she turned it down a notch. The car was an older model and she knew she'd probably be halfway home before the blown air would be warm. She sighed as she realized that she would most likely have to get out again and scrape the windows. Had she thought to put the ice scraper in her car?

"I was marveling that you actually thought you could go anywhere in this car in *this* type of weather!" Mark smiled playfully at her. Gosh, he was cute, even in the dim glow of the dashboard lights.

"Yeah, well, this is what I have," she replied, chuckling. "Hey, thanks for helping me out there. I thought you were already gone." She smiled back at him shyly, then quickly focused her attention on the windshield, pretending to watch for signs of it defrosting. With her coat on, she wasn't self-conscious about the scars on her arm.

Mark didn't answer right away. He was quiet long enough that Angie eventually looked over at him to make sure he was okay. He was concentrating on his hands, which he was rubbing together for warmth. He could feel her staring at him, so he looked up at her and tried to speak, but stopped himself. He appeared to be struggling to put his thoughts into words.

"Mark?" she prodded softly.

"Yeah?" he replied, looking at his hands.

"Are you okay?"

He looked up at her suddenly this time, a surprised expression on his face.

"Me?" he asked, incredulous.

Now Angie was really confused. Suddenly, her car seemed really tiny, with Mark sitting in such close proximity. The strange ridiculousness of the situation, that Mark Kennedy was actually sitting in her car and struggling to say what was on his mind, made her want to laugh out loud. *I wish I could tell Shawna about this — she would totally freak out!*

Instantly, the thought of Shawna brought its usual sadness and wiped away the giddy feeling as quickly as it had appeared. This time, Mark sensed the changed in her. He sat up straight and cleared his throat.

"Sorry," he began, "I'm not usually at such a loss for words. I guess I just…wanted to apologize. I didn't mean to make you feel bad earlier. I thought maybe nobody ever really asked you how you are, or maybe they never gave you a chance to talk about it. I thought you might…" He stopped and looked out the window at the storm. "Of course, who am I to butt into your business? I mean, I hardly know you. We…hardly know each other." He looked at Angie. "So, anyway, I'm really sorry, okay?"

"Oh, no, it's totally fine," Angie protested a little too quickly, taking her eyes from his face and focusing once more on the storm. "Really. The truth is I *haven't* really talked about it. To anyone. It just still hurts too much. I guess part of me is still in denial." She shocked herself with the confession; she hadn't even admitted as much to herself before now.

"Well, again, I'm sorry for bringing it up and making you upset," Mark offered. Feeling like he'd said what he wanted to and sensing that the conversation might be hurting Angie again, he changed the topic. His expression changed to one of suppressed humor, as he said, "So… this is just me, but I personally don't think you're even going to get this thing out of the parking lot, let alone home. Where do you live, anyway?"

"In Somers!" Angie groaned, leaning her head back

against the seat. "Like I said, I hadn't counted on the storm hitting so early. To be honest, it's not a drive I'm looking forward to, particularly."

"Can I offer you a ride home?" Mark suggested. "I think my rig is a little better suited to this kind of weather. It has four-wheel-drive. You could leave your car here and come back to get it when the roads are clear. I'm sure nobody would mind if you left it here for a few days."

"Really?" Angie searched his face quickly for any hint that he might not really want to do it, that he might have just said it to be nice, or that he might be asking out of pity. Coming up empty, she surprised herself by answering, "Actually, I'd really appreciate it, as long as it isn't too much trouble for you. Will your folks be worried about you?" The question made her realize that she hadn't called her own mother yet. "Shoot!" she exclaimed, pulling her phone out of her coat pocket, "Speaking of – I've got to call my mom! She's probably worried sick!" She took off one glove, and speed-dialed Theresa.

Mark waited patiently while she explained everything to her mother. Although she was grateful for Mark's offer, Theresa was nervous about Angie riding with someone whom she herself had never met. Only after convincing her mom that Mark wasn't a complete stranger would Theresa give her consent.

"Please come right home, Ang," her mom implored. "I'll be worried every second until you make it back!"

"I will, Mom, believe me, I just want to be home! Love you!" Angie barely heard her mom return the endearment before she disconnected the call. She turned towards Mark, trying not to appear overly eager. *Life is so interesting. Just a few moments ago, I was bawling my eyes out in the shower; now,*

I'm about to take a ride with my ultimate crush. Too weird!

"Okay," she managed to sputter. "I'm ready. Where's your car?"

Mark's eyes lit up. He couldn't believe his good luck. Angie Gianelli, unbeknownst to her, had been on his mind for a long time after he first met her. When was that? One of Halle's parties? He didn't remember the exact date, but knew it was in the spring a few years ago. Somebody spilled a drink on Angie's shirt and he lent her one of his. He had been impressed by her natural beauty, those big, green eyes unsullied by obnoxious layers of eye shadow and framed in long, black eyelashes. But he'd been drawn the most to her personality, to the spunk she'd shown in spite of some mean girl's attempt to embarrass her. After he got her the shirt, he was inundated with requests for music by the other party-goers, and so he and Angie hadn't been able to talk much the rest of the evening, even though he'd wanted to. He'd thought briefly of asking her for her phone number, but when he mentioned the idea to Ben, his friend had teased him, saying, "Dude, she's a freshman!" and made a few other comments that left Mark feeling like he was some kind of pervert for even contemplating the idea. So he'd let it go.

Until he saw her at the pool this evening, he hadn't thought of her in almost two years, at least not until he'd heard about the accident a few months back. Now that he'd seen her again, had actually run into her, he felt strangely compelled to get to know her, almost like his life depended on it. He felt like he was on the edge of a great precipice, and she was somehow his lifeline. He hadn't followed his instincts two years ago, but now he knew better. He wasn't about to let another opportunity slip by so easily.

He smiled widely at Angie, showing his dimples, and her heart sputtered. She laughed at the idea that it had literally "skipped a beat," and he laughed with her, although he didn't even know why. He felt so giddy all of a sudden, like he had just been granted his heart's desire, or was about to have his dreams come true. There was a tangible feeling of expectancy in the air. They both felt it, but neither knew if the other one did, and neither one wanted to break the spell. So they just went with it.

"My truck is practically on the other side of the parking lot," he grinned. "What do you want to bring with you?"

You. The thought made her smile again, which prompted another silly grin from him.

Without waiting for her answer, he fumbled around for the overhead light, pushed it on, and began grabbing things from the back seat.

"Gym bag?" he asked, holding it out to her. Angie took the bag, smiling and nodding stupidly.

"School bag?" he queried, his hand on the strap. This time he looked right at her. Looking directly into his eyes, a blush warmed her face. Her heart felt like it was swelling and would soon burst from her chest. She had to remind herself to breathe again, and to answer. Something about this whole situation tonight felt like it was so right. Meant to be. She marveled that she should be so lucky.

"Yes, please," she replied softly.

Mark pulled the school bag more slowly, all the time staring at Angie. He forced himself to look away and pull the bag to the front seat. It was weird; all of a sudden, in a single moment, he felt like he'd known her all his life, like being with her was right where he belonged. He didn't want to scare her by getting too serious right away, so in that moment, he determined to make himself take things more slowly.

"Okay," he said. "Now comes the hard part." He sucked in a deep breath, and Angie did, too, but didn't know why. For a nanosecond, she thought he was going to say he had to leave or that he couldn't give her a ride after all. The thought, although miniscule, jarred her intensely. Time and space felt like they were bending and twisting out of control. She looked at him and adopted his grave expression.

"What?" she answered, unable to muster more than a whisper.

He took hold of her gloved hand.

"Angie?"

"Yes?"

Another moment passed before he spoke again.

"We have to get out of this car and back out into *that!*" he laughed, pointing out the window at the storm.

Angie crinkled up her nose. Mark thought she was the most adorable creature he'd ever seen.

"I was afraid of that," she replied, smiling.

Chapter Six: Something New

"Piglet sidled up to Pooh from behind. 'Pooh?' he whispered.
'Yes, Piglet?'
'Nothing,' said Piglet, taking Pooh's paw. 'I just wanted
to be sure of you.'"
~ A.A. Milne

Angie sat bolt upright from a dead sleep. The dream clung to her mind, even as it dissipated rapidly with consciousness. She was covered in sweat; she had been crying, and she struggled to remember the dream before it completely dissolved.

Only pieces would form and it seemed like the harder she tried to hold onto them, the faster they slipped away completely. What is it about dreams? Why do some leave an indelible mark, leave the dreamer reeling from the emotions of it for days without ever really remembering what it was about? Angie had an impression that the dream had been about her and Shawna and the accident, but the more she tried to pinpoint details, the more they eluded her. All she was left with was an incredible sadness and a deep feeling of guilt.

The digital clock read 5:36 a.m. She wished it were a little later, because she really needed to talk to Mark. He had worked until midnight the night before, and she knew he would probably sleep until at least ten. It was too early to get up, so she lay back and tried to think about what she needed to do that day. It was Friday, June 8, and the high school had been out for the last week. Mark had finished his second semester at the local community college in mid-May, but now he was embroiled in several intense summer courses. The classes only met a couple of days a week, but they were six to eight hours long, and ever since they had begun, Angie felt like she was losing time with Mark. Besides his intense school schedule, he worked 30 hours a week at two jobs, one as a part time landscaper and the other as a pizza delivery man.

Even though it was early summer, mornings were still chilly, and Angie's room was cold. She pulled her blankets up around her head and snuggled deeper into the covers. The sun had not yet risen but a small amount of light illuminated her room and its furnishings. As she lazed in the blue-glow of the predawn, she mulled over the events of the last few months.

After Mark had driven her home the night of the big storm, he had come inside to meet her mom and Jack and ended up staying for dinner. When he left, he asked Angie if he could call her sometime. Of course, she had given him her number, trying not to look too eager but bursting with happiness.

He started calling her on a daily basis, and within a week, took her out on their first real date. They went to see a movie and he held her hand. They stared at each other more than they watched the screen, and later she couldn't even tell her mom what the movie was about. When he took her home that night, he kissed her for the first time, a slow, tender (yet very chaste kiss), and she thought for the first time in a long time that maybe she did have something to live for after all.

Since then, they had spent practically every waking second together. Angie was surprised to find that she could talk very easily with Mark about everything. She never felt like he judged her in any way and sometimes he even surprised her with his maturity and wisdom. It wasn't long before she was able to open up about Shawna. It was difficult at first, but he was a really good listener. Little by little, she allowed herself to become very vulnerable. She shared every bit of her friendship with Shawna, from the time they met until the time she died. Sometimes Mark was so moved by the intense memories of their friendship that he cried with her. Angie felt like Mark truly understood how profoundly Shawna's death had affected her. A Christian, Mark always referred to it as Shawna's "going home," like the Howsers did. As they got to know one another, Angie discovered that not only had Mark gone to the same church as the Howsers, he apparently had known Shawna for many years, as her parents were old friends of his parents. Angie found that coincidence remarkable and somehow comforting.

The emotions of the unremembered dream washed over her again. Sadness filled her heart partly because in the dream, she had been with Shawna again, and partly because she couldn't remember all of it. Suddenly, a pink hue bathed her room as the predawn shifted to dawn. Angie pushed her covers aside, got up, wrapped her comforter around herself, and stole softly over to the window, which faced due east. She gasped aloud at the beauty of the sunrise. It covered the entire eastern sky and dazzling color reflected off of some random groups of clouds and bounced off the tips of the still snow-covered mountains, which were a shadowy purple in the early light. The colors were more vivid than any she could remember ever having seen. As she watched, the clouds drifted slowly by, turning from pink to a deep sherbet orange. Edges of some clouds were tinged with brilliant yellow. Watching them intently, she started making out shapes.

It reminded her of the first sunrise she'd experienced after the accident, when she had awakened in the hospital. She'd thought the shapes looked like fairies and the thought had cheered her. Now, she thought back to some of her conversations with the Howsers. They talked frequently of the beauty of heaven and how in spite of their grief, they were sometimes jealous of what they believed Shawna was experiencing. The Howsers spoke of angels like they really believed such things existed. Mark had even admitted a similar belief in them. Now, as Angie watched the clouds performing their fiery morning dance, she was astonished when they morphed right in front of her eyes, looking for all the world like a troupe of soaring, dancing angels. One of the angel-shaped clouds even looked like it was playing a trumpet. In that moment, Angie thought that maybe angels really existed. Her eyes filled with tears of joy at the thought that maybe, just maybe, the Howsers were right and this was the sort of thing that Shawna got to see every day. *Maybe she's one of the angels playfully dancing in the sky right now!*

Angie grabbed her cell phone and took picture after picture, wanting to preserve this moment. She watched for a full twenty minutes, unable to tear her eyes away except to take a picture now and then, and the clouds continued to look like angels the entire time. When one would start to dissipate and change shape, another one would form in its place. It was magical and electrifying, and she stood immobilized at her window, riveted by the sight.

Finally, after close to half an hour, the colors drained from the sky and the morning sunlight shone on the clouds. The show was over. Angie continued to stare out the window for a few moments, feeling tremendously grateful for what she had just witnessed. But whom should she thank? The Howsers were absolutely convinced that God exists and that he truly cares for each and every human being. Angie always listened to them politely, but she wasn't sure that she even believed in God, let alone that he cared for her personally. However, while watching that incredible sunrise, she found herself overcome with the idea that God had created it just for her. "Thank you," she whispered awkwardly. She wasn't convinced anyone was really listening, but she couldn't keep the sentiment from escaping her lips.

Instantly, the birds started singing their morning songs, greeting the new day, and Angie got goose bumps. Contrary to how she'd felt a few minutes prior, she believed that she had been heard. It was a pivotal moment, leaving her deeply satisfied, like she felt when she got a bear hug from someone she loved. She remembered the inexplicable calm that had covered her like a warm blanket in the gym locker room the night Mark had driven her home in the snowstorm.

Fully awake, Angie got dressed and made her bed, and then went to take a shower. As she blew her hair dry, her thoughts drifted back to Mark. She remembered her silly, jealous rant of a few weeks ago. Even though Mark was already in college when they first started going out, it wasn't until the summer classes loomed that Angie, for some inexplicable reason, started worrying about the women Mark might meet and interact with in his classes. She worried that he would find a college girl who was more interesting or pretty or vibrant than she was, someone who didn't have ugly scars on her arm or wasn't crying every two minutes, and he would break up with her to be with the other girl. It was totally irrational, because Mark never mentioned other girls and had given her no reason to believe that he didn't want to be with her. He did his best to reassure her whenever she expressed doubts about his faithfulness.

Still, Angie let her paranoia get the best of her, and one day, she started asking him a lot of pointed questions about a particularly pretty girl whom she knew was in one of his classes. Although Mark denied every accusation and tried to comfort and console her, she let her emotions take over and ended up pushing him away and screaming at him. It was all very undignified and completely unjustified. The conversation had taken place in Angie's room while they were both studying, and Theresa had come running when the volume reached a fevered pitch. Mark hadn't shown any sign of being upset or angry with Angie; he just looked completely bewildered and hurt. Even Theresa felt sorry for him. He decided it would be best if he left and gave Angie some time to cool down.

The next morning, after spending a very silent evening in her room contemplating her behavior, Angie received a very loving text about how much he missed her, and she was ashamed of herself. He had never given her any reason to doubt his loyalty and certainly hadn't deserved what she had dished out. She had texted him right back, and they got together that afternoon to talk and things went back to normal. For a while.

Angie had taken to visiting Shawna's parents more frequently now. It wasn't that her mom or Jack were incapable of understanding her, but there was a connection between herself and the Howsers. Her mom had thought Shawna was a great person, but she hadn't spent enough time with her to truly know her and love her.

Sometimes Angie thought that she and the Howsers were the only people in the world who understood what a huge loss it was to the rest of humanity that Shawna was gone. Eileen Howser loved visiting with Angie and hearing about every detail of her life. Not that Theresa didn't care, but she worked full time, whereas Eileen only worked a couple of days a week, so she naturally had more time to spend. Plus, she got to have some "daughter time" vicariously through Angie, which she craved. The visits helped heal them both.

Eileen was a wise soul. Her graciousness had always impressed Angie, who was even more amazed at how much it still flowed out of her despite her tremendous loss. Sometimes, Eileen expressed her secret thoughts and emotions, allowing herself to cry and tell Angie just how much she missed Shawna. Angie felt honored that she was one of the few people that Eileen trusted with her deepest feelings.

When the weather cooperated, they liked to take long hikes in the woods together. Shawna had loved to hike. There was a park on a nearby bluff called Lone Pine that Shawna had loved and now Eileen and Angie frequented it in memory of her. Walking paths wound throughout the park and up and over the tree-covered hills. Short side trails along the path led to astounding views of the Flathead Valley. Angie and Eileen would rest on one of the benches placed on these offshoots and would reminisce about Shawna and about what a lover of the outdoors she had been. During her free time, Shawna was always hiking or biking or doing something outdoorsy. She would drag her best friend along, and even though Angie was more of a bookworm than an athlete, they had always enjoyed these outings immensely.

Nowadays, when Angie listened to Eileen's descriptions of heaven, of a garden paradise where there would be no more sorrow and where God himself would wipe away every tear, her heart filled with gladness for Shawna. She had no trouble picturing her out walking in sunshine-bathed, vast green meadows lined with wildflowers of every color, or of her climbing hills even more beautiful than these. Sometimes, Angie would have fanciful, Disney-esque thoughts of tiny birds landing on Shawna's shoulders and singing songs just for her, and it made her giggle. As time passed, she began to let Shawna go, a little at a time. She began to heal inwardly at the notion that Shawna still existed on some other plane, in some other universe. She even harbored a tiny, secret hope that she might actually get to see her again.

Eileen was so gracious. She never came off as haughty or "all-knowing," like some of the preachers Angie had seen on TV. She never made Angie feel silly or stupid. Angie still had many questions about spirituality and God and heaven, but Eileen patiently answered every query to the best of her ability. Admirably, she was humble enough to admit when she simply didn't have an answer. That took Angie by surprise; before these conversations,

Angie had never known an adult (besides her mother) who would admit they didn't know the answer to something. Her teachers came closest, but even as they told her they didn't know, they would point towards books and research, implying that the answer could be found there. Eileen introduced Angie to the idea that sometimes things were beyond human intellect or reasoning.

"That's really the essence of faith," she explained softly as they hiked together the afternoon of the day Angie saw the glorious sunrise. "Mankind simply does not and will not ever have all the answers. At some point, you have to decide to trust that God knows and he cares. Most of the time, that's all we really have. For myself, and for many other Christians, that is enough."

"But if God exists, why is there so much pain in the world?" Angie countered breathlessly as they climbed a hilly path. "Why do wonderful people like Shawna have to die such horrible deaths, while all the jerks and idiots get to keep on living? Why didn't he make that truck swerve away from Shawna and me? If he's all-powerful, couldn't he have done that?" Angie's voice trembled, and her eyebrows furrowed in frustration at the conundrum. She knew Eileen wouldn't think her questions were rude and that she would answer honestly. She really wanted to believe, really wanted the peace that the Howsers and Mark seemed to have in their everyday lives. But how could she trust an entity that would allow so much suffering?

"I believe he could have," Eileen began. Taking Angie by the hand, they detoured on a familiar side trail and down to their favorite bench. They sat down, and gazed at the sweeping valley view in front of them. Eileen was slow to answer. It was another thing that surprised Angie –

that someone actually *thought* before they spoke and didn't say the first thing that came to mind.

"Have you heard of 'free will?'" Eileen responded after what seemed a very long time. Her eyes met Angie's with a new intensity.

"Yeah, I guess so," Angie replied, hesitantly. She turned and gave Eileen her full attention, sensing that she was getting at something important.

"What does it mean to you?" Eileen always managed to take Angie off guard with her probing questions, and Angie admired Eileen and tried to imitate her way of weighing her words, of thinking through a question before answering, so she didn't reply immediately.

Bees hummed in the nearby trees. A squirrel scolded them from an invisible upper branch as the afternoon sun warmed them. The air was filled with the scents of spring, of fresh new grass and leaves and of the ever-present pine trees. A gentle breeze moved the tree tops. After a moment's thought, she answered, "I guess I think it means that we are allowed to think or do whatever we want."

"Exactly!" Eileen encouraged her. "So, say God has granted us free will, as a gift. If it is a pure gift, with no strings attached, then by definition, he cannot interfere. If his love and motives are pure, if he is truly perfect, as I believe he is, he must recuse himself. People, on the other hand, are imperfect, and use their free will to make decisions – decisions that oftentimes affect others. Like the day of the accident: The girl who crashed into you and Shawna had made a conscious decision to take drugs and drink. The drugs and alcohol affected her decision-making ability, but didn't remove her God-given free will. Unfortunately, in her inebriated and sleep-deprived state, she chose to drive."

"But you're always telling me that God protects those he loves!" Angie objected. "Why didn't he protect us that day?" She wanted to understand, but this wasn't making sense. "Where was God? Why didn't he stick his big hand in the way to keep us from being hit?" Her voice cracked with emotion.

Eileen could see that Angie was struggling mightily and she prayed a quick, silent prayer for help in answering her.

"Those are valid questions, Angie. I'll do my best to answer you, but as always, I must caution you – I am not some wellspring of knowledge! Believe me, I wrestled daily with the same questions for the first few months after Shawna went home. I had always prayed for her safety, every single day she was alive."

"That's what I mean!" Angie interjected impulsively. "If you were praying for her, for us…well, then why? Why did it happen?"

Eileen took a deep breath before answering. Again, Angie was impressed by her constant ability to remain composed, even in the face of difficulty, even when faced with a puzzle such as this.

"Well, let's get back to the topic of free will for a minute," she finally said. "Either we have it or we don't. If God just interjected himself into our lives without our permission or consent, if he just made things happen the way he wanted, then our free will would be a farce. He would be no more than a giant puppeteer in the sky, and we would be no more than his puppets." Eileen looked Angie directly in the eyes. Angie did her level best to just listen and not interrupt, but her legs swung impatiently back and forth under the bench. A bee was suddenly very intent on knowing whether or not the two women were flowers, and they watched it as it buzzed speedily up and over and around them, checking them out. Satisfied, it flew away and they continued their conversation.

"On the other hand, we are able to pray, and I *do* believe, whole-heartedly, that he hears and answers our prayers," she stated. Angie started to interrupt, but this time, Eileen held up her hand. "I know, Angie, believe me, I know. But please, just hear me out. I've told you numerous times about faith, right? Well, my faith tells me that there was more to the accident and its outcome than I can understand. My faith tells me that if I believe God is good, as I do, and if I believe he is *for* me and not against me, then sometimes I will just have to trust him."

"So, God can and does answer prayer, but he didn't keep Shawna and me safe that day," Angie groused, shaking her head at what she considered a glaring contradiction. She was losing patience with this conversation. Eileen wasn't making sense today.

Eileen just smiled.

"Yeah," she answered quietly, nodding her head.

Angie shook her head in frustration, and then looked away. Both women were quiet, watching the valley shadows shift as the sun moved across the sky. The fragrant air was filled with sweet birdsong. It was a beautiful day in early summer and for a few moments, they quietly enjoyed it together, not talking. Then, Eileen covered Angie's hand with her own.

"Angie? Remember that time you and Shawna wanted to go camping alone?" she asked, softly breaking the silence between them.

Angie smiled. They'd been in eighth grade and believed they were old enough to camp alone. She looked at Eileen and nodded, curious again.

"Remember how angry you were when your mom and I both said 'no'?" she continued, a smile playing on her lips. "Do remember what happened that weekend?"

"Yes," Angie admitted, remembering that the camp-ground they had planned to visit had been ravaged by a flash flood overnight. It had rained lightly on and off all day. In the evening, the rain fell heavily, and the camp-ground, located next to the Stillwater River was washed out when the river rose unexpectedly. If she and Shawna had been camping, they may well have been killed, as the flood occurred in the middle of the night. One man, a seasoned hunter, had been swept away in the flood; his body was discovered a week later, caught in a snag of logs a few miles downriver.

"Well, it's not like your mom or I knew that would happen. But we knew it was a possibility that *something* could happen, and we weren't willing to take that chance. You girls are just much too precious. So we told you 'no.' Remember how mad you were?" Eileen turned to look at her, smiling broadly at the memory.

Angie did remember and she stifled a giggle. An airplane flew overhead just then, and the noise prevented her from answering right away. Her eyes followed its trajectory and she thought about that evening of long ago. She remembered that Shawna, who was always more easy-going and flexible, had been disappointed but quietly resigned that they couldn't go. She, on the other hand, had been extremely angry and had thrown a royal fit. She screamed that they were being unfair, and cried and carried on until finally the Howsers took Shawna and headed home. After they left, she had gone to her room and flung herself on her bed and cried. Her mother followed her, scolding her the whole way for her immature behavior, and even gave her a couple of stiff swats on the behind, as she told her sternly that she would not be old enough to camp alone until she could control herself better. It was the last time she had ever been spanked. Angie blushed at the memory, embarrassed.

As the noise of the plane grew softer and eventually disappeared altogether, Angie squeezed Eileen's hand and smiled back at her.

"Yeah, okay, so what's your point?" she asked, still blushing.

"Well, if you can picture it, I actually got just as mad once. It was a few weeks after Shawna went to be with the Lord. I was alone in my room, and I started thinking about the fact that I had prayed for you girls every single day, and I got really, really angry with God," Eileen shared gently. "I was in my room thinking about it, and I just got so mad I started screaming at him. I told him I thought he had acted unfairly by not protecting Shawna, a girl who loved him so much and was willing to give her whole life, her whole being, to follow him." Eileen's voice quavered ever so slightly. Angie just sat and listened to the confession in amazed, wide-eyed silence.

"Finally, Grant came in and just held me and rocked me. He didn't say a word, God bless him. He's such a wonderful man! Sometimes I think he knows me better than I know myself," she admitted, wiping away a stray tear.

"Anyway," she said. She sat up tall, took both of Angie's hands, and looked her full in the face. "The point is, sometimes we just have to defer to God's wisdom. *I don't know why Shawna had to die, but he does.* Just as you didn't know why we said 'no' to your camping trip. You didn't like being told 'no.' Nobody does." She gently took Angie's face in her hands. "I *do* believe that God answers prayer, Angie, but I also believe that sometimes, that answer is going to be 'no' and if I truly believe he loves me, and I do, then I have to believe that he says 'no' for a reason, even if I never get to know why, at least not in this lifetime."

She released Angie's face, and sat back. They resumed watching the valley and listening to the sounds of the forest. After a moment of reflection, she asked quietly, "Angie, do you believe your parents love you? I mean, even though they got divorced?" She turned to look at Angie once again.

Angie looked at her hands. In truth, there had been times when she wondered if their breakup had had something to do with her. Oh, the idea was completely unfounded, as neither of her parents had ever said or even intimated as much. Her father had basically vanished from her life since the divorce. He still hadn't come to see her, even though it had been eight months since the accident, and he rarely even called her. Did he love her? There was a time when the answer would have been an unequivocal 'yes,' but she wasn't sure anymore.

Her mom, however, was another story. She knew her mom loved her, no matter what. Even though she worked a crazy schedule, whenever she had time off, she went out of her way to do something with or for Angie. At least, she had until Jack came into the picture. When they first started dating. Angie was resentful because she hardly ever saw her mom anymore. It wasn't until she started going out with Mark that she understood the intense pull of a love relationship and forgave her mom for being so absent those first months. Besides, at this point, her mom and Jack hardly ever made plans without consulting her and they did their level best to include her as much as possible, so she really had no room to complain.

Still, she found the question difficult to answer. Did her parents love her? She stared out at the valley and watched the cars on distant Highway 2 traveling back and forth.

Eileen, sensing her discomfort, came to her rescue. "I mean, of *course* your parents love you, sweetheart. But unless you *believe* they love you, you won't be able to trust them completely. You won't trust that they have your best interests at heart."

Angie stared at her hands. She still couldn't answer the question. For many months, she had confessed her fears to Eileen that she had somehow driven her dad away and that her mom was mad at her for it. She feared that Jack felt she was in the way of his forming a relationship with her mom, even though he had never said or done anything to make her feel that way.

Suddenly, she arrived at the crux of the matter: She wasn't sure she was even lovable. Big, splashy tears fell unbidden from her eyes and she broke out sobbing convulsively. Eileen immediately scooted to her side and took her in her arms, rocking her back and forth gently. While she rocked her, she reassured her, telling her that she loved her. Angie interrupted frequently, protesting that she was unlovable, that she was a bad person, that Shawna had been the good one, and why hadn't she died instead? Still, Eileen clung to her tightly and whispered what she knew to be the truth as Angie cried uncontrollably: That God knew exactly who she was, and that he had created her to be just who she was. That he was not disappointed in her. That he knew her better than she knew herself and accepted her exactly as she was. That he was a healer of the brokenhearted, and was loving, merciful, and kind.

Finally, she murmured that God was a father to the fatherless, a mother to the motherless, and a parent to the orphaned. As the words penetrated Angie's troubled mind, her spirit calmed and she stopped crying. Eileen continued to rock her, whispering fervent prayers for healing for them both. Finally, she let go and Eileen did, too. She sat back and wiped her eyes with her hands, and blew her nose into a tissue that Eileen provided.

"Wow!" she said, and she smiled. "I don't know where that came from!"

"I do," Eileen stated. It was unusual for her to be so forthcoming with her own opinion. "You're human, and it's human nature to want to be loved. You've had it tough, honey, Lord knows. Given all that you've been through, it's no wonder you feel unloved. But I'll tell you this: I love you. I love you dearly, with all my heart and soul. I think you're a wonderful, compassionate young woman. I'm sure your parents love you. And I know God loves you, Angie. He truly does."

"I wish I could believe that," Angie sniffed, wiping away the last of her tears. Suddenly, she brightened – she remembered the incredible sunrise she had experienced that morning, and she told Eileen all about it, including how she felt the whole thing was just for her, and how she had even said, "Thank you."

Eileen gazed at her lovingly and when Angie finished telling the story, she said, "Sounds to me like maybe you're starting to believe. Don't be scared to believe in him, Angie. He'll never let you down."

Chapter Seven: The Greatest Thing

"Eventually you will come to realize that love heals everything, and love is all there is."
~ *Gary Zukav*

"The greatest thing you'll ever learn is to love and be loved in return." ~ *Nat King Cole,* Nature Boy

Angie was full of hope after that conversation with Eileen. She didn't know the source of her hope, she just felt it. She went with it and let it carry her. For a few weeks, she was calmer than she had been in many months. Everyone noticed the change in her – her mom, Jack, even Mark. She just seemed more at peace than usual.

One day in mid-July, during a particularly hot spell, she was out on the little apartment deck sunbathing. Her mom and Jack were at work and Mark was at school. For whatever reason, she started dwelling on her dad and the fact that he hadn't come to see her in over a year. A combination of the heat and her negative thoughts left her feeling angry and dejected. Once again, she felt completely unlovable. It didn't help that this was one of the days that Mark had an eight-hour class or that his class was on a field trip up the North Fork of the Flathead River. They were going to try to identify different trees and plants they'd been studying.

Angie and Mark went to breakfast that morning at a local restaurant and then she dropped him off in the front parking lot at the college to catch the bus for the trip. Mark, well-built and darkly tanned from his landscaping job, looked so handsome it made her heart ache. His dirty blonde hair had bleached out to almost white in the summer sun. As she watched him walk to the bus, she caught a movement out of the corner of her eye. She turned and saw Brooke, the gorgeous girl who had sparked her jealous fit a few weeks earlier, sashaying towards the bus in a skimpy halter top and really tight, really short shorts. Brooke was physically very beautiful, possibly the most naturally beautiful woman Angie had ever seen in real life. She was long-legged, busty, and very fit, and she, too, was darkly tanned. Angie had always been jealous of people who could tan so well, as it seemed no matter how much time she spent in the sun, her skin refused to take color. If she stayed out too long, she burned, and she wasn't lucky enough to have the kind of skin that would go from burned to tan. Her skin just turned bright red, peeled obnoxiously, and went back to being pasty white.

And here she was, beautiful, tan Brooke, with her wavy, golden-brown hair hanging halfway down her perfect back. Beautifully built, not a scar on her perfect body. Jealousy ripped through Angie like a tidal wave as she realized that this pretty, scantily clad girl would get to spend all day with Mark. *How can he resist her? She's so drop-dead gorgeous!*

Just as these thoughts steamrolled through her mind, Mark got back off the bus. He passed Brooke without so much as a backwards glance and strode directly to the car like a man on a mission. Angie looked around the car quickly; had he forgotten something? Notebook? Sunscreen? She looked back up and he was right beside her window. She rolled it down quickly, and he bent down until he was eye-level with her.

"Did you forget something?" Angie asked him curiously.

"Mm-hmm," he murmured in the affirmative. Then he leaned in the window and kissed her, long and devotedly. Angie's heart felt like it might burst. Finally, he broke away, but he held her face lovingly in his hands.

They stared deeply into each other's eyes, and he stroked her face tenderly. She put her hands over the top of his and pressed her face into them, closing her eyes and basking in the attention. She adored him and it was easy to see he felt the same way about her.

"I forgot to tell you I love you," he said softly. Then he leaned in and kissed her again, this time more quickly and chastely. "I hope you have a good day. Don't forget to pick me up at four!" The bus driver honked the horn impatiently and he stood up and jogged to board the bus before it left without him. "I love you, Angie!" he called as he bounded up the bus stairs. Then he disappeared, the bus doors closed, and it pulled away.

Immediately, Angie realized she was being a complete idiot. To think Mark thought anything at all about Brooke or could be easily swayed by her obvious charms was ludicrous. *You'd better knock it off,* she scolded herself, *or you'll end up driving him away with your crazy jealousy! He loves YOU, you idiot!* She had a fleeting image of Shawna, shaking her head. She could almost hear Shawna telling her she was being silly, that she was beautiful too, and to stop being such a bonehead. She smiled confidently to herself, pulled out of the parking lot, and headed for home.

That had been this morning. Now, after sitting in the hot sun without a break for an hour and a half, she could feel the burn on her skin, so she got up to go inside. It was only a few degrees cooler inside the apartment, so she closed the sliding door, then went around to make sure all of the other windows were closed before turning up the air conditioning.

She could feel a headache coming on. She pulled a glass from the dishwasher, then filled it with ice and water from the fridge. Condensation formed on the glass and it almost slipped from her grip. She felt dizzy and chastised herself for staying out in the sun so long. She decided maybe some sleep would make her feel better and she went to lie down. First, though, she got a washcloth from the linen closet, took it to the bathroom, and wet it down thoroughly, running it under the cold water. She wrung it out and took it to her room, turned the oscillating fan on full power, and lay down on her bed with the cold cloth over her eyes.

Her nap was fitful. The apartment was still sticky and hot, despite the air conditioner, and her thoughts continued to spiral downward. She couldn't stop dwelling on the fact that her own father seemed to have disowned her. When she was little, she was her dad's constant shadow, following him around wherever he went. He had called her his little princess and as the only child, she felt completely adored by him. He took her places, showing her off proudly. One time he even took her out shopping for clothes for school. The trip had been totally unexpected. He came home from work one evening and announced that he and Angela were having a daddy-daughter date. Her mom had quickly washed her dirt-streaked, eight-year-old face and brushed her knotted hair until it shone, then tied it up in a ponytail with fancy ribbons.

They went to the mall, shopped in practically every store, and then had dinner at one of the diners nearby. Her dad had been extraordinarily patient, letting her try on whatever she fancied and buying her almost anything she wanted. Angie could still remember the colorful, neon signs over the shops and the heady smell of popcorn, floor wax, hot pretzels, and perfume in the mall. She remembered the thrill of riding the escalator, of hoping she wouldn't get sucked down into the crack as she disembarked. She arrived home with bags full of pretty new outfits and spent the subsequent hour putting on a fashion show for her parents, who clapped appreciatively. When her father tucked her into bed that night, she felt like the most loved little girl in the whole world.

Her elation was short-lived. The next day when she got home from school, she waited impatiently for her dad to come home from work, anticipating another wonderful evening together. Finally, when dinnertime rolled around and he hadn't shown up, she asked her mother about him. Theresa informed her that her dad had left that morning to head south for a driving job. The call had come in that morning while she was at school and he hadn't had time to wait until she got home to say goodbye. He wouldn't be back for several months. Angie was heartbroken and cried inconsolably for two solid hours. Theresa had cursed Greg under her breath as she rocked Angie and tried to calm her down.

Angie moaned against the memory. Her attempt at napping failed, and she sat up, completely aggravated, and threw the wet washcloth across the room. Her head was pounding and she actually felt like she was going to be sick. The air in the apartment, although cooler now, was stale and reeked slightly of last night's dinner, fried fish, which exacerbated her nausea.

She got up and went out into the living room. The air was much cooler in there; the apartment layout was poor and the cool air tended to pool there instead of flowing to all the rooms. Even with oscillating fans placed strategically about, the coolest air always remained in the front.

She flung herself down on the couch, turned on the television, and started watching absentmindedly. Some inane movie played, designed for housewives to watch after finishing their housework. Angie found herself completely sucked into the storyline, which centered on a couple in the midst of marital strife. The wife had caught her husband cheating on her with her best friend. and as she railed against him for his unfaithfulness, Angie's paranoia increased. She thought about Brooke and the field trip she and Mark were enjoying. She wondered what they were doing right at that moment. Had he fallen for Brooke's charms like the TV husband had with his wife's friend? Then she remembered how Mark had run right past Brooke, just to give her another goodbye kiss, and she tried to change her thought pattern.

She failed. The next thing she knew, Angie was running possible scenarios through her mind: Would spending the day in the presence of Beautiful Brooke make Mark realize how plain she was in comparison? Would he admire her slender, toned, and curvy arms and realize they were much prettier than Angie's, free as they were of ugly scars? Would they start talking and realize how much they had in common, until Mark finally decided that Brooke was the real girl of his dreams?

By the time Angie had to leave to pick Mark up from the bus, she had run so many negative fantasies through her mind that she thought it was not only possible, but highly *probable*, that he had fallen in love with Brooke during the trip and would no longer want anything to do with her. On top of that, rehashing her childhood memories that afternoon had left her with a terrible, hollow feeling. Her dad had told her many times that he loved and adored her, and yet he was able to leave without a word. He hadn't come to see her even after learning of her harrowing accident. Maybe she was fooling herself to believe that any man would ever honor his promises and not just leave her.

She pulled her car into the parking lot just as the group was getting off the bus. She watched as student after student disembarked and felt momentarily relieved when Mark leapt joyfully off the top step onto the cool green grass. He hadn't noticed her yet, and as she watched, he turned around with a big, silly grin on his face and held his hand out to someone else still on the bus. To Angie's horror, Brooke suddenly appeared and took Mark's hand. They both were laughing and chatting happily as he gallantly helped her down the bus steps. Mark let go of Brooke's hand the second she was off the bus, and they were quickly surrounded by four or five other students. The group jovially pushed each other around and laughed and guffawed at some shared joke. Mark glanced over and saw Angie there waiting for him, so he started towards her car, waving goodbye to the other students. Brooke said something and he turned to her. They shared another little joke, laughed again, and Mark turned once more towards the car. Angie heard Brooke say, "Well, see ya, Captain Uncoordinated!" and without turning to look at her, he pointed a finger in her direction and hollered, "Not if I see you first, you little instigator!" and they laughed again. Other students yelled goodbye to each other as the group disbursed. Brooke sashayed past the car and gave Angie a shy, friendly wave as she passed.

Angie didn't return the greeting. She narrowed her eyes at Brooke and fumed as she watched the girl pass. *How dare you? Don't you realize I'm his girlfriend? Have you no shame?*

Mark smiled broadly as he approached the car. When Angie did not return the smile, his own withered away. His instincts told him something was wrong.

"Hey, babe!" he said, attempting cheerfulness as he opened the door and got into the compact. "Have you been waiting long? I'm sorry we're a few minutes late! Man, it's a scorcher today, eh?" He leaned towards Angie to give her a kiss, but she ignored the gesture. She put the car into gear and started to pull out of the parking lot. Mark was immediately taken aback. He felt like a jerk. Obviously, something was really wrong. Angie refusing to kiss him? A thousand scenarios whipped through his mind at lightning speed – was her mom okay? Was Jack okay? Had her cat, Tater, been run over by a car? Tension formed a tight knot in his gut as he prepared for the bad news.

"Angie, what's wrong," he asked warily. "What's happened?"

Angie didn't answer or give him any indication that she'd heard him. Her hand was on the seat between them and he put his over hers and tried to give it a gentle squeeze, but she pulled it away roughly.

That was highly abnormal. Usually, she couldn't wait to hold his hand.

He regarded her closely as she continued to drive, watching her tense actions carefully. She still hadn't said a word to him and wouldn't even look his way. She was driving much faster than she usually did, and when she had to stop for a light, she put on the brakes so hard that they flew forward and snapped back with the momentum.

Finally, he couldn't stand it anymore.

"Angie?" he asked, more abruptly this time. He was losing patience. She continued to ignore him. "What's going on?"

She revved the engine and took off, tires squealing, and changed lanes abruptly, cutting off another motorist who expressed his unhappiness by honking his horn and extending a finger.

"That's it," Mark said, suddenly angry. He didn't know what was happening, but he loved Angie and he knew he couldn't let her continue to drive when she was so obviously upset. She was endangering both their lives. "Pull over," he ordered loudly.

She ignored him.

"NOW, Angie!" he fairly shouted. That got her attention. She glanced at him, and he pointed indicating that she should turn right into the next available parking lot.

She complied. After she turned into a parking spot and pulled on the emergency brake, Mark deftly reached out, turned off the engine, and pulled out the keys.

"What?" Angie demanded hotly, reaching furiously for her keys.

"Exactly!" Mark countered, dodging her every

attempted grab. "What indeed? Will you please tell me what is going on with you? Did something happen? You're acting like you're mad at me, but you weren't mad this morning, so I repeat: What is going on?" It took a lot to rile Mark, and he was hurt and confused. The whole situation had completely blindsided him. Moments earlier, he had gotten off the bus after having had a truly enjoyable day. "Angie! STOP it!" he yelled finally, tired of wrestling with her as she attempted to retrieve the keys. He put them in his pocket with one hand while he held her off with the other.

At first, Angie just glowered at him. Then she sat back in her seat and let out a huge sigh.

"What is it, baby?" Mark asked, more gently. He was trying to be understanding, but he was wary. Where had this behavior come from? It was reminiscent of her fit of a few weeks ago.

She wouldn't look at him, but she finally managed to spit out, "If you want to be with Brooke, I totally understand. I won't stand in your way!" She looked straight ahead, crossed her arms over her chest, and blinked back her burgeoning tears.

Mark was dumbstruck. He had never even once so much as looked at another girl since he started going out with Angie. She was his dream, his ideal; how could she not know that by now? Didn't he do everything in his power to express his devotion to her? He tried to be a good listener. He held her when she cried. He had been patient and understanding as she continued to work through the emotional pain of grief and the physical pain of therapy.

Now, he felt as if his heart was ripped in two. He

would have laughed at the ridiculous accusation, but this wasn't the first time Angie had come at him with some unfounded theory that he was falling for another girl.

His voice choked with emotion as he said, "Angie, I have never wanted and will never want another woman the way I want you. But honestly, babe, I can't take much more of this. What makes you think I want to be with Brooke?"

"I saw the way you looked at her!" Angie accused venomously, turning to glare at him. "I *saw*. I saw how you laughed together and how you helped her off the bus!" Angie was crying now. She knew she was being ridiculous. She knew that Shawna would have scolded her. *He loves you, Angie! Stop acting this way!*

"Angie," Mark tried to explain as gently as possible. "I *was* laughing with Brooke. At one point today, I slipped and fell into a creek. It was hot as blazes and Brooke took it upon herself to splash water on me and basically started a water fight. We had been hiking for hours and we were all hot and sweaty and tired and sick of trying to find stupid plants. Everybody else got involved, including Professor Fielding, and it was comical. We were still laughing about it when we got off the bus. That's *it!*" He took in a deep, trembling breath and continued. "I'm starting to wonder…" he hesitated, shaking his head slightly. Did he really want to say what he almost had said?

Angie, who had been studying her hands guiltily during his explanation, looked up at him through her tears. "Wonder what?" she demanded acidly, suddenly on the defensive again.

Her tone was so harsh and sarcastic, it cut him to the core. He loved her, but this wasn't a healthy relationship anymore. Maybe it never had been. He sighed a deep, weary sigh and looked at her sorrowfully.

"I think it's time we took a break from each other," he finally choked out. He could feel his own tears building but fought against them. He didn't want her to drop her wild accusations just because she felt momentarily sorry for him. Either she really loved him or she didn't, and if she did, then she would have to learn to trust him.

"Fine," Angie replied crisply, staring straight ahead.

"Fine," he echoed her sadly. A huge lump formed in his throat. How could this be happening? Just this morning, they had each proclaimed their love for one another. Angie didn't move or look at him. Finally, he grabbed his backpack. He opened the car door abruptly, got out, pulled her keys roughly from his pocket, threw them on the seat, and slammed the door shut. Angie jumped at the slamming of the door, but otherwise didn't move or look at him. He hesitated for one more moment, hoping she would say something or stop him. When she didn't move, he bolted away from the car as fast as his legs could carry him. He ran until he reached the college grounds. The bus had left and everyone on the field trip was gone. Nobody else remained because it was the weekend. He was very glad, because he ran to a private spot between two of the buildings, dropped to the grass, put his head in his hands, and cried.

. . .

A few days passed before Theresa finally noticed that Angie hadn't left the apartment and there had been no sign of Mark. Usually the two of them were attached at the hip.

Theresa felt guilty for not noticing sooner, but what could she do? Her job had kept her so busy the last few months. She had used all of her vacation hours in the days immediately following the accident and had been forced to take an extended leave without pay after Angie got out of the hospital. Her boss was very understanding about the time she'd needed. She hesitated to ask for more, but she had decided she and Angie needed to de-stress and do something *fun*, even if it was just for a couple of days. So she had asked for another week off at the end of the summer. She'd figure out the bills and lost income sooner or later.

Incredibly, when she made the request he had consented, assuring her it would not affect her good standing in the office. Shortly after the accident, her mother had sent her a little money, and even though she was behind on all the bills, Theresa had put it in her savings account, so there was that money. Additionally, three of her coworkers each generously donated one of their vacation days to her, so the time off would not put such a dent in her paycheck. Theresa had been moved to tears by their compassionate gesture.

She hadn't said anything to Angie yet; she didn't want to get her hopes up and then have the trip fall through. Just today, all of the pieces had fallen into place. Jack would be able to take the same week off and was going to join them! During the drive home from work, she had bounced happily in her seat like a little kid. She and Jack were going to surprise Angie – all of them were going to Silverwood and would spend their evenings at a cottage on Lake Coeur d'Alene! Silverwood is an amusement park just across the Montana-Idaho state border, with water rides and a reputedly great roller-coaster. Jack rented a cottage in nearby Coeur D'Alene, right on the lake. He had texted Theresa photos of it. It was beautiful, nestled in a thick forest, and they were going to rent paddleboats and eat at fancy restaurants and sleep as late as they wanted to. Theresa and Jack had even decided that Angie could ask Mark to come along. With two adults present, she didn't think it would be inappropriate as long as they carefully coordinated sleeping arrangements. The bungalow had two bedrooms, and the boys could sleep in one and the girls in the other.

In spite of her excitement, as Theresa had pulled into the apartment complex parking lot, she finally noticed that Angie's car was exactly where it had been when she left for work that morning. She realized that it hadn't moved in days. Angie had come home a few days earlier very distraught over something and had parked crookedly in her haste to get out and go hide in her bedroom. The car remained in the same position she'd left it in then.

Theresa always tried very hard to respect her daughter's privacy. She'd asked Angie what was wrong that day, but Angie hadn't been willing to talk about it then, so Theresa had let her be. Still, she worried about her. In the past few months, with her recovery almost complete, Angie had been back to her usual self, flitting about like a busy hummingbird, always on the move and generally in a cheerful state of mind. So, two days of her not leaving her room except for meals (and she had to be coaxed to the point of harassment just to get her to join them) were a blaring indicator that something was really bothering her.

Theresa's excitement about the trip quelled. She

unlocked the apartment door and Tater immediately wound around her legs and mewed and purred. After taking off her pumps and throwing them and her purse into the front closet, she walked, stocking-footed, to the kitchen to see if the cat had been fed. Both of her dishes were filled, so it wasn't that the cat was hungry. She deduced that Tater was lonely. Theresa glanced down the hallway and noted that Angie's door was firmly shut, as it had been for the last several days. As much as she hated to butt into her daughter's business, she resolved not to let her wallow any further. She sighed, then went to her room and changed out of her uncomfortable, polyester work suit and into some shorts and a t-shirt. She hung the suit up neatly in the closet, tossed her pantyhose in the hamper, and then made a beeline for Angie's room.

"Angie?" Theresa said softly, knocking lightly on her bedroom door. She waited a moment. When she received no response, she knocked harder and called out her daughter's name a little more loudly. Suddenly worried that Angie might have hurt herself, she was very relieved when she heard her daughter respond.

"Come in," Angie mumbled. When Theresa opened the door, she found Angie curled up in the fetal position on her unmade bed, her back facing her mother. The blinds were closed and the curtains were drawn, so the room was fairly dark; however, when Theresa opened the door, the light from the hallway illuminated it. The room was stuffy, having been closed off from the air conditioning. It was also uncharacteristically messy, with clothes and books strewn around the floor, on the dresser, and on the easy chair.

"What on earth…" she began, intending to scold Angie

for not keeping her room up. Before she could start in on her, though, she noticed Angie's shoulders were shaking. She made a beeline around the messy bed and sure enough, Angie was lying there, crying without making a sound. Theresa sat on the bed next to her distraught daughter. She tugged on her and Angie relented, allowing her mom to pull her up to sitting and to wrap her arms around her.

"Hey! What's the matter, honey?" she asked her tenderly. She reached with one hand and brushed her daughter's damp, dark hair out of her eyes, gently tucking it behind her ears.

Angie didn't answer. She threw her arms around her mother and held on tight. Theresa crooned and rocked her the way she had when Angie was in the hospital, and Angie cried harder, sobbing into her mother's neck. After a few minutes, she quieted, and the two of them just kept rocking back and forth. Theresa knew there was no point in prodding. Angie would tell her what was going on when she was good and ready, and not a minute before then.

Finally, Angie let go and so did Theresa, although she continued stroking the side of Angie's face gently. Angie grabbed a tissue off the nightstand, then lay back and looked up forlornly at her mom.

"What's wrong with me, mom?" she asked, sniffling and wiping her eyes with the tissue. Her nose was stuffy from crying. "Why do I repel the men in my life?"

"What are you talking about?" her mom responded, baffled. She stifled a sudden urge to laugh, she was so completely taken off guard by the question.

"I drove daddy away!" Angie wailed. "And Mark and I broke up!" She began crying again. With Theresa's gentle prodding, Angie unleashed all of her pent-up fears of abandonment. Eventually, Theresa was able to get her to calm down enough to talk rationally. They talked for over an hour, and of all Angie's revelations, Theresa was truly stunned to learn that Angie had been harboring the idea that she had driven her father away.

"Angela, I am so sorry!" she exclaimed when Angie finally stopped talking. "Why didn't you tell me this sooner? You aren't responsible for your dad's absence, honey! He and I decided we couldn't live together anymore, but it had nothing – absolutely *nothing* – to do with you or his love for you!" Theresa shook her head, slightly dazed at the turn of events, and then continued. "I feel terrible, because leaving him ended up making it harder for you to see each other. Maybe we should have stayed in Missoula, but I was selfish." She shook her head. "I wanted a complete break. I didn't want to have to worry about running into him."

Angie stared at the clock on the nightstand absently.

"Hey!" Theresa said a little more loudly. Angie looked like she wasn't fully buying what she was telling her, so she took her daughter's face in both her hands and forced her to look at her.

"He isn't avoiding you, Angie!" Her voice took on a new urgency and she looked Angie directly in the eyes. "His job just keeps him very busy. Since our breakup, he has taken on more driving jobs than he used to. I think being on the road has helped him to get through the hard times." She stopped, sighed, and slapped her knee with one hand. "Well, I feel totally responsible for this mess! Obviously, you need to see him, and I'm sure he needs to see you, too. In the morning, we'll call him and we'll figure out a way for you to see him. *Soon*. Okay?"

Angie sniffled and nodded. Then she started crying all

over again. She rolled to her side, dragging her pillow over her head in an attempt to hide. Theresa gently removed her grip on the pillow and set it aside.

"Mark?" her mother guessed, taking Angie's hand in hers.

"Oh, mom! I'm such an idiot!" Angie blurted through her tears. She told her mother all about the day of the breakup.

"I think I've ruined everything! Why did I act that way? He said he didn't like her, that he loved *me,* and I didn't believe him! He got so mad…I've never seen him so mad. When he got out of the car, he just ran away like he never wanted to see me again!" Fresh tears flowed down her cheeks, and her chest heaved with sobs. "He hasn't called or texted me or anything since then. I love him, Mama, but I was terrible to him! I really wouldn't blame him if he doesn't ever want to see me again!"

Theresa sat quietly, holding Angie's hand, not knowing what to say. From her perspective, it was suddenly very clear to her how Angie's thought processes had led her down this path, and she felt culpable and horribly guilty. Obviously, Angie had deep-seated feelings of rejection and abandonment, which she had projected onto her relationship with Mark. Theresa was so caught up in her own life and her new romance that she hadn't noticed what her own daughter was going through. She resolved instantly not only to pay closer attention, but maybe even look into some counseling for Angie.

She struggled to know what she could do to help now, in this moment. Suddenly, she remembered an email she had received from Greg earlier in the week. She stood up abruptly, letting go of Angie's hand in the process, and proclaimed, "I'll be right back!" Then she bolted from the room and down the hallway to her own bedroom.

Angie, surprised at her mother's sudden, strange behavior, sat up on the bed and called after her.

"Mom?"

"Be right there!" Theresa called.

Angie could hear her typing furiously on the computer keyboard. The apartment had limited space and Theresa's room was the largest, so they had agreed to keep the computer there. Whenever Angie had homework or a paper to write, it usually meant doing so in Theresa's room. They had purchased a small, three-way folding screen and had erected it as a partition so that Angie could work on the computer at night while Theresa slept.

A moment later, Angie heard the printer's gears spinning and whirring, and she listened as a paper moved its way through the machine and was ejected.

Then, almost as quickly as she'd gone, Theresa was back with the paper in her hand.

"Come on!" she said firmly. She took Angie's hand and tried to drag her to her feet. It wasn't that Angie didn't want to comply, but she was so puzzled by her mom's behavior that it took a moment for the request to sink in. She remained seated on the bed.

"Come *on!*" Theresa fairly ordered, tugging on her hand again. "Let's go!"

"What?" Angie sniffed, wiping her eyes on the back of her hand. She allowed her mother to pull her up and followed her hesitantly. "Where are we going, Mom?"

"We're going to town and get you a new phone!" Theresa stated, excited, as she pulled Angie to the front door. She started pushing her feet into her sandals while she motioned for Angie to do the same. She folded the piece of paper and shoved it in her shorts' pocket. "I don't know why I didn't think of this sooner! Jack has a smart phone and he uses it to talk to his brother in Miami all the time – it has a built-in camera and he downloaded an application that lets them not only call each other, but see each other, too!" She and Angie still used the old-fashioned, flip cell phones.

"What are you talking about, Mom?" Angie stuck her feet into her sandals obediently and watched, red-eyed and confused, as her mom fished her purse out of the front closet and dug out her car keys. "What does this have to do with me?" Theresa took her by the hand again and pulled Angie out of the apartment. She closed the door firmly and locked the deadbolt. Then she towed Angie in the direction of her car.

"Angie, a few days ago, your dad emailed me to say he had gotten a new phone, a smart phone, and that it had a web cam. You probably don't remember, but he's always had one of those cheap flip phones that you have to continually buy minutes for. Anyway, I was distracted and didn't even think about why he would tell me that. He never was very good at just speaking plainly." Theresa stopped halfway between the apartment and her car and turned to look at Angie, who had stopped dead in her tracks about twenty paces behind her. She stared at her mother, waiting for a complete explanation. Theresa fished the piece of paper out of her pocket and took it to Angie, who opened it up and began reading it while her mother resumed her explanation.

"Well, maybe he doesn't speak plainly, but I feel like an idiot for not understanding what he was telling me," she said, looking at her daughter sheepishly. Pointing at the paper in Angie's hand, she tried to explain her thought processes. "I think he was trying to let me know that if we had a similar phone, he could talk to us and we could see each other. Or more specifically, he could talk to *you* and you two could see each other."

Theresa turned and continued on her trajectory towards the car, while Angie just stared after her, dumbfounded. She unlocked the passenger door and motioned for Angie to get in.

"Come on!" she encouraged, trying to hurry Angie with her waving hand.

Angie shrugged and furrowed her eyebrows. Theresa patiently explained, "Ang, we're gonna go get you a better phone and a plan that allows you to converse with your dad, face-to-face!"

"Really?" Angie squealed, as understanding finally hit her. She marveled at the turn of events. She ran to the car and got in. As they pulled out of the parking lot onto Boon Road, she gazed at her mother appreciatively. "Thank you, Mom! I'm so excited!" It was the first time in days that she felt hopeful.

It was late July and the weather had been mostly sunny and hot. Today was a beautiful day. Sparse, fluffy, white clouds floated occasionally across an otherwise perfect, blue sky. It was around six-thirty in the evening and the traffic was light, as most of the valley's residents were somewhere enjoying themselves on a lakeshore or at a park. It was too late for rush-hour traffic and too early for people to be heading home from a day of fun in the sun. Angie's spirits were buoyed, and she smiled to herself as they drove in silence. But a few moments later, as they were turning onto Highway 93 to head into Kalispell, she sighed deeply.

Out of the corner of her eye, Theresa could see Angie fiddling with a knot on the front of her halter top, looking troubled. As they approached the first stop light, Angie glanced up at her mother, her expression one of pain.

"What?" Theresa coaxed, shifting her eyes between her daughter and the light.

"What if you're wrong?" Angie murmured softly. "I mean, what if we do all that and I call him, and he doesn't really want to talk to me after all?"

The light turned green and Theresa focused once more on the road, but she shook her head.

"No, I'm positive I'm right, Ang. Why else would he tell me that? It's not like he has any desire to talk to me!" She shook her head again and laughed. "No, you're just going to have to trust me on this one – he wants to talk to *you*."

Angie allowed her hopes to rise again during the remainder of the drive. Her spirits were higher than they had been in many months. As they picked out a phone and a plan, she allowed herself to become excited at the prospect that she might actually see and talk to her dad this very evening, as soon as they got home. The salesperson, Ricky, assisted them in choosing just the right phone, one that would be compatible with her dad's (at least, according to the details he had given in his email message). He helped them set up the face-time app, and showed them how to use it and many other common apps, too.

Theresa was delighted to find out that Angie's old flip phone could be used as a trade-in. In her impulsivity, she hadn't really thought about the cost of this whole venture until they reached the store, but by then, she knew that she would have to figure out a way to afford it. There was no way she would back out and let Angie down now.

As it happened, both the phone and the plan were more affordable than she would have guessed. Angie, realizing that the new monthly plan might be a stretch for Theresa, offered to find a part-time job to help pay for it. Theresa had accepted her offer and was struck by how mature and gracious her daughter was becoming.

The drive home was quietly pleasant, with Theresa and Angie embroiled in their own thoughts. Occasionally, they turned to each other and smiled. Theresa was pleased with herself for coming up with the plan in the first place, and Angie was full of excitement and nervous anticipation at the possibility of talking to her dad that night.

When they finally reached the apartment, Angie bounded from the car and fairly raced to the front door. She couldn't wait to try to call her dad and was even more excited at the prospect of seeing his face, which she had not seen in over a year. She tapped her foot anxiously as her mom unlocked the door, and once inside, she bolted to her room to try to call Greg. Ricky had also helped her export her contacts to her new phone, so her dad's number was already in it.

Once she was inside her own room with the door closed, Angie took the phone and carefully inserted the charging jack into the side of it. Then she plugged the other end into the wall socket. Ricky had started charging the phone in the store but had also said that she could use it while it finished charging. Now that it was all plugged in, set up, and ready to go, Angie had a moment of panic. What if she still couldn't get hold of Greg? Of course, she'd had her dad's number for years, but when she called him in the past, more often than not she got his voicemail. Only rarely had she actually gotten him to answer. She always left him messages, and a couple of times, he had called her back but because his calls always seemed to come in while she was at school or in therapy, they would end up playing phone tag. She had tried to get him to learn to text, but he never answered any of the texts she had sent him. He told her once in a voicemail that he found texting to be inconvenient and that he was "too uncoordinated and old" to learn how. They did exchange emails once in a while, but he didn't own a computer, and since he was almost always driving, his access to internet cafes was limited.

Finally, Angie sighed. She had the new phone and she knew what to do. Now she just had to muster her courage. Glancing at the clock, she did some quick mental math to figure out what time it was in Georgia, where Greg was now. She quickly surmised that he most likely would have stopped driving for the day and would be parked somewhere along the interstate at a truck stop or rest area. She tapped the icon for the phone and found her dad in the contacts. After a moment's hesitation, she hit the video call button.

The number rang three times and she almost lost her nerve. She was just about to hang up, when suddenly, Greg answered. Like magic, there he was, clear as day, on the screen.

"Hello?" he answered in his gravelly voice.

"Dad?" Angie said tentatively. He hadn't shaved in many days and his hair was a mess, but it was definitely him.

For a brief moment, Greg looked confused, holding his phone out and staring at it like he'd forgotten what it was. Suddenly, recognition swept over him. His expression lightened and became more animated.

"Angela?" he fairly shouted, a silly grin breaking out across his face.

"It's me, Dad!" she beamed. "You don't have to shout. I can hear you just fine! Can you hear me okay? Can you *see* me, daddy? I got a new phone…"

Although the screen was much smaller than a computer's, she could see him tear up and wipe away a few that escaped down his cheeks.

"I can see you, baby girl!" he answered, his voice trembling with emotion. "How's my princess? I've missed you so much!"

Angie smiled widely and her own joy spilled from her eyes and down her cheeks.

Chapter Eight: Love and Healing

"When you forgive, you love. And when you love,
God's light shines upon you."
~ Jon Krakauer, Into the Wild

Weeks had passed since Angie had gotten her new phone, and in what she considered nothing short of a miracle, she talked to her dad almost every day. Greg offered to add her account to his plan, so they could talk to each other as much as they wanted to without worrying about using up their minutes.

At first, after having spent so much time not communicating at all, their conversations were a little stilted. Now, however, they talked and laughed as if they had never been apart. At Eileen's urging, Angie had even found the courage to confront her dad about his absence and how much it had hurt her. Greg had taken full responsibility, admitting that part of the reason he hadn't called was because of his own hurt and anger at Theresa – he didn't want to call the apartment and take the chance that he might have to talk to *her*. When Angie pointed out that she'd had her own cell phone for over three years, and asked him why he hadn't called her personal phone more often, he could only say that having not seen her in such a long time, he was afraid of her reaction, that she might be hostile towards him. It wasn't until she called him on the new phone and he could see her face that he realized how foolish he had been. He had been a coward, he admitted to his daughter.

Eventually, Angie was bold enough to share her fears that she had driven him away, and although she had sensed all along that her feelings were distorting the truth, it made a big difference when her dad assured her (just as her mother had) that it was between the two of them and that their break-up had nothing to do with her. Hearing the words from Greg's mouth seemed to carry more weight than they had when she'd heard them from Eileen or her mom, and she began letting go of her deeply rooted fears of rejection and abandonment, a little at a time. Every conversation healed her a little more.

Angie and Greg's connection soon became strong enough that she even confided in him about her relationship with Mark, and about how her fears had caused her to preemptively reject him, because she was so sure he was on the verge of doing so to her. Her dad had sympathized and encouraged her to try to reach out to Mark. She told him she would think about it.

At the moment, her focus was on her newly restored relationship with her dad. She was unbelievably happy. They started making plans to see each other at the end of the summer, which was only a few weeks away.

Angie's spirits were higher than they had been since before the accident. The icing on her happiness cake was when her mother revealed that before school started, she, Jack, and Angie were all taking a vacation. She was happier than she'd been in months.

. . .

*O*n a blisteringly hot August Saturday, Theresa and Angie decided to go do some shopping for their trip. The temperature had hovered around one hundred degrees for several days; there was no breeze and the air was stiflingly hot. The air-conditioning barely made a discernible difference in the muggy apartment.

As such, the two women couldn't wait to get into the much better air-conditioned stores, and once inside each one, they shopped leisurely, trying on different bathing suits, sundresses, and shorts outfits, in no hurry to return to the heat outside.

The extreme temperature created mirages on the roads as they drove to practically every store in the nearby city of Kalispell. Finally, they reached their last destination before they would head home, a newer shopping area on the northern end of town. Stores of every type dotted several acres of asphalt; huge, accommodating parking lots were broken up intermittently by lovely, landscaped islands covered in deep green grass and pink and red flowering bushes. Restaurants were scattered about between the stores, and the women had decided to visit a couple more shops and then stop for an early dinner. They had been shopping for hours and both were exhausted and hungry. The back seat of the car was overflowing with evidence of all the great sales they had stumbled upon, and the floor in back was littered with empty water bottles and drained Frappuccino cups.

As Theresa pulled the car into the parking lot of the biggest discount store in the complex, Angie's attention was drawn to a nearby grassy island, where two young men were hard at work, pulling weeds and trimming the rose bushes. One of the men, deeply tanned and hair bleached white, looked up at the car as the women swung the doors open and disembarked. As their eyes met, Angie realized it was Mark. She started to wave, but Mark immediately looked back at the ground, pretending he hadn't seen her.

Theresa watched quietly from her side of the car. During the first weeks after Mark and Angie broke up, Angie refused to answer his calls or texts, so he had called Theresa to see if she could help. She inevitably ended up telling him (per Angie's orders) that although she was sorry, there wasn't anything she could do. He had sounded so dejected it made her heart ache, but no amount of cajoling would make Angie take his calls. After a week he had given up, and neither woman had heard from him since. Theresa knew he loved Angie and that he was deeply hurt by the whole situation. She longed to be able to do or say something that would bring the two back together, but she'd always felt like her own mother had been such a busybody when she was a teenager, and she was loathe to interfere in the same manner. She stood by mutely for a moment, wrestling with her conscience, and then she changed her mind. Maybe they just needed a push.

"Angie?" she said softly. Her daughter stood like a statue, staring at the two men, unsure of what she should do. She missed Mark like crazy but knew that she had brought the whole break-up upon them both, and now she struggled internally. *What's the right thing to do?* She still loved him and suspected that he loved her as well. Through numerous conversations with her dad, mom, and even Eileen, she realized that she had projected her fears onto Mark, and in the process of avoiding his rejection, she had hurt *him* instead – deeply. Should she just leave him alone? Did she have a right to try to reach out to him now?

The sun beat down on the parking lot and the heat reflecting off the asphalt and the cars was stifling. Angie felt lightheaded and dizzy, unsure and confused.

"Honey, what are you going to do? We can't just stand here – it's hot as blazes!" her mother wheedled her impatiently. She wiped at her forehead with a tissue she retrieved from her purse, but it made no difference. Her face immediately remoistened with sweat. The heat was making her nauseous.

"Go on, Mom," Angie said firmly, suddenly resolved. "I'll be there in a minute." She had created this mess and it was up to her to try to fix it. If he didn't want her anymore, that was fine, but she missed him terribly and she had to try to make things right. She was sure that he wouldn't want to date her anymore, but she couldn't stand this enmity between them. They both deserved better. After all that they had been through together and knowing how much he had supported her during the hardest thing she'd ever faced, suddenly her greatest desire was to try to salvage their friendship. At the very least, she knew he deserved an apology. Whether or not he accepted it, she realized, was something she couldn't control, but she had to try.

"I have to go talk to him, Mom," she explained as Theresa eyed her curiously. She squared her shoulders and felt a bead of sweat run down her back between her shoulder blades. The sun beat down on them mercilessly.

Theresa nodded her head encouragingly and smiled tenderly at her daughter.

"I know," she confirmed. "Why don't you invite him to come over tonight to talk? Don't stay out here too long; you know how you get when you're overheated!"

"Yeah, I do," Angie agreed, amused. She acknowledged inwardly that she had been "overheated" the day she and Mark had their fight. She smiled back at her mother. "Go ahead, Mom. I won't be long."

Theresa nodded and smiled again, and then hurried into the store and out of the heat. Angie turned slowly, took a deep breath, and headed towards the island where Mark was feverishly hacking at an obstinate rose branch that was encroaching on the walkway. He didn't notice her approach – or didn't appear to – until she was almost right next to him. Then he looked up suddenly. His expression was unreadable.

"Oh. Hello," he said, without a trace of emotion. He went right back to cutting the branch.

Angie caught her breath; she had forgotten how handsome he was. Immediately, though, the tone of his voice caused her to take a step back, and she regarded his face cautiously. Despite his efforts to look blasé about the situation, she could see that sadness had taken up residence in his eyes. She noted that he had lost weight. His face was so skinny it was verging on haggard. It nearly broke her heart.

The other young man who had been furiously pulling weeds beneath the bush suddenly stood up, and when he saw Angie, he grinned widely. His mahogany skin was tanned the color of espresso, and he had long, coffee-colored dreadlocks and big, brown eyes.

"Hey! Angie! How are you?" Recognition washed over Angie. She was amazed to realize it was Ben Shafer. She hadn't seen him in years. His family, missionaries like the Howsers, had moved to Thailand the summer after Halle's birthday party. Mark spoke of him often. They had stayed good friends via social media and email.

"Ben? HI!" Angie gushed enthusiastically. She rushed over to give him a giant hug, ignoring his protests that he was dirty from working all day. "How are you? When did your family get back?" They both laughed with delight at the unexpected reunion, and for the next few minutes, they chatted like they were old buddies. As Mark's best friend, Ben knew all about the relationship between them and felt an affinity towards Angie. Likewise, Mark had spoken so often and so fondly of Ben that she felt like they were good friends, too.

After a minute or two, they realized that Mark was no longer standing beside them. Shielding their eyes against the sun, they scanned the parking lot and the front of the store for Mark. Angie spotted him first, sitting on a bench in the shade near the store's entrance, about fifty feet from where they were standing. As they watched, he took a long drink from a water bottle he was holding. Then he sat back nonchalantly and watched the shoppers scurrying in and out of the store, acting like Ben and Angie didn't exist. Angie looked at Ben questioningly.

"He's really hurting, Angie," Ben stated gently. A bee buzzed around his head; he swatted it away, mopped the sweat from his forehead with his hand, and then continued. "He's hardly told me anything about what happened. When I try to ask him, he changes the subject. But he used to talk about you nonstop…"

"I want to talk to him," Angie interrupted clumsily, "but I'm afraid. He has every right to hate my guts, but I want things to be…better." What was she trying to say? She shook her head. "I don't know what to say to him," she admitted, embarrassed. "Stupid, huh?"

"Do you love him?" Ben asked pointedly. His candor caught her off guard, and she almost protested that it was none of his business. Ben just looked at her, kindly, without a trace of malice, and she realized that he wasn't trying to trip her up or make her feel bad. Suddenly, her heart melted, and her dark green eyes pooled with tears.

"Yes," she fairly whispered. "But I broke us apart. *I'm* the one. I'm not sure I have the right to…"

"If you don't, who does?" Ben replied softly. "He loves you so much, Angie, he's just…well, his pride is wounded, you know?"

Angie nodded and looked over at Mark. He was leaning back on the bench with his arms stretched out across the back of it. One leg was crossed over the other, his foot on his knee. He looked like he didn't have a care in the world as he continued watching the passersby.

She took another deep breath, let it out, and exclaimed quietly, "Well, here goes nothing!" She looked up at Ben, who was smiling. "It's been great seeing you, Ben."

"You, too," he answered jovially, as he took her hand and pulled her into another friendly hug. "Think I'll take a break now, too." He glanced over at Mark, then back at Angie. "Go. Don't be afraid," he encouraged. He turned and started walking towards the store's entrance, digging his wallet out of his back pocket as his sandals slapped the hot pavement.

Mark caught the movement out of the corner of his eye. He stood up and started to call after Ben, but Angie beat him to the punch.

"Mark?" she called tentatively. He stopped and turned towards the sound of her voice. She waited for a few cars to pass by, and then stepped off the curb of the island and began walking towards him. As she drew closer, their eyes locked. It seemed to Angie that his expression softened, if only by a few degrees. Making her way across the fire lane to the sidewalk, she stumbled clumsily on an uneven patch of pavement. Mark's face broke into a grin, and Angie instantly matched his, but he stiffened and his expression became serious once more. Her smile faded, too, and she regarded him cautiously. Amused by the awkwardness of the situation, he gave her another tentative smile, and her heart skipped a beat, just as it had when they were sitting in her car during the snowstorm last winter, before they officially started dating.

This smile was fleeting, too. As she approached him, he stood and crossed his arms over his chest, a wordless gesture of self-protection which belied his true emotions. His expression was guarded. He didn't want her to know that his heart was buoyed in her presence; in fact, when he had first spotted her as their car pulled up, it had leapt for joy. For an instant, it was almost as if nothing had gone wrong between them. Only for a moment, though, and then the dagger of her rejection pierced him again.

"Hey," she said shyly, when she was just a few feet from him.

He felt his resistance melting at the sound of her voice.

"Hey," he responded noncommittally. Sweat rolled down his nose, and he wiped it away impatiently with his hand. "Frick, it's hot!" he exclaimed to no one in particular.

"How are you?" Angie asked, ignoring the comment on the weather. Now that she had mustered her courage, she wasn't about to settle for small talk.

Mark, startled by the question, was instantly conflicted. He abruptly sat back down on the bench and leaned forward, placing his elbows on his knees and clasping his hands together, almost wringing them. Over the past couple of weeks, his feelings had morphed gradually from unbelievably hurt to intensely angry to numb. He gnawed subconsciously on his fingers while he mulled her question over. In fact, it had only been in the last couple of days that he had begun to have any sense of peace about the break-up. He had started to call her many times, but his pride always stopped him. He had almost convinced himself that he didn't need her.

Now, here she was standing right in front of him, asking him how he was? He dropped his head into his hands, rubbed his face tiredly, and sighed. Part of him wanted to lash out at her, ask her how on earth she *thought* he was, dish back some of the pain she had dealt him. Simultaneously, though, he was flooded with love for her and didn't want to hurt her, in spite of how much she had hurt him. *What do I do, Lord?* he implored silently. Above all, he didn't want to succumb to sheer emotion, to what he considered to be his petty humanity. He wanted to take the high road, to respond in a manner worthy of his faith. He had been taught about forgiveness his whole life; now, here was a chance to walk the talk.

But she hadn't asked for forgiveness – she had just asked him how he was.

Looking back up at her, he kept his expression as nonchalant as possible while he answered, "Oh, okay. How about you?" He cleared his throat nervously, glancing out at the nearby traffic. Then he tried to smile at her, but it didn't reach his eyes.

Angie was taken aback at his indifferent response. Suddenly, she wasn't sure why she was trying to talk to him. She searched his eyes, those intense blue-green eyes, for the man who had only weeks before proclaimed his everlasting love for her.

"M-me?" she stammered, surprised that she could find her own voice. "I'm…okay…too?" Her response came out more a question than a statement. She shook her head a little and regarded him cautiously, like he was a snake about to strike.

"Good," Mark blurted, forcing his voice to sound more pleasant than he felt. "That's good. I'm glad to hear it." He nodded at her, then forced his attention away from her as he opened the water bottle and took another long drink. Some water escaped out the side of his mouth and dribbled down his chest. He wiped it away quickly with his hand and swiped at the drips on his mouth and chin, embarrassed, still not looking at her.

Angie smiled and teased him. "Drink much?"

He chortled mirthlessly, but the sound was music to her ears. She missed his laughter. "Spaz!" he chided himself quickly, rolling his eyes. Then he became serious once more. He felt her watching him and he cautiously returned her gaze. She was smiling at him lovingly, like she used to, like nothing had happened between them. This felt too familiar, too friendly, given the events of the past month. Once again, he felt the need to guard himself.

"What do you want, Angie?" he asked more sharply than he intended.

His changed demeanor felt like a slap in the face, but Angie knew that it was no less than she deserved, so she bravely answered, "I…I'd really like to talk to you. Can you come over tonight? Like, around seven?" Unbidden tears stung her eyes and she fought them off. She started to reach out to stroke his face, an old habit, but caught herself. "Please," she implored, dropping her hand but not taking her eyes from his.

She looked so sad and forlorn that his heart ached, and he just wanted to take her in his arms, to hold her, to rock her, to kiss her like he used to. Her eyes, her beautiful deep green eyes, filled up with tears, and part of his favorite scripture suddenly flowed through his mind: *Love keeps no record of wrongs.*

"Why?" he asked her more gently. *Love always protects, trusts, hopes, and perseveres.*

A couple of tears spilled over and down Angie's cheeks.

"Because I'm sorry," she whispered. A few more tears escaped. "Because I miss you." *Love always hopes, trusts, perseveres.*

In a flash, all of the sadness and pain of the last month melted away in Mark's heart and was replaced with hope. He had thought he could resist the pull of her, but he was wrong. He realized he had never stopped loving her at all – he had only been kidding himself. He reached up and tenderly wiped one of her tears away with his fingertip.

"Why?" he asked again, his voice brusque with emotion. His eyes burned with his own burgeoning tears and he blinked to keep them at bay. He *knew* why, but he was afraid. He was afraid to hope. He was desperately afraid that she wouldn't say the words.

But then she did.

"Because I love you," she said plaintively, as tears began streaming down her cheeks. She looked him straight in the eyes and he knew she was telling the truth.

Joy burst through his being, wiping away the desolation of the last month. As his own tears began to fall, creating streaks in his dirty face, Mark stood again. He reached out and stroked her hair and wiped her tears with the backs of his fingers.

"I love you, too, Angela. So, so much. More than you'll ever know," he declared, and pulled her into his arms and held her tightly.

. . .

Mark went to Angie's that night, and after sharing a jovial dinner with Jack and Theresa, they excused themselves to go to Angie's room. There, they sat on the floor and talked, cried, laughed, held each other, and talked some more. Angie told him about getting back in contact with her dad. She opened up about all of the fears she had been harboring for years about her parents' break-up. She had convinced herself that she was unlovable, and so had been unable to believe that Mark could love her.

The sun set around nine-thirty that evening and the night brought mercifully cooler temperatures. They sat out on the deck, rocking gently back and forth on the swinging bench, and talking quietly into the early hours of the morning, long after Jack had gone home and Theresa had gone to bed. While crickets and frogs serenaded them, they reaffirmed their love for one another. And as a gentle breeze stirred up the fresh scents of a mid-summer's night, of flowering trees and newly cut grass, they sealed their renewed commitment to each other with a tender kiss.

Chapter Nine: Not Goodbye

"Goodbyes are not forever, Goodbyes are not the end,
They simply mean I'll miss you
Until we meet again." ~ Author Unknown

A few days after Mark and Angie had made up, Angie received a phone call from Eileen Howser. Eileen informed her that the headstone for Shawna's grave had finally been completed. The stone mason would be bringing it out to the cemetery the next day, and Eileen was arranging an impromptu ceremony. Just a few of Shawna's closest friends and family were invited, she explained, to observe the stone being set and to pay their respects. Angie had been in the hospital and unable to attend Shawna's funeral, and Eileen knew that she needed the closure such a service would provide.

Eileen asked her if she wanted to play her guitar and sing at the small service. Angie, while completely honored at having been asked, was hesitant. Although she continued to practice every day, and had regained much of her ability, she still struggled with her hands going numb. What if she messed up during such an important occasion?

Finally, Eileen convinced her that Shawna would have wanted her and nobody else to sing for her. If Angie made any mistakes, Eileen said, she should just picture Shawna there laughing with her. It would only be in front of a few people and nothing that Angie should be nervous about.

So, on a beautiful, sunny Wednesday in August, a small ensemble of Shawna's best and closest friends and her loving family gathered in the Little Cemetery behind the Little Brown Church that Shawna had attended her whole life, whenever the family had not been away on a missions trip. The stone mason, a friend of the Howser's, brought the stone out about an hour before the guests arrived and by the time Angie, Mark, Theresa, and Jack got there, he had already planted it firmly and lovingly at the head of Shawna's grave.

Angie knelt down carefully in her flowery sundress and traced the elaborate inscription in the smooth, cold, purple granite with her finger, while she silently read the words. "Shawna Elizabeth Howser, Beloved Daughter." Below that, the dates of Shawna's birth and death were carved, and just below that, in beautiful script, was the following Biblical quote: "Blessed are the pure in heart, for they shall see God, Matthew 5:8." On either side of the inscription were carved flowers and ribbons. She thought it was a lovely headstone, although she'd never seen one up close before. The whole scene was surreal to her. Months had passed and she thought she was coming to grips with the loss of her best friend. She couldn't fathom that the stone had anything to do with Shawna. She didn't want to even think about her friend's body lying just a few feet below them…

Angie stood back up quickly and Mark was at her side in a flash. They held each other tightly, and Angie, not sure what she was feeling, remained surprisingly dry-eyed. It wasn't really sadness, for through many conversations with Eileen, she had come to believe that Shawna was alive in heaven, whatever heaven might be. Angie wasn't sure what or where heaven was, but she was comforted by the idea of Shawna dwelling forever in a place of happiness, beauty, and peace, no longer troubled by the world and its problems.

The pastor invited everyone to stand in a circle around the grave and opened with a heartfelt prayer for the Lord's presence and peace to be with them all. Then he spoke very briefly about the uncertainty of life, the sureness of death, and the comfort available to those who placed their hope in God. He said that those in Christ didn't ever have to say goodbye, only farewell. Finally, he drew an analogy of how each person's life, compared to the whole universe and all of eternity, might seem like a small, insignificant pebble, but if you dropped a small pebble into a pool of water, ripples formed and spread out to the edges of it. The meaning was clear: Even though Shawna's life was relatively brief and seemingly insignificant, she had made a big difference in the lives of the people who knew and loved her, and she would never be forgotten. It was a very sweet message, unlike anything Angie had ever heard. Although brief, his speech was loving and sincere. When he finished, Eileen asked everyone to take hands, and she invited each person present to say a little something about what knowing Shawna had meant to him or her.

Angie was nervous, unaccustomed as she was to public speaking, but when her turn came, she found it surprisingly easy to tell the group about the difference Shawna had made in her life during their short time together. By the time each person had said what he or she wanted to say, they were all passing around tissues and sniffling and wiping their eyes. Clearly, Shawna *had* made a tremendous difference in all their lives and had been a blessing to them all. She had only lived seventeen years, but in that short time, her beautiful soul had had a tangible effect. Angie believed that if the "pebble" of Shawna's life had only made one, small ripple, those ripples surely reached out into eternity.

After the last person spoke, Eileen told everyone about how much fun it had been to watch Angie learn to play the guitar, and how privileged she had felt as she and Shawna had tried their hand at songwriting and shared their creations with her. Then she invited Angie to play and sing, and while Angie retrieved her guitar, Eileen told the small group about the injuries Angie had sustained and praised God for the miracle that she could still play.

Angie approached the group, smiled timidly up at them, and pulled the strap over her head, positioning her guitar to play.

"I'm not sure what to say," she told them, strumming quietly on the strings and adjusting a couple until the guitar was tuned to her satisfaction. "I've never played for anyone but my family. Well, and Shawna's family. Well, they ARE my family…" she stammered, frowning at her inability to be articulate. Eileen, Grant, Mark, Jack, and her mom smiled at her, and a few people chuckled softly. She hadn't been nervous until now, and she realized she was babbling. "Um…I don't know any religious songs. I hope that's okay?" she asked no one in particular. It didn't really matter whether those gathered approved or not, she justified herself internally. She only knew a few songs, and Eileen *had* only asked her to sing just yesterday, after all.

"Anyway," she smiled bravely at the waiting group.

"This is for you, Shawna." Angie played a very simplistic version of a song that she had loved as a child and had taught herself, Christine McVie's "Songbird." It had been a favorite of both girls.

Her voice was as strong and sweet as it had ever been, and she closed her eyes and imagined singing the words to Shawna alone. Although she stumbled over the lyrics a few times and couldn't hold down the strings tightly enough for the chords to ring out as clear and true as she wanted them to, she played bravely on to the very end. When the last note hung on the air, she opened her eyes, and everyone was crying again. She heard a few people say, "Amen!" and "Beautiful!" as she took her guitar and put it away. Mark stared at her like he'd never seen her before, awed by her talent, which in her insecurity she'd kept hidden from him until that moment. Then they all took hands again and the pastor offered up a final prayer, asking God to bless each one to live their lives in a way that would bring honor to him and to the memory of Shawna.

As the small group disbanded, Eileen moved over to hug Angie.

"I'm so proud of you, Angie, and I know Shawna is, too," she whispered through her tears.

"Thank you, Eileen," Angie whispered back. Eileen kissed her on the cheek.

"I love you, Angie," she said, smiling.

"I love you, too, Eileen," Angie smiled back.

Everyone was invited to stay and have cake and tea in the little church afterwards, so, with the ever-gracious Eileen leading the way, people meandered down the little path and around to the front doors of the church.

"Oh, honey, that was just perfect!" Theresa gushed, sidling up to give Angie a quick little hug.

"Well, it wasn't perfect, but it seemed to fit, eh?" Angie smiled.

Jack came over next, put his arm around her, and gave her a loving squeeze. "You're a miracle, you know it? I'm your doctor – I know what you've been through physically. Bravo, kiddo, bravo!"

"Thanks, Jack," she said self-consciously, as she hugged him back. Then he and Theresa turned and left to join the others heading into the church.

Mark came up behind her just then. He wrapped his arms around her, put his chin on her shoulder, and whispered, "Wow!" She placed her arms over his, and they stood there, rocking quietly back and forth, staring down at the gravestone and at all of the flowers people had brought and placed around it. The temperature had dropped to a much more comfortable seventy-eight degrees, and there was a nice, cool breeze blowing. It was a perfect day. Mark let go a little and moved until he was standing side-by-side with Angie. He kept his arm around her, and she put hers around his waist. Still, neither one spoke. They looked out at the grassy prairie that stretched out to the very edges of the mountains ringing the Flathead Valley, broken only here and there by a smattering of houses and barns.

The breeze bent the tall, yellow prairie grass back and forth, and whooshed softly as it fingered its way through it, creating ripples and waves. Overhead, a red-tailed hawk let out a single screech, catching their attention, and they watched as it soared by on an invisible wave of air and then did a sudden nosedive, coming up with a small varmint in its mouth and flying quickly away. Scents of hothouse roses and carnations wafted around them, mixed with the pungent smell of the wildflowers and grasses drying out in the field under the summer sun. Hummingbirds buzzed in and out of some nearby bushes, jockeying for position around the flowers and voicing their angry threats in tiny squawks and tweets. Occasionally, there was the muted sound of a car passing by on the adjacent highway, but otherwise the stillness of the peaceful afternoon was unbroken.

"What are you thinking about?" Mark finally murmured in Angie's ear.

Angie didn't react or indicate she had heard him and he was just about to repeat the question, when she suddenly and quietly replied, "I'm thinking about life. And death. And heaven." She stared out across the pasture to the mountains. Mark tightened his arm around her as Angie continued. "I'm thinking about Shawna, about how young she was and how much she still had left to do here on earth."

"Mm-hmm," Mark agreed, resting his head sideways on top of hers. They continued to rock side-to-side, slowly and steadily, not speaking.

"I'm not sad, which is weird, you know?" Angie asked suddenly. She stopped rocking, dropped her arm from Mark's side, and turned to face him. "I mean, of course I'm sad, and I will always, always, *always* miss Shawna so much," she continued, looking at him earnestly. "But there is something stirring in my heart. What the pastor said, that thing about there being eternal life in Christ Jesus... do you think that's true?" She wrinkled up her eyebrows at Mark and before he could answer, she resumed her train of thought.

"Because I'm starting to think…it *could* be true. I mean, I want to believe, but I'm scared. I want to believe there's a chance I'll see Shawna again. And I really, really want to see her again, you know?" She sighed. "I don't know what's happening to me." She shook her head a little and then looked up at him.

Mark had been listening to her quietly, and now he smiled at her.

"Don't just smile at me, say something," she laughed, giving him a small, playful shove.

"I'm scared, too, Angie," he said. "On the one hand, yes, I do believe it's all true. On the other hand, I've tried very hard not be…well, overly religious when I'm around you. Would you consider me a freak if I told you that I think what's happening to you is spiritual? That I think it's God, speaking to your heart?" His expression indicated he thought she might scream or run away.

Instead, she just nodded at him.

"Oh," she said seriously, nodding again. "Hmm." She turned and stared out at the grassy plains and the mountains again. Mark put his arm around her again and they stood there quietly for a time, just listening to the birds calling to one another and to the bees buzzing in the flower arrangements.

"No, I wouldn't," she finally said, softly.

"Wouldn't what?" Mark smiled at her obtuse way of expressing herself.

Angie turned slightly so she could snuggle into his chest. He pulled her into a fierce hug, burying his face in her hair. He smelled shampoo and soap and sandalwood, her favorite fragrance. He had missed her so much and was just so happy to be here with her now.

"Wouldn't what?" he murmured once more.

"Wouldn't think you were a freak," she whispered into his neck. "At least," she laughed softly, "not more of one than I already do!" She felt him laugh with her, but he kept her within his tight hold.

"Actually," she continued, "I think...or at least, I'm starting to...think it's true, too."

Chapter Ten: Dreams

"The only person you are destined to become is the person you decide to be."
~ *Ralph Waldo Emerson*

"Sometimes the dreams that come true are the dreams you never even knew you had."
~ *Alice Sebold,* The Lovely Bones

Now that she was down to having therapy only once a month, Angie missed Chloe in between appointments. Over the previous ten months, their relationship had become more than just that of therapist-patient; it was a friendship. Sometimes it was hard to focus on her exercises, because she always wanted to pick Chloe's brain about things that were going on in her own life. At twenty-six, Chloe really wasn't all that much older than Angie and she had grown very fond of her patient. She felt very protective of her, almost like a big sister. She was honored that Angie always asked her advice or told her secrets.

Angie admired Chloe on many levels. She liked her style and her independence. Chloe's hair was cut short and dyed black. She had tattoos and piercings, and liked to wear black, giving her the appearance of a total rebel. In reality, though, she was one of the most grounded and kind people Angie had ever known.

At her first appointment after the small ceremony at the Little Brown Church, on another blistering day in late August, Angie gushed to Chloe about having played the guitar for the small group and how well-received she had felt. As she listened, Chloe led her over to a little table with a black, padded top and patted a short stool on one side, indicating Angie should sit. She moved to the other side, sat down on an identical stool, and started massaging Angie's fingers while she congratulated her for having the courage to go through with it. Since Angie wanted to play guitar well again, Chloe focused that day's therapy on strengthening the small muscles of her hands. She was pleased to know that Angie was picking her guitar up and practicing daily.

"Just the simple act of playing through a few chords is wonderful exercise," she commended Angie while she worked each finger from the base to the tip.

The therapy arts building was air-conditioned; the room they were in was blessedly cool that afternoon, and the massage was so relaxing that Angie started getting droopy-eyed. Chloe, not wanting to put her patient to sleep when there was so much work to be done, ended the massage. She got up, walked over to a cupboard and grabbed a large piece of a blue, clay-like substance. Then she returned to the table and guided Angie through some small exercises designed to strengthen her hands. As she alternately squeezed and released the blue clay, Angie complained that her hands were going numb.

"It's the most frustrating part of trying to play my guitar!" she lamented. "I can usually play through a whole song now, but by the time I get halfway through another, my hands, especially my left one, start going dead." At Chloe's prodding, she described the sensation she felt when she tried to play, pointing to exactly where her fingers went numb.

Chloe listened to her carefully, interjecting occasionally, saying, "Hmm," or "Really?" At last, she nodded. "You know, I don't know why this didn't occur to me before. I guess a few months ago, you weren't really playing your guitar very much *because* of the numbness, and I just assumed it was because your hands still had some healing to do," she said. She manipulated Angie's hands a little more, and asked her to move them several different ways, all the while pushing her to be as specific as she could be about her symptoms.

"Angie," she remarked finally, putting Angie's hands down softly on the therapy table. "You have the classic symptoms of carpal tunnel syndrome." She explained what she knew about the condition, stating that it usually occurred from overuse of the hands and wrists and was common in people whose jobs involved a lot of repetitive motion. "It just occurred to me that it can also be brought on by an injury – *Hello, Chloe!* I can't believe I didn't think of this before!" She shook her head at herself, exasperated.

She ran to a small, steel desk in the corner of the room, grabbed a pen and a small notepad from the center drawer, flipped the notebook open, and began scrawling on it furiously. Then, she tore the sheet out and brought it to Angie, who could only stare at her, bewildered.

"That's the name and number of a terrific orthopedic surgeon here in town," she said, pointing to her writing. "If it turns out she can help you, it should be covered under the insurance that's covering all the medical related to the accident. There's no denying that your hands and arms suffered the most damage when you were hit," Chloe explained, excitedly.

When Angie still didn't react, she said, excitedly, "Angie! I'm saying that it's possible that your condition can be corrected with carpal tunnel surgery! It's a pretty straight-forward procedure. You'll probably have to have both of your wrists operated on, and they usually only do one at a time, for obvious reasons. You'll have to have more therapy when it's over, but you're no stranger to therapy – you're a hard worker and it'll be a piece of cake for you. And when you're all healed up, there's a chance that the numbness will disappear. Forever!" She waited expectantly for the information to penetrate Angie's brain.

She could tell when it did, because Angie's face suddenly lit up like a Christmas tree.

"You mean, gone? *Gone* gone, like, permanently?" she asked, incredulous. Chloe nodded.

Impulsively, she stood and hugged Chloe tightly.

"Thank you!" she whispered, her eyes misty with tears.

"Well," Chloe laughed, hugging her back. "Don't thank me yet! You still have to consult with the doctor. She's the one who will ultimately decide if the surgery is right for you. Then, you'll have to *have* it! And *then*, you'll have to endure more pain and therapy." She laughed again as Angie's face fell slightly.

Taking Angie's hands in her own, she leaned in and whispered, "But I think it's gonna work!" As Angie hugged her again, she laughed and said, "You're welcome!"

. . .

t dinner that night, Angie could hardly contain her joy and excitement as she shared Chloe's diagnosis with her mom and Jack. She was nervous about telling Jack, afraid that as a physician, he would know something Chloe hadn't and shoot the whole thing down before they even looked into it. So, she was delighted when he agreed wholeheartedly, and he even offered to attend a consultation with her if she wanted him to.

"I know Dr. Thompson. She's an excellent surgeon and a really great person," Jack remarked, as he passed the Italian dressing to Theresa. He noticed her iced tea glass was almost empty, so he got up, retrieved the pitcher from the fridge, brought it to the table, and refilled her glass. He motioned for Angie to hold her glass out and filled it, too. Then he put the pitcher down and raised his own glass, saying, "I propose a toast. Here's to a successful surgery and a complete healing for Angie!"

Angie and Theresa both responded with a hearty, "Here, here!" and they all clinked their glasses together. Theresa took in Jack's actions with doe-eyed affection. He smiled at her lovingly, then went back to spreading mustard on his hoagie roll. It was still hot enough that nobody wanted to cook, so they ate a simple dinner of homemade sub sandwiches and salad. The table was covered in the necessary accoutrements. There were jars and bottles of condiments, plates full of cold cuts and cheese, sliced, juicy tomatoes, spicy-sweet pickles, zesty banana peppers, cool, crisp lettuce, and a couple open bags of chips. They ate in amicable silence, with only the sounds of their breathing, chewing, and of ice tinkling in their glasses until Angie's phone rang.

Angie looked over at the counter where her phone was

lying, and back at her mom, whom she knew didn't like interruptions during the dinner hour. She tried to ignore it, as her own sandwich was only half-eaten, but finally she blurted out, "Maybe it's Dad!" She stared at her mother expectantly. Theresa sighed and waved her consent for Angie to leave the table.

"Thanks, Mom!" she yelled as she bolted from the table. Theresa rolled her eyes and she and Jack smiled at each other as Angie exited. She snatched up her phone from the kitchen counter and ran with it to her room.

"Hello?" she answered breathlessly, touching the screen to connect the call as she closed her bedroom door behind her. But instead of her dad, it was Mark. A smile spread across her face. He was the only one besides Greg that she was ever anxious to talk to.

"Hey, gorgeous!" Mark gushed. "What are you doing? I'm calling to see if you want to go to the lake with me. The church is hosting a barbecue for the high school and college kids at Somers Beach, and they're setting up a volleyball net and everything! Do you want to go?"

"Wow," Angie remarked, deflated. "Really? Somers Beach..." She hesitated. She hadn't been to Somers Beach since last summer, when she had gone with Shawna, she reflected glumly. "Well, we're kind of in the middle of dinner..."

"It's a barbecue, silly! You can finish eating there!" he joked. Then he begged, "Come on, Ang! Summer's only going to last a little longer, you know! We *do* live in Montana – we could get a snowstorm tomorrow!"

Angie giggled, brightening a little. "Well...I guess so. I'll have to go ask my mom. Can you hold on a minute?"

Mark said he would wait and she put down her phone.

She knew she could take the phone with her, but she wanted time to think. She contemplated pretending to ask and then telling him she couldn't get permission but hated the idea of lying to him. She just wasn't sure. That particular beach had been the girls' primary summer hangout for the last five years. Angie knew every inch of the place. She knew the water like the back of her hand, where it was shallow and where it suddenly dropped off into murky blackness. She knew where the ground was soft and sandy and where there were sharp rocks to be avoided. She couldn't dredge up a single memory of that beach that didn't include Shawna.

Still, it was a really hot day, and she hadn't been swimming anywhere all summer except at the pool. She loved the water. When she was small, her parents called her their little water baby, because they couldn't keep her out of any kind of water. She even got in trouble once for splashing around in an icy puddle to the point that her winter boots were soaked inside and out. Her punishment had been that she couldn't go outside until they dried completely, which took a good two days. They'd had to stuff them with newspaper, and place them on the heating vent…

Angie shook herself back to the present. She knew she was stalling, and Mark was waiting, so she went out to the dining room to ask for permission to go.

Her mom and Jack were finished eating and the table was mostly cleared, although her own plate with its half-eaten sandwich remained. Jack was in the kitchen putting the condiments away. She could hear the jars clinking against each other as he made room for them in the crowded refrigerator. Theresa was stacking plates and glasses and getting ready to take them away when she noticed Angie.

At the look on Angie's face, she put the plates back on the table, grimaced, and asked pointedly if it had been Greg on the phone, expecting to hear that he'd broken his promise to come see her already. Angie explained that it was Mark and Theresa relaxed. She listened patiently as her daughter asked for permission to go to Somers Beach with him. Theresa's motherly intuition was on full blast. She sensed that Angie was hesitant about going and she instantly gleaned the reason.

"It is hot, Angie, and you haven't been swimming anywhere but the gym this summer," she encouraged softly. Seeing the pained expression in Angie's eyes, she said simply, "I know." She and Angie just looked at each other for a moment.

As Angie regarded her solemnly, Theresa nodded. Her ability to read her daughter was a thing of legend in their household, but it still took Angie by surprise when she hit the nail square on the head.

"I know you haven't been there since last summer. I know it's another first. That's the hardest part of losing someone you love, honey: All the firsts. You've been so brave up to now. If you don't want to go, then don't, but realize that you're only putting off the inevitable."

Angie continued to stand there staring at her, until Theresa smiled a little and asked, "Is Mark still on the phone?"

At that, Angie's eyes opened wider and she exclaimed, "Oh! Yeah!" She looked at her mother almost apologetically and said, "I think I'm gonna go." Theresa just smiled after her and shook her head slightly as her impetuous daughter turned and trotted out of the room and down the hall. Moments later, as she watched Angie bounce around, looking for her towel, trying to find her beach bag, and moaning that she'd lost her flip flops, Theresa reflected for what seemed like the millionth time in the past ten months on how fortunate she was to still have her daughter.

She wasn't a religious woman by any stretch, but she thought of the pastor's words at the little ceremony they'd attended recently. She'd been experiencing some weird coincidences lately – feeling an inexplicable peace come over her whenever she was stressed, receiving a unexpected refund check in the mail the day after they'd picked up Angie's new phone, stuff like that – that had her wondering if God really did exist. The word *blessing* often came to mind lately. She thought of Eileen and without really knowing what she was doing, she offered a silent plea that Shawna's family would continue to heal and be comforted. Then she frowned as she caught a glimpse of herself in the mirror hanging above the buffet chest. *Was that a prayer, Ms. Gianelli?* She shook her head at herself and went to finish tidying up the kitchen. She wasn't sure if it was or not, but it felt right to think it, and she sensed that the thought had been received and acknowledged.

A few minutes later, there was a knock at the door. Angie was still in her room looking for her flip flops. Jack answered the door and let Mark in. The two men shook hands, greeting each other enthusiastically. Jack really liked Mark and thought him very mature for his age. He had started feeling a little protective of Angie in the months he'd been seeing Theresa, but he always felt as though Angie were safe whenever she was with Mark.

For his part, Mark also thought the world of Jack. He appreciated his wacky sense of humor; the two were constantly reciting hilarious lines from Monty Python movies to each other in British accents. Jack had a nice house in Lakeside a couple blocks from Flathead Lake and he had hired Mark and Ben to do his landscaping. He paid them very well and gave them extra perks, like ski lift tickets for the coming ski season or gift cards for nice restaurants so they could take their girlfriends out. Angie knew Ben had recently started seeing someone but hadn't met the girl yet. Mark had been unusually quiet about this particular subject. Maybe she would be there tonight?

"Mom!" Angie hollered from her room. "I still can't find my sandals!"

"Did you look out on the deck? That's the last place I remember seeing them…" her mother called from the kitchen.

Angie came sailing down the hallway with her beach bag and towel draped over her arm. She flew straight over to Mark, reached up on her tiptoes to kiss him quickly, said, "Hello!" and then abruptly shoved the bag and towel into his arms. "Hold these, please!" she half-ordered, half-asked.

She crossed the living room to go look for her sandals on the deck. Mark said, "As you wish, your grace!" adopting a stiff-backed, straight-legged pose and using his best British butler accent. Jack smirked. She turned her head and batted her eyes at him like a femme fatale from an old movie, and then opened the door and peeked out at the deck.

"Oh, yep, here they are, Mom!" she started to yell, but as she picked them up and turned back around, she almost ran smack into Theresa, who had come from the kitchen and was standing right behind her. "OH!" She jumped and they both grinned. Theresa jokingly answered her, yelling, "OKAY!!" and Angie jumped again.

"Funny!" She wrinkled up her nose at her mom and remarked drily, "I'm surrounded by funny people!" Theresa burst out laughing, and Mark and Jack snickered.

"You know you wouldn't want it any other way!" Mark teased. "Are you ready? The barbecue might be over before we even get there!" He ducked when she tossed one of her flip flops at him, and it flew over him and slapped into Jack's chest. It didn't hit hard, but it made a surprisingly loud *smack!* upon impact.

"Ow!" he yelled melodramatically, clutching his chest and stumbling around. "I'm hit! I'm wounded! Medic! Medic…oh, wait, I'm a doctor…" He laughed heartily at Angie's exasperated expression and handed back the shoe.

"Like I said," Angie deadpanned. "Funny people."

Her expression was so amusing that everyone else cracked up laughing, and she finally broke down and joined them. Then she and Mark said goodbye and left to go to the lake.

When they got there, Angie was suddenly nervous. She saw a ton of people, but not very many that she recognized. Of course, she knew Ben, whom she saw standing near the water with a pretty, blonde-haired girl. It made her happy that she would get to see him again. She kept her nervous insecurity to herself and bravely got out of the car. She and Mark gathered their bags and towels and headed down the few feet from the parking lot to the beach, which sat just off the highway.

Flathead Lake is the prevailing geographic feature of

northwest Montana. Many miles of the two main highways from Polson to Kalispell run right along its edges, making for a lovely drive whether you take what locals refer to as the "west side" or the "east side" of the lake when traveling. The east side highway is bordered on one side by the lake and on the other by beautiful, heavily forested mountains. The west side was equally pretty with fewer views of the water, but it wound through scenic, forested hills. Having a place like Somers Beach as a hangout was like having a personal resort.

Several people shouted their greetings to Mark and he waved back at them. He and Angie snaked through the coolers and small klatches of people until they were right by the water. He spotted a place big enough for the two of them and they claimed it by laying their towels out. It was only around six-thirty in the evening. The sun wouldn't set for another few hours, and at the moment, the temperature was still a toasty eighty-eight degrees. The two teenagers sat on their towels for a few minutes, getting situated. While they did, another couple meandered by and Mark introduced them as Brad and Sabrina Jones, the youth ministers at their church. They were very friendly and welcoming, telling her they were glad to meet her and were happy she could join them. Angie wiped the sweat from her brow and tried to be gracious, but in truth, her stomach was in knots.

Her prevailing thought was that in all the times she had previously been to this beach, she had been here with Shawna. One memory in particular stood out: During the summer between seventh and eighth grades, on one of their many trips here, they had brought a giant floatie, as big as a raft, and the two had climbed aboard it and had paddled themselves a good distance from the beach, so they could lay out and tan and talk without anybody else interrupting them. It had been one of their most memorable trips there.

Angie lay back on the towel and closed her eyes, letting the sun soak into her skin, which she had slathered generously with sunscreen. She loved the smell of cocoa butter lotion; it relaxed her – a cheap aroma therapy. She listened to the sounds around her. Birds twittered, cars passed on the highway. She could hear the sound of a volleyball thumping and of people scuffling to return the hit. Laughter and splashing came from the direction of the water.

"Phew! It's hot!" Mark exclaimed. "I'm gonna take a dip! Do you want to go with?" he asked Angie.

Without opening her eyes, she replied, "Not yet. I'm feeling a little nappish." She yawned reflexively.

Even though her eyes were closed, she noted that it was suddenly much darker, like the sun was being blocked. *That's odd. I don't remember seeing any clouds on the way here.* She opened her eyes and Mark's face was just inches above hers. He peered down at her with a look of pure adoration.

For a few seconds, they just stared at each other. *How did I ever get so lucky?* she mused. She reached up and stroked his face, thinking she had never seen a more handsome man, and he closed his eyes and pressed his face into her hand. He, too, marveled at his good fortune in knowing her and having her in his life.

He opened his eyes again and leaned in and kissed her. He gave her a quick peck, and another. Then, he looked intensely into her eyes, and brought his lips to hers more fervently. Angie moaned reflexively, reaching both arms up and wrapping them around his neck, and Mark placed his hands on either side of her face as their lips moved together in passionate synchronicity. They closed their eyes, momentarily lost to the world, when suddenly, somebody cleared his voice just above them, and they stopped and turned to see Ben standing there, grinning down at them.

"This *is* a church function, you two," he scolded them, amused. "Maybe you should get a room!"

Mark jumped up then, and the two began wrestling, each trying to push the other one into the water. Angie leaned up on one arm and watched them, smiling at how much they resembled two little boys. Then she laid back on the towel and closed her eyes again. The heat made her incredibly sleepy.

She could hear the boys rough-housing and splashing, and her mind returned to the day she and Shawna had been out on the giant floatie. That day it had been just the two of them. Other people were at the beach, of course, but the two of them were there just to spend time with each other and nobody else.

. . .

They had paddled themselves out about fifty feet from shore and then just lay on the raft, stretched out, trying to catch some rays, and talking. The beach was within walking distance of Shawna's house. Angie had spent the night with her, and when they had awakened, they had hastily consumed a small breakfast of fresh fruit (at Eileen's insistence), and then had headed immediately to the beach. They were looking forward to a whole day of fun in the sun.

Once they reached the beach, they found a quiet little spot under a tree and set up a little camp of sorts, laying out their colorful, striped beach towels and anchoring them against a small breeze with their beach bags. The bags contained water bottles, sunscreen, snacks, and clothes in case the weather turned or they just wanted to change. After everything was arranged the way they wanted, they hit the water. They both sucked their breath in sharply as their feet entered the ice-cold, glacier-fed lake, but the sun bore its intense heat down on them and they knew from experience that once they swam, their bodies would quickly adjust to the water temperature. They were looking forward to alternating their time between sunbathing and cooling off in the frigid lake. It was stiflingly hot, but a slight breeze stirred up small waves and the floatie rocked gently as they lay back and closed their eyes. Nothing could ruin the perfect day ahead.

Or so they had thought. After about an hour on the water, Angie started feeling her skin burn and a headache coming on. Determined not to let it take hold and ruin their outing, she and Shawna agreed to take a small break. They would go back to their spot and drink lots of water and take a little nap in the shade under the tree. They laughed and joked as they paddled the awkwardly shaped floatie way back to shore.

But their conversation came to a screeching halt as they neared their spot. From about fifty feet away, they could see Callie, Bridget, and Alexis lying on towels there instead. The girls all had their eyes closed like they were asleep. Shawna and Angie had looked around the beach and back at each other quizzically. Were they crazy? Wasn't this the spot they had set up?

They stole quietly around the tree, searching for their towels and bags, and found them about twenty feet behind the tree. Their towels were balled up and they couldn't even see their bags. They unrolled the towels and found the bags wadded up inside. The towels, bags, and their clothes (bunched up inside the bags) were soaking wet and covered in mud, like they had been dragged through the sludge at the lake's edge. Their water bottles were still there, but they were empty and crushed up, and their snacks were gone.

The girls stared at each other, completely flustered. Without even talking, they both knew good and well it had been Callie and her friends. Angie's temper flared; she furrowed her eyebrows, balled up her fists, and started heading around the tree to give them a piece of her mind, but Shawna stopped her by placing her hand on Angie's shoulder. Silently, she brought a finger to her lips, and then pointed at the nearby water fountain. A large, blue, plastic pail was there for people to use to give their dogs a drink. It was dirty and dog-chewed. Shawna smiled an uncharacteristically wicked smile, her gaze bouncing quickly between the pail and the girls, and Angie stifled a giggle as Shawna's plan became clear.

The girls tiptoed through the patchy grass and saw that the pail was full. The water had not been refreshed recently. It had dirt and dog fuzz floating on the surface, and there was a little algae growing on the bottom of the bucket, along with a couple of water-logged weeds.

"Perfect," mouthed Angie, and Shawna covered her mouth, stifling a giggle. But as Angie bent down to pick up the pail, Shawna suddenly reached out and blocked her access to it.

"Um…yeah…I don't know…" she whispered. Her countenance had changed, and she now seemed contrite. "They teach us at church that we shouldn't get revenge when people do mean stuff." She looked honestly concerned that she might be taking part in a very un-Christian-like retaliation and crinkled her golden eyes questioningly at Angie. "What about the Golden Rule: 'Do unto others as you would have them do unto you?'"

Angie regarded her friend appreciatively, beads of sweat rolling down her face. She marveled at Shawna's very mature and "un-teen-like" ability to think ahead and not just react. For a moment, they both just stood there, eyes flashing between the pail of stagnant, nasty water, Callie's group, and each other.

Finally, Angie shrugged and murmured emphatically, "Well, *I* don't go to church and I'm *sick* of her! You stay here; I'll take care of it." She bent to pick up the bucket once more, and as Shawna watched, slack-jawed, she stole over to where Callie, Bridget, and Alexis were still lying quietly. Birds squawked overhead; little kids splashed and squealed at the water's edge as their mothers sat nearby in chairs or on blankets, reading or watching their children play. An airplane soared high overhead, leaving jet stream in its wake, the sound of its passing too far away to be fully audible. Angie watched the girls for a moment and gleaned they were sleeping, a conclusion drawn from their stillness and the way their chests moved up and down.

Without another thought, she brought the bucket up over her head and back down again forcefully, splashing the cold, nasty water all over the girls' faces. In that moment, she wouldn't have cared if they had drowned. The next minute, the air was filled with their shrieks and cries. They sat up abruptly, coughing and sputtering. Shawna's expression was one of horror mixed with controlled glee. She put her hand over her mouth in disbelief. Angie stood over the girls triumphantly, bucket still in her hand.

"What are you DOING?" Callie screamed, jumping to her feet. She pulled soggy dog hair and wet weeds off her skin. As she touched her hair, she squealed, "It's slimy! Ew!"

"Ew! Gross!" Bridget and Alexis cried, jumping around, trying in vain to get the slime off their skin. They didn't want to use their towels but finally realized they would have to in order to clean the disgusting water off of themselves. The head of the blanket they had been lying on was soaked and dirty.

Without warning, Callie rushed at Angie. She flew into her full-speed and knocked her roughly to the ground. Before Angie could get back up, Callie was on top of her, punching her in the face with all her might. Her friends stood by and yelled encouragement.

"Get her, Callie!"

"Beat the crap out of her!"

Angie, surprised but unafraid, pushed against Callie and kicked and flailed, and the two rolled until Angie was on top and she had Callie's arms pinned to the ground on either side of her head. Angie's lip was bleeding and she suspected she would have a black eye, but she held firm. Her back was scraped from rocks that were on the ground where she had fallen. The wounds stung, but she ignored the pain. She hadn't intended to get into a fist fight. She had just wanted to get even for what she knew the other girls had done to their stuff.

While all this was happening, Shawna, horrified, had come over to try to help. She didn't really know what to do; she hadn't even wanted to confront the girls verbally, and in a physical fight, she was completely out of her element. She yelled at Callie to knock it off and at the other girls, telling them to stop encouraging the fight. Finally, Callie tore herself away from Angie, rolling sideways and throwing Angie off of her. She stood up. Except to pin her arms, Angie hadn't laid a finger on her, but she was crying.

"What the heck?" she blubbered. "What did you do that for?" She brushed dirt off the back of her butt and legs, her face contorted in horror. Her wet hair was matted with dirt and grass.

"You know doggone good and well," Angie spat. Not a teardrop had even formed in her eyes. She had her hands balled up, ready for round two. "You took our spot. But worse, you got our stuff all muddy and you drank our water and took our snacks!"

"We did NOT!" Callie retorted hotly, wiping a tear away angrily, but Angie pointed down at the blanket on which the girls had been lying. There were a couple of empty plastic sandwich bags, and one still had a few of the cut-up apples that she and Shawna had brought with them. The evidence was fairly incriminating.

Callie scowled at Angie, speechless. She had been caught red-handed, yet she stood her ground, staring back at her defiantly. "Well, we didn't know that was YOUR stuff," she offered as a weak explanation.

"Even worse!" Angie said adamantly, taking a step toward her. Callie, still a good two inches taller than Angie at that point in time, took a step back. "Why would you take things that obviously weren't yours? And why drag our towels and clothes through the mud? That was just plain *mean!* What exactly IS your problem, Callie Simmons? I'm about sick of you and your nastiness! You are evil!"

Callie cried harder, but she turned to her friends and spat out at them viciously, "What are you two staring at? Help me pick this stuff up!" She gestured toward the blanket and their towels, lying on the ground, partially soaked in the nasty dog water.

Skinny, fair-haired Alexis protested, "What? Where are we going?"

"I'm not ready to go home!" wailed pudgy, red-headed Bridget. "My mom will just make me do chores!"

"Shut up, stupid!" Callie yelled harshly. She stopped crying abruptly. At the venomous words, Bridget reared back as though she had been slapped. "We're not going home! We're going to my apartment and make my mom drive us to Foys Lake. It's not as crowded as this beach!" She gave Angie and Shawna a dirty look.

Angie wasn't about to let Callie off the hook so easily. "Wait a minute! How about an apology?"

Callie regarded her incredulously. Shawna started to interject that they didn't need one, but before she could speak, Callie blurted rudely, "Are you crazy? I mean, seriously, are you mentally deranged? I don't owe you a thing!"

Angie took another step in Callie's direction, but Shawna stopped her. "Don't, Angie, she's not worth it!"

Callie turned on Shawna, "And you! You're nothing but a chicken…" Callie let go a steam of profanities that would make a sailor blush. Shawna's eyes widened and her face reddened at the ugly vitriol. Angie stepped closer to Callie until they were face-to-face, and said, "Get out of here, Callie. I've had all I can take of you for one day!"

Callie turned away and she and her friends resumed picking up their things, feigning bravery, although Bridget and Alexis eyed her warily. When they had all their belongings in their arms, they turned to make the long walk to Callie's apartment.

Callie said, over her shoulder to nobody in particular, "You'd better watch your backs! This isn't over! Not by a long shot!"

Angie and Shawna had heard this exact spiel from her numerous times before and remained unfazed by her threats. They rolled their eyes at each other, then they picked up their own stuff and headed back to Shawna's house. Eileen fussed over them both, washing the blood off Angie's face and bandaging her cuts and scrapes, while they told her animatedly what had happened.

. . .

"Wake up, Sleepy Head!" Mark shook Angie gently until she opened her eyes, awakened from her nap. She hadn't realized she'd fallen asleep, and she was disoriented. "They're building a bonfire! We're gonna jam out!" He was soaked from swimming and playfully shook water from his hair onto her.

Angie yelped, "Hey!" as the cold droplets hit her bare, hot skin, and Mark laughed. He took her hands and pulled her to sitting. She sat dazed, momentarily unsure of where she was.

Mark laughed again. "Wow, you were really out, huh?" He pulled her to her feet and took her in his arms, rocking her gently while she woke up. She held him tightly, basking in the coolness of his skin, breathing him in. He smelled so good, of sunshine and water and warm sand combined. As the dream dissipated, she slowly became aware of her surroundings again.

"What time is it?" she yawned, noting that the sun was a lot lower than it had been when they arrived. The temperature was cooling, too, but it was still warm, hovering around seventy-five degrees.

Mark reached into his bag and pulled his cell phone out, glanced at the time, and tossed it back in. "It's seven-forty-five," he announced. "Are you hungry? Thirsty? There's still a lot of food on the table, and there are sodas and water in coolers right over there." He pointed and she followed the direction with her eyes. She spotted the picnic table, which was indeed still covered in paper plates, napkins, plastic ware, paper cups, condiments, and platters of burgers and hotdogs. Then she searched briefly for the coolers. As she did so, she saw Ben sitting with his blonde friend. They waved at her and she waved back. The girl looked familiar somehow…

"Hey, there's Ben," Mark said enthusiastically. "Let's go sit with him!"

Angie looked back at Mark's face, so manly and yet so boyish, and smiled. She reached out and brushed his long, bleached bangs away from his darkly tanned forehead, and leaned in and kissed him. He pulled her closer and pressed his lips to hers earnestly. When the kiss ended, they were both slightly dizzy. They stood for a moment, just gazing at each other, and then Angie let go and backed away.

"Go save us a seat," she encouraged. "I'll be right there. I just need to go to the shack first." The "shack" was what all the kids called the old outbuilding that housed the restrooms.

"Okay," Mark answered. "Don't take too long – I'll miss you!"

Angie rolled her eyes and smiled a half-smile. "I'll only be a few minutes!" she chastised. She turned and started walking quickly to the ladies room.

The restrooms were really old. They had probably been there for thirty years or more, judging by the fixtures, but they were neatly kept up by a little old lady who lived across the highway. Nobody asked her to and she didn't get paid. She just did it because she *could*, figuring that if her family or anybody else she knew used the facilities, she wanted them to be clean. Still, the stalls were ramshackle and the bolt latches didn't work. The sink had an old faucet, not an automatic one like so many newer rest areas have, and there was a roll of paper towel sitting on top of the dispenser. Angie guessed they probably didn't even make the kind of paper that fit the dispenser anymore. The room smelled musty, like dirt and old paint.

Just as she was exiting, the blonde girl who had been sitting with Ben opened the door suddenly, startling her.

"Oh!" Angie jumped. "You scared me!" She laughed self-consciously. Amused, she quickly sized up the other girl. She could swear she knew her from somewhere.

"I'm sorry," the too-familiar girl apologized politely. She scrutinized Angie for a second, and then she bit her lip. She stared at Angie tentatively. "Angie?" she asked.

Suddenly, Angie recognized the blonde: It was none other than Callie Simmons. A hundred emotions ripped through her in an instant. She hadn't actually seen Callie in a couple of years, and frankly, she hadn't missed her.

"Callie?" Angie responded, suddenly on the defensive. She regarded her old arch-nemesis curiously, unsure of what to say. Callie looked so…different now. Softer. Finally, she asked, "So, are you with Ben?" It wasn't the first thing she wanted to ask her, but it was what popped out first. She really wanted to ask her how her life as a witch was going but couldn't bring herself to be unnecessarily rude when they hadn't seen each other in such a long time.

"Yes, I am," she responded softly, smiling shyly. "I'm one lucky girl! And you're with Mark?" she inquired, exceedingly politely once again. Angie continued to wrack her brain, trying to figure out what was different about Callie, besides the fact that she was being so nice. Meanwhile, she remained wary, waiting for the proverbial shoe to drop. In times past, Callie had only feigned courtesy right before she attacked. And yet, Angie sensed inexplicably that she wasn't going to attack this time.

"Um, well…yeah," Angie stammered her answer. It reminded her of how Shawna had always replied to questions. A stab of pain pierced her heart momentarily.

She struggled to know what to say next, but Callie smiled at her and said, "That's wonderful! They are both the sweetest guys, you know? I mean, besides being incredibly *hot*." She blushed and looked quickly at the floor and then back at Angie. "Well, um, hope you'll excuse me, but I really need to go!" She shrugged sheepishly, pointing at the restroom interior and continuing through the doorway. Then she turned quickly and said, "I'll see you down there? I'd love to talk to you some more…"

"Uh…yeah. Yeah, of course. See you down there,"

Angie said, shaking her head. She was completely blindsided by this whole interaction. Callie smiled at her obvious confusion, then went ahead into the shack.

Suddenly, it occurred to Angie what was different about Callie. She realized that she had never seen her smile, except contemptuously (after she had just hurt or upset someone) or sadistically (right before). This new Callie had seemed genuinely glad to see her, and her smile had been sweet and sincere. Angie marveled at the change and at the news that it was *Callie* Ben was dating. How could she not have known this? Did Mark know? Was he trying to protect her?

By the time she rejoined Mark and Ben at the fireside, the jam fest had commenced, so she couldn't ask him about Callie. A couple of people had brought guitars, shaker eggs, and rhythm sticks, and accompanied the group as they sat on logs and rocks by the fire and sang through lots of lively songs Angie had never heard. At the beginning of the second song, Callie returned quietly and sat next to Ben. Angie struggled to keep from staring at her. She was so different. Aside from the fact that she was older and more mature looking, there was something else unusual about her, something intangible, and Angie couldn't quite pin it down.

The songs continued, and although she had never heard a single one of them before, there were several that she really liked. She couldn't wait to ask Mark about them, as she wouldn't mind acquiring some of them to listen to on her mp3 player, if possible, or even obtaining the sheet music so she could learn them. They were all about God and his love, but unlike any "church" music Angie had ever heard. Instead of slow and syrupy, these songs were upbeat and fun. At one point, as she was leaning into Mark and listening to him sing, she looked over and noticed that Callie, leaning similarly into Ben, was singing as well. Several people closed their eyes and lifted their hands to the sky; others looked around and sang for the pure enjoyment of it. Since she didn't know any of the words, Angie just listened, quietly enjoying watching everyone else. All of them reveled in the happiness to be found in such simple pleasures as a bonfire and a sing-along by a calm, blue lake on a pretty summer's evening.

As they sang, the sun dipped silently below the western horizon. The sky, still free of clouds, was a deep indigo melting down into pale yellow on the horizon and tinged along the bottom edge with fiery orange. In the burgeoning twilight, Angie reflected that Callie was truly a beautiful girl. Her blonde hair hung halfway down her back and was streaked from the sun. She was very fit and tanned. But as Angie watched her, she realized it wasn't those things that made her seem beautiful. It was her countenance. She seemed like a totally different person from the one with whom Angie had had so many unpleasant run-ins. She suddenly realized what the big difference was: Callie looked *peaceful*.

When the songfest ended, some people got up and began packing up the table and taking things to their cars. Others continued to sit quietly and watch the fire, Angie, Mark, Ben, and Callie among them. Angie was completely blown away by this new Callie and was bursting with curiosity about what had happened to change her so drastically, but didn't want to embarrass her by asking her a lot of pointed questions in front of other people. As the group members came and went, hauling coolers on wheels or boxes of food and utensils away, the others sat enjoying the calm evening. A couple of times, Angie looked up and noticed that Callie was looking back at her. They would make brief eye contact; then Angie would quickly look down or out at the water or at the fire. She was uncomfortable. Her frame of reference regarding Callie continued to make her wary, even though each time their eyes met, Callie would smile at her shyly.

Finally, the last car pulled away, leaving just the four of them at the fire. After all the activity of the evening, it was suddenly very quiet. The fire, which had been crackling and popping loudly, was dying down. Ben took the opportunity to introduce his girlfriend to Angie.

"Oh, hey, Angie? This is my girlfriend, Callie," he said enthusiastically. He glanced down at Callie lovingly and she beamed at him. She turned towards Angie and Mark, smiling, still shy.

Angie was caught off guard.

"Um…yeah…um," she stammered. "We actually just met in the shack. I mean, we actually know each other. I mean, well…" She bit her lip, at a complete loss as to what to say. Mark looked curiously back and forth between Angie and Callie. Of course, he knew about the history between the two girls from his conversations with Angie, but he hadn't made the connection between that girl and Ben's Callie. He seemed to have forgotten about the incident at the skating rink. As for Ben, he had been there that night, too, so Angie couldn't fathom why he was introducing her like she was somebody new that Angie wouldn't know. She also didn't know why Mark hadn't told her. The whole encounter had Angie baffled.

Callie, recognizing Angie's discomfort, uncharacteristically came to her rescue. "Yes, Angie and I have known each other for a while, since sixth grade, isn't that right, Angie?" she said softly, smiling at Angie, who was frozen like a deer in the headlights. There was no trace of malice in her voice, so Angie attempted to smile back, but she knew it didn't reach her eyes. She nodded stiffly.

"Actually," Callie continued, "we haven't seen each other in a long time. The last time we were around each other was before all the radical changes in my life," she explained to Ben. She turned her gaze back to Angie and continued quietly, "I'm sure the last time I saw you, I was horrible to you. I'd like to apologize for being the way I was back then and beg your forgiveness. I was a really unhappy kid back then…" Her voice trailed off and Angie stared at her, dumbfounded, until Mark nudged her and she realized she hadn't responded. A couple of cars passed by on the highway, one with a really loud engine, giving her a tiny reprieve.

"Oh! Ah…yes. I mean, you were," Angie said at last. She struggled to know how to respond to the unexpected admission of guilt and request for absolution. This was such a departure from any other interaction the two girls had ever had. Callie looked down quickly at her hands. She fiddled with her fingers and looked as uncomfortable as Angie felt. Her expression actually tugged at Angie's heartstrings, and she hurried to say something positive. No one had ever *literally* asked her for forgiveness before.

"But," Angie responded quickly, "Well…I mean, we were kids then, right? People change, don't they? I know I'm not the same person I was a few years ago." Callie looked back up at her hopefully. Angie shrugged and smiled tentatively at Callie, who smiled brightly in return.

"So, anyway," Angie barreled on rather tactlessly, "if you don't mind me asking: What happened? To make you change, I mean?"

Callie's smile amped up to brilliant as she answered, "Well, a lot, actually. More than I could say in one sitting." She beamed at Ben again, and his answering expression was one of sheer admiration.

As this uncomfortable exchange occurred, Mark sat quietly, his gaze shifting between Angie and Callie. He had been introduced to Ben's girlfriend several weeks ago. When they met, he'd had the feeling he knew her from somewhere but hadn't been able to pin it down. He had almost asked Angie about it on a few occasions, but something in his subconscious warned him to leave it be.

Now, as he listened to the girls' stilted conversation, he suddenly looked up at Callie in amazement. "Wait a minute," he began slowly, as recognition dawned on his face. "I remember now! You threw your drink on Angie at the skating rink that one time!" He shook his head in disbelief. "Man, I've been trying and trying to figure out where I'd seen you before. You were *that* girl? No way! You are such a nice person now; I don't know that I would have ever made the connection if it weren't for tonight and this conversation!" He grinned at Ben. "Do remember that night, Ben?"

Indeed, Ben did remember, and he and Callie had had conversations about it. He gave Mark a warning look and shook his head slightly, as Callie looked back down at her hands, flushing with embarrassment and biting her lower lip. She looked like she might cry. He tightened his arm protectively around Callie's shoulders.

Mark realized his blunder and responded gently, "Oh!

I'm sorry, Callie! I'm not trying to make you feel bad. I'm just flabbergasted. You are *so* not that girl anymore. Now that I remember you, I'm just astonished at the lovely person that you have become!"

Callie looked back up at Mark and Angie. Then she looked at Ben questioningly, and he nodded encouragement to her, so she began speaking again. The fire had died down to embers. Her face glowed red in its fading light. The night was still relatively warm and they could hear the gentle rhythmic sound of waves lapping on the shore of the lake. Loons called hauntingly to each other across the water, as the quarter moon shone its soft light down on them. Ben stood up and threw a few more pieces of wood on the fire. Flames immediately began licking their way up the logs and soon the fire was crackling merrily again.

"Would you be interested in hearing about how God changed me? I mean, I'll try not to make it a long story," Callie offered, as Ben sat back down and wrapped his arm around her again. She looked at them earnestly and waited for a response.

Angie answered perhaps a little too hastily.

"Absolutely! I'd really like to know!" She softened her tone a little and gave Callie an encouraging look. "Please," she added kindly. Mark nodded his agreement, too.

Firelight danced off of their faces and they appeared to glow in anticipation.

Callie smiled shyly and glanced at Ben, who also nodded his encouragement. So, she began telling them about herself, why she had been the way she had, and what had happened to change her heart.

"I don't really know where to start. My life has changed so dramatically these last couple of years." She drew in a deep breath, then blew it out, saying, "Up until a few years ago, my life was really lousy."

. . .

*F*or the next hour or so, Callie told the small group of friends about her horrific upbringing. She had never known her father, who had left the family when she was only three months old. Her mom had always struggled. Besides having to support herself and a baby, she carried emotional baggage from her own lousy childhood, combined with mental illness, which she had tried, unsuccessfully, over the years to keep locked away. She had never had the money nor the inclination to seek professional help for her problems. Instead, she self-medicated. Alcohol was her drug of choice and she was drunk almost all the time.

Her insecurities and addiction only exacerbated her problems, of course. She had never been able to keep a job for more than a year. Additionally, she sought relief from her life in a series of unhealthy relationships. Callie had seen numerous men come and go. When one guy moved out, it was only days before another moved in. Some of them had abused her physically and emotionally. A couple of them had even abused her sexually. Some of them had insisted she call them "Daddy," so her impression of fathers in general was colored by the behavior of some really terrible men. Only a few of the boyfriends were ever really nice to her, and those ones didn't seem to stay around too long, as her mother's neuroses or drunkenness quickly drove them away.

Callie stopped talking momentarily and Mark got up and threw another couple of logs and sticks on the dwindling fire. In seconds, it sparked back to life and was popping and cracking cheerfully, its light lifting the mood around the fire pit, which had definitely become heavy. As the flames licked up the logs, their faces became visible once more. Callie's expression was one of resolve, and the others remained silent, giving her space to process her thoughts. Angie was horrified and stunned by the information. Callie looked at Ben, silently trying to ascertain whether or not she should continue.

"Go ahead, baby," he whispered, his arm still wrapped around her shoulders tenderly. "If it's helping, keep talking." She glanced at Angie and Mark, who nodded encouragement as well, so she resumed her story.

Surprisingly, her mom hadn't been nasty or unkind to Callie as she grew up. She was just mentally absent. She knew on some level that her problems and relationships made things difficult for her daughter, but instead of ever really spending any time with her or talking to her, she lavished gifts on her – clothes, music – anything she wanted, she got. Callie reflected that she hadn't even wondered where the money came from, since her mom could barely keep a job. She had only recently discovered that her mom carried a horrendous amount of credit card debt.

Her room as a child had been decked out in some of the nicest furnishings, she said, and she got all the clothes she wanted, no questions asked. Angie thought back to the outfit Callie had been wearing the first day they had met – the skimpy, bejeweled top and miniskirt – and how it had seemed a little risqué for a twelve-year-old. She remembered Callie being forced to wear her gyms shorts the rest of the day and saw the whole scene in a different light. How humiliating it must have been for Callie! She'd said she had to call her "dad" that day and that she was going to "get it later." Angie shuddered at the realization that the man, whoever he was, not only wasn't Callie's real dad, but may well have been one of the really abusive boyfriends. Mark scooted closer and put his arm around her and she leaned gratefully into his shoulder.

To make up for the abuses of her boyfriends, Callie's mother gave her too much freedom at too early an age. Callie shared that she had been allowed to stay out as late as she wanted to, starting when she was about eight years old. Of course, most of her friends had parents and rules and curfews, but she had learned early on how to lie very convincingly. Through sheer luck (or lack thereof, she reflected humorlessly), nobody had ever questioned how a little girl was allowed to spend the night at friends' houses during the school week or for entire weekends. She had only been nine when she started smoking and drinking, stealing cigarettes and liquor from her mom and her parade of boyfriends.

Living without love, Callie had also begun shoplifting at an early age. She had discovered that she could gain emotional gratification from it, even though it was temporary. Her mom bought her so many things that she never noticed if Callie had something in her room that she hadn't purchased herself. No matter how many things she stole, it never satisfied the inner longing she felt. It didn't fulfill the need to feel loved and accepted.

As for friends, she confessed that until recently, she had never had any real ones. She had surrounded herself with people whom she could control, not allowing anyone close who might call her on her bad behavior or discover her terrible secrets. Imitating her mother, by age ten, she began having relationships with a series of boyfriends, and was sexually active by the age of eleven. Her lack of social skills combined with her young age meant that none of the relationships lasted very long, of course.

As Angie listened, dumbstruck, to Callie's life story, she thought back to the little groups of "cronies" that had always followed Callie around. She had known back then that they weren't true friends of Callie's. Many of them could be heard in the girls restroom or out on the playground talking trash about Callie when she wasn't around. At the time, she had felt it served Callie right. Now, all she felt was immense compassion for that little girl who was never loved. And sex at eleven? She shook her head, disbelieving. *At eleven I was still playing with Barbie dolls!* She and Mark had been together for the better part of a year and they still hadn't gone all the way. Several times during Callie's confession, Angie's eyes pooled with tears. Mark, Ben, and Angie listened quietly, glancing at each other occasionally and shaking their heads sadly at what Callie had been through.

. . .

"But," Callie said cheerfully, "that's not the end of the story, fortunately!" She looked up at the group and her face reflected the peace Angie had seen earlier in the evening. The fire crackled merrily.

"A few years ago, on a Friday night, I overheard some

kids at the mall talking about a youth group 'lock-in' that they were going to. I was still my old, hate-filled self, and after I heard where it was going to be held, I decided I was going to crash the party and see what kind of mischief I could get into," she said, shaking her head with embarrassment at the memory.

"So, I got my mom to give me a ride to the church where it was being held. I didn't even bring a sleeping bag! Of course, I didn't know what a 'lock-in' was! I just inserted myself into a group of kids as they went through the doors. I didn't see anybody I really knew, and nobody knew who I was or that I hadn't been invited.

"I had never set foot in a church before, and I was curious, so I quickly separated from the rest and wandered about. There were some stairs, so I followed them down to a little hallway. There were little rooms off the hallway, and I walked through each one, scoping them out. They looked like classrooms to me, with chairs and tables and colorful bulletin boards. As I wandered, I read all these posters on the walls with sayings about God and his love. In the nursery, I actually sat and read some picture books with Bible stories in them. All of those, too, made out that God was this great being who created all of us and loved us. I had never really thought about God before, but I remember feeling really skeptical about that – the love part. I was so full of self-loathing. I felt like if there was a God, he certainly didn't love everybody the same. If he did, why had my life been so crappy?

"I got so angry and sad that I started thinking about doing some really destructive stuff, like breaking pictures and throwing paint on everything and then sneaking out. But just as I was entertaining the thought, I heard music coming from the sanctuary, where all the other kids had gathered. Of course, I didn't know it was called a 'sanctuary' then. What an apt name."

Callie smiled briefly before continuing. "I was curious, so I followed the noise back upstairs and peeked in through a window in one of the sanctuary doors. All the kids were on their feet. I saw what looked like a band playing on the stage, and the kids and leaders looked like they were rocking out and having a really good time. I remember suddenly feeling more alone than I ever had in my whole life, and I didn't know why. All the mean intentions left my mind and I started crying. I wanted so badly to be in that room with those other kids, having a good time.

"Just as I started crying, a voice behind me scared the ever-living poop out of me!" Callie laughed out loud at the memory. "One of the group leaders had been in another part of the church and had come up behind me. I was so enrapt, watching the kids sing and then crying, that I didn't even hear her. I almost had a heart attack!

"She asked me if I was going to go in. I jumped and then I turned and looked at her. I'm sure I had guilt written all over my face. I expected her to ask me who I was, and I knew that when she found out I wasn't invited, she would throw me out. I was even scared for a minute that she might call the police.

"But instead, as soon as she saw I was crying, her expression became unbelievably kind. Without asking who I was, she just said, 'Oh, sweetheart! Can I give you a hug?' Needless to say, I was shocked. But for some reason, I let her hug me. She held me tightly and I just started bawling my eyes out. I didn't even know why I was crying, but I couldn't stop. She just kept holding me, whispering that everything would be okay.

"For some reason, her kindness just broke my heart. I couldn't stop crying! I must have been pretty loud," she continued with a wry smile on her face, "because another leader – another woman – came out to see what was going on. The two women invited me to a nearby office to talk, and the next thing I knew, I was telling them all about myself. I didn't know them, but I couldn't help it – it was like a floodgate had been lifted. I told them every sordid detail of my life. The most amazing part was that they both just listened and let me talk. They didn't interrupt, and most importantly, they didn't judge. In fact, when they found out how I had come to be in the church that night, they both smiled big smiles and said something to each other about how great God was and how he worked in mysterious ways.

"Of course, I didn't have a clue what they meant. When I finally felt like I had said everything, they started asking me questions about whether or not I had ever thought about God. Even though I know I got defensive and snarky at their questions, they still didn't judge me. They listened to my remarks patiently. For some reason, I quickly lost the desire to be my usual, smart-alecky self, and I started asking them some genuine questions I had.

"Nobody had ever talked to me or listened to me like that in my whole life. We must have talked for hours. At one point, one of the men came to find out where the ladies had gone and what was going on. Rachel, the first woman, the one who had hugged and held me while I cried, went out to the hallway with him for a minute. I could hear them talking but didn't hear what they said to each other. And then Rachel came back, and she and

Leah, the other lady, and I kept talking.

"I didn't realize it then, but that night was pivotal. For the first time, I felt like there were two human beings on the planet who really cared about me. They invited me to stay for the rest of the lock-in and provided me with a sleeping bag and some toiletries. I will never forget their kindness.

"I was really scared to join the rest of the group – petrified, in fact – but it was about one in the morning and everybody else was already asleep, which was a relief to me. We were all tired, so they led me back to the sanctuary and helped me find a place to sleep near them. I don't think I ever really slept that whole night. My mind was overflowing with all of the events of the previous few hours and with all the things that Rachel and Leah had told me about God and his unconditional love for me.

"The next morning, they introduced me to the rest of the group. I saw a couple of kids from school then, kids I had been mean to. I felt so guilty, I couldn't even look them in the eye. We were led to a little cafeteria and they fed us breakfast. I sat with some girls I'd just met and they, too, were really nice to me. Then I saw some kids I knew from school get up and go over to one of the leaders. They pointed at me as they talked to the leader. I looked up and they were all staring at me. I was so embarrassed. The leader said something to them, and the kids went back to their table.

"Then, I saw Rachel go up to the leader. They talked for a minute, and then they came over to me. I was mortified, terrified that they were going to ask me to leave. Instead, Rachel introduced me to Phil, saying he was the Youth Pastor. He shook my hand and said, very sincerely, that he was glad to meet me. He wondered if I would mind if he introduced me to everyone at the morning meeting. I was absolutely dumbstruck, but I agreed.

"So, a little while later, when everyone gathered in the sanctuary again, he introduced me to the group. For the most part, the kids welcomed me enthusiastically. I glanced over at the kids I'd seen talking to Phil at breakfast. They were looking back at me dubiously. I gathered up all of my courage and asked Phil for the microphone and he gave it to me. I was so scared, my voice was shaking. I admitted that I had crashed the lock-in and had originally had some very destructive plans. I stammered a lot because I had never spoken to a large group of people before, let alone with a mike, and I didn't know how my confession would be received. I plunged ahead, driven by some strange feeling that it would be okay. I told everyone about how Rachel had discovered me in the hallway, and how she and Leah and I had talked into the early hours of the morning.

"Looking straight at the kids who had ratted me out to Phil, I said that the last 24 hours were unlike any I had ever lived through. I told them how Rachel and Leah had listened to me in a way nobody else ever had, ever, in my whole life. I told them that I didn't fully understand what was happening to me, but I felt like I was a different person from the one who had arrived at the church the previous evening. I said I hoped that they would allow me to stay. I assured them that I didn't want to hurt anyone; in fact, I was just really tired, but I wanted to stay and listen, if it was okay with them. Then I handed the mike back to Phil.

"Imagine how astonished I was when the whole group stood up and started clapping! Even the tattletale kids were clapping! They all smiled at me and yelled encouraging things like of course I could stay and how glad they were that I was there."

Callie looked up then at Angie, eyes filled with tears, and she said, "That weekend changed my life, Angie. I started going to that church. It wasn't very long after that that I invited God into my life, and things have never been the same." She smiled tentatively. Angie's heart had melted, listening to Callie's story, and she realized that she was no longer feeling wary of Callie, only deep respect. She smiled back at her encouragingly.

"Not long after I started going to church, my mom got her second DUI." Callie continued staring at the fire which was dwindling again. "She was forced to go to Alcoholics Anonymous as part of her sentence, and she had to wear an ankle bracelet. During the time she spent under house arrest, she started to change, too. One of the first things she did was to kick out her most recent boyfriend. She and I started actually talking to each other. She started reading self-help books. Through a friend at her workplace, she found a counselor who was willing to meet with us for a very small fee, one that my mom could afford. We still see her once a month.

"Since then, my life has changed radically. My mom doesn't go to church; she's still full of questions. But she doesn't drink anymore, and she listens when I talk to her about God. She's more open to the idea than ever. I know that part of it is that she sees the change in me." Callie stopped talking, shaking her head in wonder.

The four teenagers sat in silence then for a few moments, just watching the fire.

"Wow! I'm sorry!" she apologized suddenly. "I've

really hogged the conversation tonight!" She laughed self-consciously.

"Not at all!' Angie said softly. She stared at Callie, her expression full of blatant admiration.

"I really am sorry, Angie," Callie gazed back sorrowfully. "I know I have done some awful things to you. Can you ever forgive me?"

Seconds ticked by in uncomfortable silence. Angie raised her eyebrows and shook her head, dumbfounded. Mark removed his arm from her shoulders. He folded his arms across his chest and his eyebrows furrowed at her in angry confusion. Ben also looked at her critically. Her eyes popped open wide as she realized they had misinterpreted her actions. The firelight masked her deep blush.

"No!" she almost shouted at the disapproving boys. "You misunderstood me!"

Turning to Callie, who was looking at her like a beaten puppy, she said, "I was shaking my head because there is nothing to forgive, Callie. *Nothing!*" Her voice trembled with emotion, and the boys' expressions relaxed. Mark uncrossed his arms, smiled sheepishly, and shrugged at Angie apologetically.

"Don't jump to conclusions," she murmured, as she backhanded him playfully in the chest. "Have a little faith in me!" She shook her head at him sternly, but then couldn't help but giggle at his chagrined face.

Turning back to look at Callie, Angie thought about Shawna and how unbelievably accommodating she had always been where Callie and her hateful actions were concerned. She remembered Shawna remarking that night at the skating rink how Callie must be one of the most miserable of all God's creatures. It was while they were in the bathroom, when Angie had been changing out of her wet shirt.

Her eyes filled with guilty tears as she reiterated, "No, nothing to forgive. Can you forgive *me*, Callie?"

Callie's eyes welled up, too, and she looked at Angie quizzically. "For what?" she asked, incredulous.

"For being a kid who couldn't see beyond herself, beyond her own life? For not having more compassion?" Angie responded, her voice shaking. Mark pulled her close again and kissed the side of her face. "I'm so sorry for all that you've been through, Callie. And I'm so, so happy that things are turning around for you."

Impulsively, Angie stood and moved over to sit by Callie. As their boyfriends looked on, wide-eyed with surprise, the two girls looked at each other briefly, then Angie reached her arms out. Callie hesitated for only a nanosecond, and then two girls were hugging.

"Thank you, Angie," Callie whispered through her own tears. "Thank you." She and Angie rocked gently back and forth for another minute, then both let go and they sat back and smiled at each other shyly.

The boys started fidgeting, uncomfortable with all the expressed emotion, and suddenly, Ben jumped up and asked, "Okay, wow! That was intense! Does anybody want to go swimming?"

The teens all grinned at each other, and Mark also jumped to his feet, yelling, "Last one in is a rotten egg!" He sprinted for the water with Ben close on his heels.

Callie and Angie looked at each other and shrugged. Like two little girls, they jumped up and ran into the lake, squealing as their bodies fell forward into the cold water. An epic splashing contest ensued, followed by an enthusiastic game of 'Chicken.' Angie rode on Mark's shoulders and Callie was astride Ben's, and the girls giggled, shouted, and wrestled each other furiously until both couples fell over in the water. Four heads emerged seconds later, and all four laughed heartily.

They played in the water for another half hour or so, then realized it was getting really late. Angie and Callie exchanged phone numbers, then hugged goodbye and promised to call each other very soon. Then they hopped into their cars and headed for their respective homes.

As they drove the short distance to her apartment, Angie leaned her head sleepily on Mark's shoulder. She turned the events of the evening over and over in her mind, marveling at how things can change so rapidly and unexpectedly. *Shawna wouldn't even be surprised*, she reflected, thinking back on her many conversations with her best friend. She smiled at the realization that for the first time, the memories did not cause her pain. Instead, she had an uncanny sense that Shawna had been there with them that evening and was cheering them on.

Chapter Eleven: Welcome Surprises

"Happiness is a perfume that you cannot pour on others without getting a few drops on yourself."
~ *Ralph Waldo Emerson*

The next day happened to be Angie's eighteenth birthday, and she woke to a glorious scent wafting through the apartment. Crepes! Her mom traditionally made her a birthday breakfast of homemade crepes with fresh, succulent strawberries, powdered sugar, and whipped cream, and she had seen the strawberries in the refrigerator the night before. Even though it wasn't a surprise, she still hopped out of bed, grabbed her fuzzy purple bathrobe, and ran to the kitchen excitedly, like a little child.

"Hey, Mama!" she burst out enthusiastically as she caught sight of Theresa sliding the third crepe off the pan and onto the waiting platter. She placed a piece of parchment paper over the crepe and popped the platter back into the oven. Then she grinned up at her boisterous daughter.

"Hey, yourself, baby! Happy birthday!" she intoned warmly. Setting the spatula aside, she gave Angie a giant hug and a kiss on the cheek. Then she turned and poured batter for another crepe into the heated skillet. It sizzled as she swirled the skillet round and round to form the crepe. The air in the kitchen was filled with the delectable scents of warm vanilla, sugar, and butter.

"Mm! It smells heavenly in here!" Angie sighed, inhaling deeply.

She peeked around the corner at the dining table. It was already set with her mom's best tablecloth (a pretty white eyelet lace), her grandmother's silverware, and her parents' wedding china. Angie adored her mom's china. She didn't know what kind of flowers were on them, but thought they were silky blue cornflowers. In addition to the table settings, presents were piled artfully on the nearby buffet, along with some cards and a big spray of purple, green, and blue balloons. A cheerful banner hung across the sliding glass door to the deck announcing the occasion.

"Mom!" she cried. "When did you do all this? It looks so beautiful!"

"Last night, after you went to sleep," Theresa smiled. Adopting an expression of mock-consternation, she scolded playfully, "You guys got in kind of late, didn't you?"

"Um, yeah…sorry about that, Mama. We kind of lost track of time," Angie shrugged, sheepishly.

"Honey, I'm kidding," she reassured. "It was only a little after midnight, and you are eighteen now, after all." She shook her head in disbelief. "I was up finishing a book, anyway. So, did you have a good time?"

"Oh, Mom, it was incredible! You won't believe it when I tell you!" Angie pulled a carton of orange juice from the fridge, poured herself a glass, put the juice back, and launched into a detailed summary of the previous evening's events, as her mom continued making crepes.

Starting with her nervous arrival, she told Theresa about napping on the beach and her dream about Shawna and Callie, and how later, incredibly, she ran into her at the barbecue. She shared her astonishment at discovering that Callie was Ben's new girlfriend.

Theresa's head snapped up at the mention of Callie's name. She was well aware of Callie Simmons and doubted she could ever forget the horrible things she had done to Angie. A knot formed in her stomach as she anticipated a new horror story starring Callie. She had no love lost on the girl and didn't expect she would ever amount to anything. She almost flat out said so to Angie, but something stopped her. Following her intuition, she held her tongue, and listened silently as Angie relayed the life-changing experiences Callie had shared. Theresa's expression turned from wary to amazed as Angie revealed that the four of them had all ended up playing in the water and having a great time.

"That poor girl," Theresa murmured sympathetically, as she carefully slipped the last crepe onto the hot platter and put it back in the oven. She turned off the stove, set the skillet in the sink, and turned to look at Angie, who gulped down the last few drops of her orange juice.

"What an awful way to start your life!" she continued, shaking her head. "You know, the one time that I went over to their apartment to take issue with her mother over something she'd done to you, I sensed that all was not well in the Simmons household, but obviously, I had no idea it was so bad." She looked at Angie shrewdly. "Are you sure you can trust her? She always was a skillful little liar…"

"Mom," Angie interrupted gently, "it's fine, honest. She is one hundred and eighty degrees from that mean little girl. In fact, we exchanged phone numbers. We're going to try to get together to go shopping for school clothes."

Theresa raised her eyebrows, her mouth set in a skeptical frown.

"Okay, if you say so, honey," she allowed, "but, please, be careful. I don't want you getting hurt."

"Don't worry, Mom, I honestly think she's changed," Angie replied. She took a deep inhale and let it out, saying, "Are those crepes ready yet?" Her stomach growled loudly, accentuating her question, and she and Theresa both laughed.

"Geez, I guess I'd better feed you before the monster escapes! Why don't you go get dressed? Jack's on his way over," Theresa suggested. The words were no sooner out of her mouth than there was a knock at the door. Angie yelped and scampered down the hall to her room, slamming the door behind her. Theresa went to let Jack in. He carried a big bundle of purple mums and had Mark in tow; Theresa had asked him to come to Angie's birthday breakfast as a surprise.

The men each hugged her silently, grinning deviously, and then walked over to put their presents on the buffet with the others.

"What can I do to help?" Jack asked, after planting a sweet kiss on Theresa's waiting lips. Mark turned away from the couple discreetly and ran a finger down one of the genuine silver knives.

"Wow!" he remarked to no one in particular. "I can see myself in this knife!"

Theresa and Jack laughed, and then Theresa said, "Jack, would you mind getting out the juice and strawberries and putting them on the table? I just want to go change."

She had worn an old t-shirt while making the crepes and flour trailed down the front of it. "Mark, go ahead and sit at the table. Angie will be out in a few minutes, and then we'll eat." She turned and hurried down the hall to change.

Jack headed for the kitchen and took the orange juice, bowl of sliced strawberries, and whipped cream out of the fridge. Balancing them carefully in his arms, he made his way to the table and placed each item in the center of it. Then he picked up the pitcher of orange juice and began filling the juice glasses. As he was filling the last glass, Angie opened the door to her room and came bounding out to the dining room. Her espresso-colored hair was tied up in a neat bun, and she was wearing a fitted, purple and green floral sundress. She was barefoot and sporting some color from the previous day's sun. She looked radiant.

Mark stood up to greet her, and when she saw him, she squealed and ran to give him a hug.

"I didn't know you were coming! Yay! I'm so glad you're here!" she beamed. Then, she turned and gave Jack a hug, too. He squeezed her back and said, "Happy Birthday, pretty girl!" He planted a kiss on her forehead, and she fairly hopped around the table to sit down by Mark.

"Your mom told me about your birthday a week or so ago," Mark replied happily. "I really don't care, 'cause I don't really like you all that much," he joked, "but when I found out about your traditional birthday breakfast, I figured I could deal with being around you again for a little while."

"Oh, nice!" Angie retorted, slapping his upper arm. "Thanks a lot!"

"I'm kidding, you silly girl," he said sweetly. He

leaned in to give her a kiss and instantly knew he'd been forgiven. She wrapped her arms around his neck and kissed him back fervently, until Jack cleared his throat. She dropped her arms and stepped back, turning crimson with embarrassment. Just then, there was a knock at the door.

Theresa came down the hall in a hot pink, frilly blouse, white capris, and sandals. She looked gorgeous, her black hair perfectly complimented by the brightly-colored top. Jack silently appraised her and smiled adoringly at her.

"Who could that be?" she wondered aloud, noting Jack's stare and smiling self-consciously as she made her way to the front door. She put her eye to the peephole in the door for a second and then jumped back in surprise.

"Oh. My. Lord!" she exclaimed, looking over at Angie. "Angie, I think you'd better answer the door!"

Jack, Mark, and Angie, who were all seated at the table, looked up in unison at the tone of Theresa's voice. She stared at the door like she'd seen a ghost.

"Mom?" Angie asked anxiously, as she stood and walked over to the door. "What's going on?"

Theresa backed away slowly, smiling and holding her arm out like a game show hostess, inviting Angie to open the door. Jack, sensing that something was amiss, immediately came and stood beside her.

"What's wrong?" he whispered in Theresa's ear. She kept smiling, her eyes never leaving Angie's.

"Nothing," she stage-whispered back, shaking her head incredulously. Turning to Angie, she repeated her directive. "Happy birthday, Angie. What did you want more than anything? Open the door."

"What on earth…" Angie shook her head at her mom. "Mom, you didn't order a singing telegram, did you? I'll be so embarrassed if you did!" Theresa only shook her head, grinning like a Cheshire cat.

There was another knock at the door, a little louder this time.

Angie took a look in the peephole, then she gasped and threw open the door.

"DAD!" she yelled as she flew into Greg's arms. She and Greg both squealed and laughed like little kids. He grabbed her up and twirled her around on the landing to the apartment, then set her down to look at her. His eyes welled up with tears.

"Happy birthday, Princess!" he whispered, hugging her tightly again, one hand clutching a shiny blue gift bag. Then he held her out at arm's length again. "You're so... grown up!" he marveled. "Did I miss the crepes?" he asked, looking up at Theresa, and he and Angie laughed together again.

Jack glanced quickly down at Theresa, who shrugged at him.

"I had no idea," she mouthed. She leaned into him and he tightened his arm around her.

Greg silently gazed at his ex-wife, noting, of course, the tall, rather well-built, handsome man standing with his arm around her.

"Hey, T," he said softly. "Sorry to just barge in on you like this."

"Don't be silly," Theresa said graciously. "You're her father. You have every right to be here."

The adults appraised one another briefly. Theresa had no trouble remembering how she had fallen for Greg as a senior in high school. Although his face reflected the passing of the years, with crow's feet deep around his eyes and worry lines in his forehead, he still had almost boyish good looks. His blonde and salt-and-pepper hair curled softly away from his face and down the back of his neck. He seemed fit, considering his job involved a lot of sitting at the wheel. She noted a sadness had taken up residence in his eyes and felt momentary guilt for her part in putting it there.

As she made her quiet assessment, Greg straightened up and faced Jack and Mark. The men regarded each other curiously.

"Oh! I'm sorry, where are my manners?" Theresa chided herself. "Won't you please come in, Greg? I'd like you to meet my boyfriend, Jack Halverson, and Angie's beau, Mark Kennedy." She opened the door wider, allowing him access to the room, arm stretched out again cordially.

Greg entered the apartment and shook both men's hands firmly. Then they all stood awkwardly for a moment, not knowing what to do or say, until Angie finally piped up.

"Well, perfect timing, Dad! Let's have breakfast!" Her glowing eyes never left her father, and she put her hand in the crook of his arm and led him to an empty space at the table next to her. "You can put my present there, next to the others, Daddy."

"This?" Greg swung the present back and forth on one finger. "What makes you think this is for you?"

"Dad!" Angie intoned with mock-exasperation. Greg grinned at her and set the bag on the buffet next to the other gifts. As he did so, Angie noticed the beautiful bouquet of mums.

"Oh, look at the flowers! Oh, they're so pretty!" she gushed. "Are they from you, Mom?" she asked, looking over at her mother. Her fingers tenderly brushed the soft, deep purple blooms.

"Those are from Jack," Theresa said, as she crossed to the buffet and deftly pulled open the top drawer.

Angie wound around the table to Jack, and murmured, "Thank you, Jack! They're beautiful!" Jack grabbed her up in a big hug, then set her back down and kissed the top of her head.

"You're welcome, kiddo! Happy birthday!" he smiled down at her.

Theresa, silently pleased at the show of affection between Angie and Jack, and almost shamefully pleased that it had transpired in front of Greg, smiled to herself as she collected another linen napkin and table service from the buffet, while Mark went to the kitchen to gather another juice glass. Jack took another pretty floral china plate, cup, and saucer from the hutch. In less than a minute, they had everything set up in front of Greg, who thanked them appreciatively. If he was jealous or otherwise put out at the display between his daughter and his wife's boyfriend, he didn't show it. Theresa smiled again, this time reminding herself that in an age where there can be so much drama amongst members of mixed families, she should be grateful that Greg didn't overreact.

Finally, she retrieved the crepes from the oven and brought them to the table. Then she sat down and surveyed the oddly mixed assembly in front of her. Angie and Greg just beamed at each other, while Mark and Theresa watched the interaction happily. Jack, unsure what to do or say, kept looking from face to face, then back at Theresa, grinning. Theresa interrupted the group's reverie.

"Eat up, everyone. Or as my mama from the old country would say, *Manga!*"

They wasted no time digging in, and the next half hour was filled with the clinking of dishes, tinkling of silverware, and happy, bubbling conversation. Everyone kept complimenting Theresa on the light and crispy crepes, or exclaiming over the sweet, juicy strawberries and cool, sweet whipped cream. Greg asked Angie and Mark dozens of questions about how they met, were they serious, etcetera, and even embarrassed Angie when he proclaimed that as "The Dad," he realized it was his duty to ask Mark what his intentions were toward his little girl. All conversation stopped momentarily then. Theresa and Jack glanced at each other, surprised. There was an awkward moment as Mark, totally unprepared for such a question, stammered rather stupidly, until Greg burst out with his loud, boisterous laugh and assured him he was just kidding. Then everyone let out a collective sigh of relief and the jovial conversation continued as it had been. When everyone was stuffed with food, they all pitched in to clear the table.

"Don't worry about the dishes," Theresa said. "Jack and I will get to them in a while. Let's do presents! Bring your coffee cups, everyone, and let's go sit in the front room." The apartment was stuffy, so on her way to the living room, she popped the sliding door to the deck open. The sweet sound of birdsong floated in on the fresh, cool morning air.

Angie fairly burst with excitement. She didn't necessarily like being the center of attention, but she loved getting presents. With mock humility, she announced that she would "try to bear the embarrassment" of having to open gifts while everyone stared at her. Mark started scooping up her presents in his arms, saying that he wanted to spare her feelings, and he would happily toss them off the deck, until she tugged at his shirt, stopping him in his tracks.

"You put those down right now!" she ordered playfully. Unable to resist her, he complied, piling the presents on the coffee table. Jack brought the coffee carafe from the kitchen and served everyone a cup of coffee. Then they sat around the room, some on the floral sofa and some in the fluffy side chairs, and got comfortable. The midday sunlight filtered in through the patio door, laying a solid beam of warmth across the living room floor. Tater basked lazily in its glow, flicking her tail and regarding them haughtily.

Angie took a couple of pictures of her presents with her phone, and then grabbed the first package wrapped in pretty purple and green foil wrap and turned it over until she found the tag.

"To Angie, Love Mom and Jack," she read. "Thanks, Mom! Thanks, Jack!" She tore into the present like an exuberant little girl and squealed with excitement as the wrapping fell away. Inside, she found a box from a familiar shoe store which contained a pair of really cute, lime green, indoor/outdoor sandals that she had been wanting for over a year. The sandals were designed to be worn hiking or in the water – just about anything one could do recreationally. They were made of strong woven nylon and designed to stand up under years of wear and tear. They were expensive, which is why her mom had never agreed to buy them for her before, but given the events of the past year, and how close she came to losing her little girl, the expense now seemed negligible.

"Jack helped me pay for them," her mom answered her

quizzical expression, grinning. Jack just blushed, slightly embarrassed.

"Hey, I'm just glad I can serve some purpose here," he quipped, and he winked jovially at Greg, who smiled back. It was an interesting and new experience for Greg, watching the woman he had been married to for almost fourteen years flirt with the new man in her life. Still, enough time had passed that he held no animosity towards her. Greg was genuinely happy for Theresa.

"Aww!" both Angie and Theresa intoned at once, and then both women burst out laughing, as Theresa tossed a pillow at Jack. Angie jumped up quickly to give each of them a hug, whispering her sincere thanks as she did so.

The next package, also decorated in the same green and purple foil, with a pretty, bouncy purple, green, and blue curling ribbon, was just from her mother. It was a small box filled with all kinds of inexpensive, super cute jewelry from Claire's in the mall. Angie adored silver, and there were funky toe rings, pretty earrings, and a couple of plain, sterling silver chain necklaces.

"Thank you, Mama! I love them!" Angie gushed, jumping up to give her mom another quick squeeze.

"You're so welcome, baby," her mother whispered, thinking she would happily have given her daughter the moon, thankful as she was that Angie was alive. "I'm glad you like them." Another present, also from Theresa, contained the prettiest, softest, deep purple chenille sweater Angie had ever seen.

"Mom! It's gorgeous! But it's still eighty degrees outside!" Angie got up and hugged her mother tightly again.

"It's Montana – winter's coming!" Theresa intoned

flatly, causing the group to burst out laughing.

Greg had brought her some peach marmalade from Georgia, and some beaded necklaces and a cd of Dixieland music from New Orleans that he had picked up during a couple of his deliveries to the South. The Howsers, who were on a missions trip, had brought by a box and left it with Theresa the week prior. It was a sweet, carved little wooden treasure box. Inside was a beautiful, round silver locket with pictures of Shawna and Angie inside, which made both Theresa and Angie cry a little as they turned the beautiful piece over and over and admired the intricate designs on it and the delicate chain attached to it. They both thought the locket looked antique; its intricate filigree designs harkened back to another era. The pictures were from the first year Angie and Shawna met, during sixth grade, and they both giggled a little at how awkward and gawky the girls had looked during their adolescent stage. She immediately put it on, and as she fastened the clasp, Angie knew she would treasure it for the rest of her life.

Mark presented her with his gift, a cd that coincidentally contained many of the songs Angie had said she liked just the night before. As she hugged him tight and thanked him, he whispered that he had one more present for her but wanted to wait until they were alone to give it to her. She pulled back to look at his face, trying to glean some kind of unspoken meaning behind why he was waiting, but his expression gave nothing away.

"You're just going to have to wait," he smirked, and then he leaned down and gave her a peck on the cheek.

Finally, Angie opened a card her grandmother had mailed from Arizona. In it was a check for two-hundred dollars. Her grandma had written a lovely note telling her to spend the money on whatever her heart desired, and that she couldn't wait to see her again. With the gifts all opened, everyone relaxed back into the chairs and sofa and started discussing what needed to be done before their family excursion to Silverwood.

"Are you coming with us, Dad?" Angie asked.

"Not this time, honey," Greg answered. "I have to be in Georgia again by the first of the month. Maybe next time," he offered, when she expressed disappointment. "When is your surgery again?" he asked.

"As soon as we get back," Angie told him. "We get back on the fifth of September, and my surgery is set for the following Monday, the ninth."

"Are you nervous about it?" he asked. "I sure wish I could be here for that." He affectionately ruffled Angie's hair.

"Greg, if it's any consolation, Dr. Thompson is the best orthopedic surgeon in the valley. Jack went to the consult with us," Theresa informed him. "She said although in the past, it was a risky procedure that could easily go wrong, with modern developments, it's now almost foolproof. The good news is that she only has to have her left wrist done. Dr. Thompson thinks Angie can heal her right wrist through continued exercise and therapy.

"Why are you having this done, again?" Greg asked Angie, furrowing his eyebrows at Theresa. Although he wasn't religiously opposed to surgery, he felt that any type of invasive procedure should only be done when absolutely necessary.

"Because she needs it!" Theresa blurted, exasperated. She suddenly found herself losing patience with Greg and his questions. *What was he asking for?* she fumed. Did he suppose they had made such a decision lightly? In spite of the magnanimous feelings she had been having for her ex all morning, she was flooded with the familiar anger that caused her to leave him. He always questioned her decisions and opinions and it offended her.

"Mom, it's okay, I've got this," Angie soothed. Turning towards her dad, she held out her wrists. "Dad, I'm having it because I put my hands through the windshield when we got hit. The previous surgeries I had while still in the hospital corrected the broken bones of my arms, but didn't address the micro abrasions and crushing that my wrists suffered. My arms started to heal okay, but I'm still experiencing weird pins-and-needles sensations in my wrists, and my fingers go numb whenever I play my guitar. My therapist thought I should get checked for carpal tunnel because she said if that's what it was, it was treatable. And that's the whole story."

She stood up a little bit taller and finished her explanation by proclaiming, "And I, for one, believe it's going to work, and who knows? I may even become a world-famous guitarist." She put her nose in the air with false pride. "And I will try to remember all the little people when I make it big."

Mark swept in from the side and tackled her into the couch, then began pummeling her gently with one of the soft decorator pillows. Tossing the pillow aside, he started tickling her, and when she begged for mercy, he said, "And who exactly are these little people of which you speak, your highness, huh? Who? Me? Do I seem small to you?"

"Stop! I'm gonna pee!" she shouted, and he finally relented, while Theresa, Jack, and Greg looked on, laughing.

"Okay, thank you for explaining it to me," Greg said,

when they had settled down again. He shot Theresa a quick look. "Well, thank you for breakfast," he said, standing. "I've got some things I need to do, so I'm going to head out. Happy birthday, Princess," he added, hugging Angie tightly.

"Dad, how much longer are you going to be in town?" Angie asked.

"I have to leave day after tomorrow," Greg answered. "But I would love to take you two kids to dinner tomorrow night, if you're up for it?"

Angie glanced at Mark, who nodded in the affirmative. "Thanks, Dad, we'd love to. Just shoot me a text or call with the where and when."

Greg smiled, then turned to shake hands with Mark.

"Mark, good to finally meet you." They shook hands firmly. "I'll see you tomorrow night."

Finally, he shook hands with Jack, stating he was also pleased to have met him, and then he turned to Theresa, who still looked miffed.

"Hey," he said calmly, "Don't be mad, T. I wasn't trying to question your motives, I just wanted to know what they were going to do. Thanks for allowing me to share in our daughter's birthday celebration. And the crepes were fantastic as usual." He opened his arms for a hug.

Theresa hesitated only a moment, and then relented, leaning in to give him a quick squeeze.

"I know. I know you only want the best for Angie," she conceded.

"And for you, too," he whispered, before she let go. "Jack's great. I hope you guys have a great life."

Theresa released him with a grateful smile. She wasted no time moving back to Jack's side and putting her arm around his waist.

"Well, 'til tomorrow, kids!" he enthused, and then he exited through the apartment door without any more fanfare.

After the door closed behind him, Angie turned to her mother.

"Mom! That was amazing! Did you know Dad was coming?"

"No, honestly, I didn't even know he was in town. He didn't tell you he was coming out this way?" Theresa answered.

"No, not a word." Angie shook her head, marveling at what a great surprise it had been to have her father show up.

"That was pretty cool," Mark said, adding his two cents' worth. "I look forward to getting to know him a little better before he has to leave again." He smiled down at Angie, who sidled up to him and put her arm around him.

"Well," Theresa interrupted quickly. "I know you two kids probably have something fun to do on this beautiful summer day, so let's get all our ducks in a row for the trip and you can both skedaddle!"

So, they all went back to sit in the living room and made plans for the trip. While Theresa jotted notes on a stenographer's tablet, they hammered out all the last minute details about when they would visit the park, when they'd take the boat ride, what they would bring to cook and which days they would eat out.

"Mom, Jack," Angie gushed, "I'm SO excited about these sandals! I know a couple of people who have them and they swear that they are the most comfortable shoes they've ever worn! They'll be great for the trip!" While she talked, she methodically tore off the sales tags and bit through the plastic string that held them together. She put them on hurriedly and then proclaimed, "Oh, my gosh! They're right! These fit perfectly!" She stood up and walked around the living room in them. "It's like walking on clouds, they are so comfortable!"

"Well, I'm glad you like them, honey," Theresa stood and kissed her cheek. Jack smiled and winked at her.

"I do, I do! And thank you for my birthday breakfast, Mom! You always make every occasion so special. I love you!" Angie hugged Theresa hard, and suddenly her throat felt like it was swelling shut. Big tears began falling from her eyes and a sob burst forth from her chest. Theresa held her tightly.

"I know, honey, I know," she crooned, as she gently rocked Angie back and forth.

"She should be here, Mama," Angie cried into her mother's shoulder. "She should still be here." Suddenly, she was sobbing. Mark and Jack quietly excused themselves and headed to the kitchen to do the dishes and give the women some space.

Theresa held Angie close, murmuring comfort into her ear and rocking her until the sobbing subsided moments later, almost as quickly as it had begun. Mark appeared miraculously with a tissue. He handed it to Angie, who accepted it gratefully. She straightened up and dabbed at her nose and eyes.

"Wow, sorry, everyone," she apologized. "That sure came out of nowhere."

"There is absolutely no need to apologize, Angela," her mother said. "This is another first, you know? I'm actually surprised that it took so long for you to recognize it. I think you're healing, even though you may not realize it. But don't ever feel badly when these moments hit you. Just go with them. They are a part of the process, and I can guarantee you this won't be the last time something makes you miss her. It won't be the last time you cry."

"I hope not," Angie sniffled. "I mean, not that I want to be a crying basket case every time I turn around, but... but I kind of feel like if I stop crying it will mean I've forgotten her."

"Not at all, sweetheart," Theresa said emphatically. "You know how devastated I was when Grandpa died. Remember? Remember how long I cried? And now, when is the last time you saw me burst into spontaneous tears? It's been awhile, hasn't it? Do you think that means I don't miss my father every day?"

"No?" Angie answered slowly.

"No." Theresa replied firmly. "I find that grief is cyclic. It comes and goes, and each time it cycles back around, it stings again. Over time, the circles get bigger and the pain hits less frequently. But never do we stop missing the person we grieve for. Never do we forget about them. Occasionally, when memories of Grandpa cycle around again, I find myself tearful, missing him terribly. Most recently was when you had your accident. It hadn't hit me that hard in years, but as you lay comatose for the first few days, I found myself crying more than once for my daddy. I didn't want to face such a hard reality without his loving guidance. I still had Grandma to lean on, but it was hard, nevertheless."

"Thank you, Mom," Angie said, wiping the last of the tears from her eyes. "When did you get to be so wise? I hope I inherit that from you!" She smiled widely.

"Oh, Lord!" Theresa exclaimed. "I don't know that I'm all that wise. Just things I've observed over time and as I have weathered a few of my own storms. You've weathered a huge storm, baby, and you've emerged with some wisdom of your own." She smiled back. Mother and daughter hugged tightly again, and then Theresa said, "Now, you two kids, get out of here! The day is wasting! Jack and I will finish the dishes, and then I think we're heading to town to see a movie. What are you two up to today?"

"I actually don't even know," Angie shrugged and giggled, looking at Mark. "What are we doing today? What time is it?"

"It's just noon," Mark chimed in. "I thought we might go hike up Lone Pine and try out your fancy new sandals. And then Ben and Callie were wondering if we wanted to get together and do something. I told them I'd have to check with you." He smiled at her and shrugged. "It's your birthday. It's up to you."

"Sure, that sounds like fun," Angie answered enthusiastically. Turning back to her mother, she said, "I guess that's what we're doing!"

Theresa and Jack laughed.

"Alright, but be sure to take plenty of bottled water with you," Jack cautioned. "It's supposed to be a scorcher today!"

So, while the adults finished cleaning up the kitchen, the teenagers scrounged up a small cooler from the storage closet off the deck and filled it with ice and bottled water. Angie grabbed a box of crackers from the cupboard and some savory summer sausage and sharp cheddar cheese from the refrigerator and stuffed them inside the cooler as well. Then they headed out into the bright sunshine.

. . .

The day did turn out to be outrageously hot. They had planned to hike all the way to the top of Lone Pine, to the lookout, but ended up feeling completely exhausted and drained by the time they reached the first turnout. They meandered over to the benches and plunked down, to take a break and enjoy the view. They each drained a bottle of water, then leaned back against the bench and surveyed the scenery below them. They could see and hear the small amount of traffic moving east and west on Highway 2. They heard the echoing, rhythmic pounding of a house under construction in the distance. Birds twittered and chattered; bees buzzed. It was too hot to lean into each other, so they simply sat as close as the heat would allow, lazily soaking up the sunny afternoon.

Angie was drowsy and thinking how much she'd love to go home for a while and take a nap, when suddenly, Mark spoke, and she jumped a little.

"Angie?" he asked. His voice was thick with emotion. "Remember how I told you that I had another present for you?"

Angie sat up a little and turned her full attention to Mark. She nodded. She was suddenly nervous, although she didn't know why. She took a deep breath and gave him her full attention.

"Yes," she answered. She trembled nervously.

"Angie," he started again. "We've been going out for about ten months now. I know that in some peoples' eyes that doesn't seem like a very long time. But I know what I feel, and what I feel is this: I can't picture myself ever being with anyone else. Maybe it's too soon to think about forever, but I want you by my side for that long. For forever." He stopped, stuck his hand into one pocket of his cargo shorts, and produced a small ring. As she watched, flabbergasted, he rose from the bench and got down on one knee.

Angie gasped. Mark continued, holding the ring up for her to see. She couldn't take her eyes off of it. Its design was two tiny, delicate intertwining vines made of white gold.

"I love you, Angie. I realize you still have your senior year of high school to get through. Truth be told, I want to at least get my associates degree before we get married. So this isn't an engagement ring, it's a promise ring. But this is still a proposal. Angie, when you get out of school, you would make me the happiest man on the planet if you would agree to be my wife." Mark finished his speech and Angie made herself stop staring at the ring. She forced her eyes up to meet his and saw that they were beautiful, turquoise, and filled with tears.

Her deep green eyes welled up and without a second's thought, she blurted out, "Yes, yes! Of course, I will. I love you, too!" Big, happy tears trickled down both their cheeks.

Mark slid the ring onto her left hand. They both stared at it there, and he said, "Perfect." Angie couldn't take her eyes from the ring on her hand. It was so beautiful.

"I love it, and I love you," she whispered.

Chapter Twelve: Hope

"Faith has to do with things that are not seen, and hope with things that are not at hand." ~ Thomas Aquinas

The next month and a half sped by in a flurry of activity. First was the trip to Silverwood, which couldn't have been better, they all agreed. The weather was as perfect as it possibly could have been. Early September in Idaho emerged with a sudden show of fall colors, brought on by cool, crisp evenings and lovely, warm, sunny days. Their days were filled with roller coasters and cotton candy at Silverwood, and shopping and eating out at the many malls and restaurants in nearby Spokane. The house on Lake Coeur d'Alene was beautiful and private, with big rooms, lush furnishings, a steam room, and a hot tub on a secluded deck. It was surrounded by huge, fragrant evergreens, and the wide private beach sported a dock big enough that they could bring lawn chairs down in the evenings and sit and watch the sunset from it.

On one particularly beautiful, warm evening, as they watched the last of the recreationalists docking their boats in the mirrored distance and rehashed the events of another wonderful day spent together, Jack emerged from the bungalow with a big smile on his face. In one hand, he held an ice bucket filled with ice and a bottle of champagne; in the other hand, he held four champagne flutes upside down, by the stems. Ignoring the flurry of questions, he set the bucket and glasses down on the little café table. Then he turned, got down on one knee in front of Theresa, and pulled an ornate ring box from his pocket. He opened it, revealing a gorgeous white gold ring with a single, large, princess-cut Yogo sapphire set in the center. Montana is famous for its Yogo sapphires, which come in an astonishing array of colors. This one almost mimicked a mystic fire topaz; it was mostly green, but in the twilight, it refracted a dozen other colors, depending on how the light hit it. It was stunning, and Theresa sucked in a big breath, and then started to cry. She blurted out that she would love him forever and would definitely marry him almost before he finished asking, and as he slipped the ring on her finger and they fell into each other's arms, all four of them were crying and laughing with joy. Jack then popped open the champagne and they all had a glass. Even though Mark and Angie were under age, Theresa decided it would be okay for them each to have a half a glass, since they were being supervised.

That special evening turned out to be the highlight of the whole trip. They had taken dozens of photographs, and when they got home, each downloaded and printed the pictures from their own phones with a photo printer Jack bought. The Friday after they got home, Mark came over to the apartment, as did Jack, and they spent a fun evening putting together one, large family vacation photo album. Theresa liked to scrapbook, although she really didn't have the time or money to get into it full bore, and she happened to have a pretty, fall-themed album and some stickers and decorations stashed away in her overstuffed closet, which she produced for the project. They laughed at some of the shots and had a blast putting speech bubbles with funny stuff next to some of them. When it was completed, they all agreed that not only had it been the perfect trip, they now also had the perfect keepsake to remember it by.

The following Monday, Angie finally had the long-awaited carpal tunnel surgery on her left wrist. Compared to all of the surgeries she'd had while in the hospital after the accident, she judged that this surgery could not have gone better. It went so well that Dr. Thompson believed she would heal without any problems whatsoever. She went home the same day, and except for some minor achiness, had no ill effects. She waited as patiently as she could for the day they removed the bandages and she got to find out if it had worked or not. Even before the surgery, she had gotten back in the habit of picking her guitar up and fiddling around with it every day, fighting through the annoying lack of sensation. She couldn't wait to see if the surgery worked and the numbness disappeared.

A month later, during the first week of October, she had her post op appointment. She held her breath while Dr. Thompson unwound the bandages surrounding her left wrist. She warned Angie that she would still need to wear a wrist guard for a while and would need to do daily exercises to gain back strength in the wrist.

Finally, the last of the bandages fell away. She showed Angie where she had made the incision and Angie was amazed at how tiny it was, considering all the doctor had done, scraping away scar tissue and clearing a path for her nerves. She gave her a ball of putty like the one Chloe had given her in therapy, and showed her different exercises to do with it. She also showed her some exercises she could do without any equipment Then she produced a printout of the exercises she had just shown her and told her how many times a day she should do each one.

"And that's it!" she exclaimed. "Do you have any questions for me?" She smiled at Angie.

"Really?" Angie replied. "That's all? It seems too easy," she laughed. "I guess I do have one question: When can I start playing my guitar again?"

Dr. Thompson smiled at her. "I'd like for you to do your exercises for a couple days first. Then I'll leave it up to you. Are you a right-handed or left-handed guitarist?"

Angie pantomimed playing and showed her that she used her left hand for holding the neck and forming chords.

"Well, I play a little guitar myself, and I know that holding down the chords is going to put a little extra strain on that wrist. So, like I said, give yourself at least a few days of just doing the exercises. Then, when you start playing again, pace yourself. Play a few chords and then stretch your wrists and see how they feel. Okay? Any other questions?" she asked.

"Um…no," Angie said, shaking her head. "I can't think of any."

"Well, that's it then! You're done! Keep in touch and let me know how things go, okay? If you experience any numbness or tingling in that wrist, I'd like you to come right back in, because there shouldn't be any." She stood up and Angie followed her.

"Good luck, Angela," she smiled, and held out her hand for Angie to shake.

"Thank you so much, Dr. Thompson," Angie gushed. Outside of Jack, she was the kindest doctor she had dealt with since the accident. "I really appreciate all that you've done."

"You're welcome," she said, escorting her back to the waiting room with one hand on her shoulder. "Let me know when you have your first concert and I'll be there."

Angie blushed. "I will," she giggled. Dr. Thompson turned to walk back down to her office, and Angie lingered for a moment in the hallway just before the waiting room. On the wall, she saw a bulletin board overflowing with thank you notes and testimonials from patients, all gushing over how much better they felt and how nice Dr. Thompson was. She felt confident that her wrist was going to be completely healed and couldn't wait to try playing her guitar again, although she had every intention of following the doctor's order to wait a few days.

The weather outside was cool. The trees were in the late stages of change. Many still displayed their pretty red, orange, and yellow fall foliage, but quite a few had lost their leaves already. It was early October, only a couple weeks away from the one-year anniversary of the accident and losing Shawna. Angie didn't tear up at the thought, which surprised her. As she walked to her car, she inhaled the crisp autumn air a deeply. She loved the comforting smell of burning leaf piles and wood stoves. In a few weeks, or possibly sooner, winter would arrive in Montana again, like clockwork. She always got a little melancholy in the fall, even though it was her favorite season. It felt like everything was shutting down and going into hibernation. She had often thought that she should have been one of those creatures who hibernated, because she wasn't a huge fan of winter.

When she got home, the apartment was filled, as it so often was, with the delightful scents of her mother's home cooking, this time cheese manicotti and garlic bread. Italian food was Angie's absolute favorite and she reveled in the smells. The apartment air hung heavy with the scents of tangy tomatoes, savory garlic, and sautéed onions. She took off her jacket and tossed it in the front closet, then carried her book bag down the hall and threw it onto her bed. She went back out to the dining room to join her mom and Jack, who had all but moved in since they had gotten engaged. His presence no longer irritated her; in fact, she appreciated it and like her mother, felt somehow more secure when he was around. Angie had come to adore Jack. He was perpetually cheerful and encouraging. He was like a big, goofy puppy, with his silly sense of humor. She still thought he was a total hottie, but no longer blushed when he spoke to her. That had long since passed, as soon as she had started dating Mark. At that point, she had suddenly seen him as an older guy, someone her *mom's* age, and she couldn't believe she had ever nurtured a single fantasy about him.

She removed the splint she had been sent home wearing and showed them both the incision. Just like she had, they marveled at how tiny it was for so much work to have been done. Angie stuck her exercise regimen on the fridge with a magnet. She told them she couldn't wait to play her guitar, but that the doctor had admonished her to wait a few days and build up some strength.

"I'll bet you're chomping at the bit to get back in the saddle again, huh?" Jack joked, mixing metaphors on purpose and playfully punching her softly in the arm.

"You said it," she responded enthusiastically. "I can't wait! But I've come this far, so I'm going to be a good girl and fight the urge to pick it up until I've gotten a few days' exercise under my belt, like the doctor said."

Theresa, who had gone in and added some extra cheese to the top of the manicotti, now came back out to the dining room table where they were sitting. She put her arm around Angie and gave her a squeeze.

"Don't hate me for saying so. I'm not trying to be condescending, I'm really not. But I'm *so* proud of you! You may not realize it, but you have matured so much in this past year. I love you." Theresa's voice broke a little as she spoke the endearment.

"Aw, Mama, I love you, too," Angie blushed, embarrassed. "And by the way, YUM! That manicotti smells fantastico!" she said, trying to change the subject. Like a stereotypical Italian, she put her fingers to her lips, pulled them back quickly and made a noisy smacking sound with her lips. "Ima gonna eat me a ton o' that-a, you can bet your sweet-a bippy!" She used her best Italian accent, mimicking Theresa's mother's accent.

Theresa laughed and Jack, attempting to add his two-bits' worth, joked, "Hey, that's-a spicy meat-a ball-a!"

Theresa looked at him blankly. "There aren't any meatballs in it," she stated, feigning confusion. She and Angie stared at him with deadpan expressions, but glanced at each other sideways, eyes twinkling. It was so much fun to tease Jack.

Jack grinned sheepishly, "Oh, ha ha, well, that's about the extent of my Italian…" He blushed with embarrassment.

Angie and Theresa responded with loud peals of

laughter and Jack realized they'd been putting him on. "Oh, you guys!" he said, jumping up and grabbing them both in a squeeze. They hugged him back.

Just then, the doorbell rang. Angie hopped up and ran to get it. Mark was also a regular fixture at the Gianelli apartment. He had always hung around a lot, but since giving the promise ring to Angie, tended to eat dinner with them every night that his schedule would allow. He usually stayed as late as possible afterwards, helping Angie with her homework or just talking and listening to music. The four of them often watched movies together, too.

Theresa and Jack had been a little apprehensive when Angie came home on the evening of her birthday sporting a ring. She had just turned eighteen that day, her mother had argued. Jack was also concerned about their relative youth and about making such a big commitment. They had calmed down considerably after she explained how he had presented the ring to her. Yes, he wanted to marry her, but he, too, was cognizant of their relative ages *and* that Angie still had another year of high school. It was only a *promise* ring, not an engagement ring, she had explained. It really didn't mean anything more than they were committed to each other on a level just a little higher than boyfriend/ girlfriend.

At that point, her mom had felt compelled to ask about whether or not they were being "safe." Angie told her that she and Mark had made a commitment months earlier to remaining abstinent, partly because of Mark's faith, which she respected, but partly because they both believed that they would be married one day and they wanted to have a "real" wedding night. That proclamation had blown both Theresa and Jack away, and they had stopped giving her grief about the ring. In private, they marveled that any two kids in this modern era could have the will power to see such a commitment through. They knew if anyone could, Angie and Mark were that couple. Theresa was filled again with tremendous pride in her daughter's wisdom and maturity.

Angie swung the door open wide.

"Hi!" she exclaimed happily, almost knocking Mark down in a half hug-half tackle.

"Hi, yourself!" he responded, smiling hugely. He hugged her back tightly and entered. As Angie shut the door behind him, he exclaimed, "Oh, my goodness! It smells heavenly in here!" He drew a deep breath of the manicotti-filled air and his stomach growled so loudly that it could be heard from across the room. Theresa, Jack, and Angie all laughed loudly.

"Mom, quick, is dinner almost ready?" Angie quipped, giggling. "The beast must be fed!"

At that, Theresa stood up from the table and headed towards the kitchen.

"I'm sure it's ready. Come get your plates, guys!"

Unlike on Angie's birthday, the table wasn't set. They tended to do things more casually on a daily basis, often just dishing up their plates in the kitchen and then heading straight to the living room to watch TV. Without needing a second invitation, they all followed Theresa into the kitchen. The manicotti was perfect, covered in a bubbling, golden brown cheese. Theresa was busy slicing the garlic bread, which she always made herself. She didn't make the bread from scratch, but instead of buying the premade garlic bread from the grocery store, she bought the plain French bread. Then, she roasted garlic in the oven, mixed it with melted butter, and spread the soft, delectable concoction over the bread.

Each of them loaded their plates with the gooey, cheese-filled pasta, dripping with tomato-basil sauce, and each grabbed a slice or two of the steaming hot bread. Jack pulled the tossed salad, which he had prepared earlier, from the fridge, and dished them each a bowlful. While Angie, Mark, and Theresa took turns pouring on the homemade olive oil and red wine vinaigrette, he quickly grabbed the set of four TV trays from the hall closet, wheeled it out, and started setting up trays.

In record time, all four of them were seated in the living room, watching "Jeopardy" and stuffing their mouths full of the delicious food. It was a full ten minutes before anyone spoke, except for scattered proclamations of "Wow! Delicious!" or "Yummy!"

When "Jeopardy" ended, they took their dishes to the kitchen and Angie and Mark offered to wash them while Theresa and Jack watched an old rerun of "The Big Bang Theory." Mark wiped down the TV trays, while Angie found containers for the leftovers. Laughter erupted frequently from the living room. They were finished in no time at all, and then they went back to the living room to finish watching the episode.

When it ended and the station went to commercial, Angie suddenly blurted out, "So Red Ribbon Week is almost here again. It's week after next." She looked at Mark, who gave her hand an encouraging squeeze.

Theresa muted the TV and looked compassionately over at Angie, as did Jack. The sun was setting and the room grew dim, so Jack reached over and turned on the end table lamp so they could see Angie while she spoke.

"Wow," Theresa exclaimed softly. "I can't believe it's been a year already. How are you, honey? Has the school asked you to do anything special?"

Angie fidgeted uncomfortably. "Actually, they have," she answered. She looked down at her hand intertwined with Mark's and nervously rubbed her thumb back and forth over the back of his hand. "They have asked me to speak about my experience last year. The crash. Losing Shawna. They think it will make a good public service announcement about why they preach to us kids about not drinking and driving. I just don't know if I can do it." A tear quietly slipped down her cheek.

"What did you tell them?" Theresa asked. Jack got up, grabbed a box of tissues from the kitchen, and brought it to Angie, who accepted it gratefully.

"I don't know," Angie responded, wiping her eyes and dabbing at her nose. "I mean, I see what they're getting at, but the thing is, it's not just a PSA to me. This is my life! Shawna was my best friend!" She sniffled and a few more tears escaped. "I am happy to talk about Shawna. She was the most important person in my life for five years. She was like an angel sent to earth just for me, you know? She was the kindest, truest person I've ever known, with the purest heart. So, yeah, I'm more than happy to talk about her, but I don't want her whole life boiled down to how it ended.

"I was talking to Eileen about it the other day. You know how they give out awards at school to athletes and scholars? We were thinking it would be really something if the school started giving out an award in Shawna's name, like a kindness award. Students could nominate and vote for one person each semester and the award could be given out at the traditional awards ceremonies. The Shawna Howser Award for Kindness. *That* is something I can picture myself doing."

Theresa adjusted her position on the couch so that her body was turned towards Angie.

"That's a beautiful idea, honey," she commended. "I wonder if you couldn't do some kind of a combination of both. I mean, tell everyone about Shawna, about what kind of person she was and what she meant to you, so they understand the gravity of the accident. I can understand the principal and counselors wanting you to talk a *little* bit about the accident, because that really is kind of the point of Red Ribbon Week. Kids need to understand that their actions have consequences and that they could do something while under the influence that they can never take back, something they'll have to live with the rest of their lives. I don't think talking about that diminishes Shawna's life or what she meant to you. I think it makes it more...I don't know. Special? Real?" She stammered, looking for the right way to express her thoughts.

"Here, what about this?" she suggested. "Maybe you could start by telling the facts of the accident. Short and to the point. You were both on your way to school, doing everything right, and Bam! You were hit. Shawna perished and you suffered a year of surgeries and therapy and the like. Then, you could tie it into Red Ribbon Week by explaining the irony of the accident, that the young woman who hit you was under the influence of drugs and alcohol. And from there, you could explain that you want to honor Shawna's memory by telling everyone about her and about what a wonderful person she was. Then you can spend as much time as you like (or as the school will allow) talking just about Shawna. Maybe you could put a slide show together?"

"That could work," Angie mused. "I wonder who I should approach about starting a Shawna Howser award, though? I would really, really like to see that happen."

"I'd go to your guidance counsellor," Mark suggested. "It's as good a place to start as any, and they have the ability to either take the idea to the person who can make such a decision, or they can point you in the right direction to get the ball rolling." He smiled at her then. "Have you thought about singing and playing your guitar? Something to honor Shawna?" He had been so impressed with her talent at the service they had attended over the summer.

Blushing, she admitted, "Actually, I have. I have been listening to the Christian radio station lately, and the other day, they were playing some retro music from the last three decades. I heard a song and used an app on my phone to search for the title while it played. It's called 'Friends,' a song by Michael W. Smith. It made me cry and I thought about how perfect it would be. I checked with the music store downtown and they were able to order me the sheet music. It should be here in a couple days. Of course, Michael W. Smith played it on piano, but the store associate found sheet music that includes guitar chords." She sighed. "If I can learn it, and if I can muster up the courage, I'd really like to play that."

While she had been talking, Mark looked up the song on YouTube. He played it for Theresa and Jack to hear. By the end of the song, everyone had tears in their eyes.

"I agree one hundred percent," Theresa said softly. "It's the perfect song, honey. I think you should do it. Play it again, will you, Mark?"

They all listened once more, each reflecting quietly on the lyrics. Although the song is meant as a "farewell" to friends who are moving away, it got Angie thinking about her many conversations with Eileen about heaven and eternity. If, as Eileen believed, all of humanity already existed in eternity, and if heaven was just another plane of existence within eternity, then it was reasonable to think of Shawna as having just "moved somewhere else," and it was also reasonable to believe that she would get to see her again.

There might never be any proof, but she was ready to believe it could be true. At the very least, she was already full of hope that it could be.

Chapter Thirteen: One Small Ripple

*"Doing good holds the power to transform us on the inside,
and then ripple out in ever-expanding circles that
positively impact the world at large." ~ Shari Arison*

"Those are just a few things I wanted to share with you today about my friend, Shawna Howser. They are but a drop in the bucket. She may have only lived on earth for seventeen short years, but she will live on in my heart, in her parents' hearts, and in the hearts of all those who were fortunate enough to know her forever."

As Angie concluded her speech at the Red Ribbon assembly, there was a tiny moment of complete silence, and then the gymnasium full of people burst out in thunderous applause. The gym was decked out in black and orange banners, reflecting the school colors, as well as red streamers, balloons, and of course, ribbons, to commemorate the nationally recognized week. When she had arrived at the gym that morning and had seen all the decorations, she had to excuse herself immediately to the restroom. It hit her full force that one year ago, she and Shawna had been heading into school to decorate in similar fashion, and that the drive in had been the last thing Shawna had ever done on earth. She sat alone in a stall and cried hard for a few minutes, something she hadn't done in months. Miraculously, she had almost immediately felt the warm peace come over her, the same peace that had enveloped her on other occasions when she thought her heart would literally break into pieces. She had pulled herself together relatively quickly and had gone right back to the gym to prepare for her speech.

Now that she was finished, she looked over at the group of people who had shown up to support her and smiled. Mark was there, as were Theresa, Jack, and miracle of miracles, Greg, who had been able to arrange his driving schedule so he could attend. Eileen and Grant Howser were present, too, and Angie saw them both wipe tears away many times during her presentation. Ben and Callie were there, even though Callie attended the high school on the other side of town. They all clapped loudly in support of the courage they knew it had taken for her to speak.

Angie's counsellor, Mrs. Jacobsen, walked over to join her at the podium. The applause died down.

"Thank you so much for sharing all of that with us, Angie," she said. "We know you've been through a lot this year. Not only have you been grieving the loss of a great friend, you have had your own physical healing to contend with. We're glad you are here with us today." She smiled at Angie, then reached out and gave her a hug. The audience applauded once more.

Then Mrs. Jacobsen turned back to the microphone. "A few weeks ago, Shawna's mother, Eileen, and Angie came to me with an idea for keeping Shawna's memory alive and to establish a legacy to her. They expressed their desire to see a new award added to the awards ceremony each semester, one that would be given to the person that the students and faculty felt best exemplified Shawna's gentle spirit and her uncommon kindness. The school board voted unanimously to establish the Shawna Howser Kindness Award. Most of you have seen the posters announcing the new award, and many of you nominated and voted for people whom you believe meet the simple criteria: Someone who strives to always be kind, in word and deed. Someone who sticks up for the underdogs of the world. Someone who has the self-control to turn the other cheek when confronted.

"We decided to give out the first award today at this Red Ribbon Assembly, instead of waiting until the semester awards ceremony, because it is almost one year ago to the day that Shawna's life was taken due to the carelessness of someone who chose to drive while under the influence of both drugs and alcohol. Going forward, this award will be presented during the semester awards ceremonies. If you get a chance, please visit the hallway near the front office where all the trophy cases are. You will notice that a special plaque has been placed on the wall to the left of the Spirit Awards trophy case. Each recipient of this prestigious award will have their name added to the plaque and he or she can also add having received the award to his or her resume.

"And now, without further ado, it gives me great pleasure to announce the first winner of the Shawna Howser Kindness Award. Mr. and Mrs. Howser, would you please come forward and personally present the award certificate?" Eileen and Grant moved to join Angie and Mrs. Jacobsen at the podium.

Mrs. Jacobsen continued. "Please join me in congratulating the first recipient of the Shawna Howser

Kindness Award – Miss Ally Nicholas!" A cheer went up from the crowded bleachers. Ally, smiling widely, approached the podium. Eileen and Grant each gave her a big hug, as did Angie, and then Eileen presented her with the certificate. Ally was a cute, popular cheerleader. Physically adorable, she had big, china blue eyes, naturally white-blonde hair, and a curvy figure. Her beauty wasn't what made her popular, though. She was known simply for being one of the nicest people at the school. She tutored fellow students for free. If someone spilled or dropped something and she was nearby, she rushed to help. Like Shawna had been, she was just one of those rare people who went out of her way to make everyone around her feel special and important and loved. She was the perfect choice for the first recipient of the award.

More thunderous applause broke out as she accepted her award and made her way back to her seat. Mrs. Jacobsen stood before the podium again.

"We are near the conclusion of our Red Ribbon Assembly. We hope you have each learned something new today, something you will take with you throughout your life. We, the staff and faculty of Kalispell High School, think each and every one of you, our students, are precious and special. We hope we never lose another one of you to such a terrible tragedy as the one that took the life of Shawna Howser. We hope that not a single one of you will ever use drugs or alcohol. We aren't so naïve, of course, as to believe that will be true. Statistics show that a certain percentage of our students have already tried cigarettes, alcohol, or drugs. We wish that weren't so, but it's just a sad fact. We *do* hope, however, that each one of you will take responsibility for your actions. We hope that if you ever do try any of these harmful substances, you will think long and hard before you get behind the wheel of a car.

"To close our ceremony today, Miss Angie Gianelli would like to sing a song. Thank you all for coming and thank you, students, for being such a polite and attentive audience. Angie?" She stepped aside from the microphone, rolling the portable podium away as she went to give Angie maximum exposure.

Angie had already pulled the guitar strap over her head and positioned the guitar. As she stepped up to the microphone, she realized suddenly that she wasn't nervous. She wasn't overcome with emotion as she had thought she might be. Instead, she was filled with resolve. Today was about honoring the life of her friend, taken too soon, but who would not be soon forgotten. Shawna, beautiful, bubbly Shawna. Girl with the golden hair and eyes, always shining, always smiling, always full of love. Her love had been one small pebble in the ocean, but Angie knew the ripples would continue out into eternity.

Her hands, which had not gone numb since she had the carpal tunnel surgery, were sure and steady, and her voice rang out sweetly. As she sang a cover of Michael W Smith's "Friends," she realized that her biggest fear had been that she still had to say goodbye, and goodbye seemed so final. Now, though, she suddenly realized that she didn't have to say it. Shawna would always be with her, in her heart, wherever she went and however long she lived. And one day, she believed, she would see her again, and they would laugh and dance together in heaven.

Afterword

*O*n October 26, 2006, my dear friend and colleague, Dawn Bowker, was hit and killed while she was driving to her teaching job at Somers Middle School in Somers, Montana. It was around 7:30 in the morning and she was only about another five minutes from her destination. The man who hit her was travelling home after having been up partying all night. It is unknown why his truck crossed over the center line of two-lane Highway 83; however, he hit Dawn's station wagon head-on. A seventy-mile-an-hour road, the cars collided with the power and energy of double that rate of speed. Dawn was pronounced dead at the scene. The driver who caused the accident survived relatively unscathed.

Somers Middle School was observing Red Ribbon Week. Anyone who has taught school, attended public school, or is the parent of public-school student in the last thirty years is familiar with Red Ribbon Week, a nationally recognized week in which schools focus on the perils of drug and alcohol use. It was a Thursday. Each day of that week was dedicated to some kind of fun event, and that day happened to be "Crazy Hair Day." The kids had enjoyed all of the activities we'd planned, and they couldn't wait to see what Dawn, one of their favorite teachers, had done to her hair. (I was also teaching at SMS that year; my hair was teased and backcombed into a mess, and sprayed with purple glitter.)

When Dawn hadn't arrived by the start of school, of course kids started asking where she was. One of the aides took over her homeroom class, as well as her first block of math class. I didn't have an answer for them; as far as I knew, she was just running late. Another teacher on our team, Cheryl, and I did our best to keep the kids focused on learning, confident that Dawn would show up any moment and the mystery would be solved.

It never crossed my mind that anything could have happened to Dawn, so when the other of the two aides came to relieve me at around ten o'clock, saying the principal wanted to meet with me briefly, I certainly had no inkling that it had anything do to with Dawn. I briefed the sub on what we were doing in class and headed down the hall to see what the principal needed.

As soon as I entered her office, she shut the door behind me and asked me to have a seat at the table in her office, which I did. She cut right to the chase and informed me that Dawn had been killed in an accident on her way to school that morning. I was shocked, to say the least. The news was surreal and I didn't want to believe it.

Dawn and I were both hired as sixth grade teachers in the fall of 2005. One day about three weeks before school started, we were introduced to each other in the office. As soon as I saw her, I recognized her from somewhere. Likewise, she recognized me. It only took a few minutes for us to figure out that we had taken a sign language class together at the local community college four years earlier. She was such a friendly and kind person and I hadn't forgotten her, although I was surprised she remembered me. It was the only class we ever had together, and after obtaining our Associates Degrees, I headed to the University of Montana's School of Education in Missoula, while Dawn went to the School of Ed at Montana State University in Bozeman, Montana. We were delighted to have rediscovered each other and were both so excited about beginning our teaching careers.

Dawn was twenty-five in the fall of 2005, and I was forty-four, having gone back to college as a non-traditional student when my youngest kid was a preteen and my eldest three were teenagers. Even though there was an almost twenty-year age gap between us, Dawn and I became fast friends. I admired her so much. Although she was so much younger than I, she was very mature and wise. She was a devout Christian, but here's the rub: She loved God and the Lord Jesus with her whole heart and soul and lived her life to please Him, but she was no Bible-thumper. She was down-to-earth, loving, and one of the kindest people I have ever known. I should have been advising her, but found that I could tell her things I didn't tell anyone else, and I could share my problems with her. Aside from never judging me, she always seemed to be able to say just the right thing. She willingly acted as an advisor to (and a prayer partner with) me.

Dawn had an amazing sense of humor and was rarely seen without a broad smile on her beautiful face. One of my favorite memories of Dawn is the night of our very first parent-teacher conferences. We had both prepared carefully and fretted much about this, one of our first interactions with our students' parents. The conferences took up several nights. After the last parent left on the first night of conferences, Dawn and I came out into the hallway at the same time, and as soon as I saw her, I asked her how it had gone. In mock slow-motion, she rolled down to the floor, and then rolled from side to side, waving her arms and legs in the air, doing a ground level victory dance. I howled. She was always doing things like that.

The last time I saw her was Wednesday, October 25, after school. I'd had a particularly hard day and was outside in the playground area in back of the school. I don't remember why I was back there, but I ran into Dawn, who was just returning from an after-school run. We sat on a bench and she comforted and encouraged me. We had talked many times about doing something together outside of school and finally decided to make it happen. She told me about a concert she was going to attend the upcoming Sunday, a Christian musician that she admired very much and was certain I would also enjoy. It was a date!

We firmed up our plans to meet and go to the concert. I was so excited, because she was the person I was closest to at the school. I had dreamt of becoming a teacher since I was a child, but I was having trouble settling down into the "professional" I hoped one day to be. Dawn – so many years my junior, yet miles beyond me in maturity and professionalism – never judged me in any way. Of all the people I had met at the school up to that point, she was one of the few who "got me." I had been praying that the Lord would bring me a real friend for years, because I hadn't really made any good friends since moving back to Kalispell after college. I was thrilled that Dawn seemed destined to become that friend for whom I had prayed.

Obviously, the entire school was devastated by the loss of Dawn. I felt desolate. It was the beginning of what was only my second year of teaching and I faced a situation that would prove challenging to even the most experienced among the staff. That was a hard year, but I did what I could to help our students as they moved through the various stages of grief. Dawn's mother, Irene, became very active at the school, as she also wanted to help the kids deal with their grief. Once a semester, we had a fun day where the kids could take elective classes, and Irene stepped into Dawn's role, leading a class on pie baking. I hadn't had the pleasure of meeting her until after Dawn passed away, but she has become a good friend and a very special person in my life. The character of Eileen Howser is modeled after Irene, who is a very beautiful and gracious Christian woman. I love you, Irene!

Irene worked with the administrators at Somers Middle School to create the Dawn Bowker Award for Kindness. SMS began awarding it to one person – student, teacher, or staff member – each semester, starting with the very semester that Dawn died. Voted on by classmates and teachers, the recipients are those who best exemplify the type of person Dawn was, someone gentle, loving, respectful, and kind. I checked with Irene and at the time of this writing (March 2020), the award is still given out.

The driver at fault was given a ten-year prison sentence. He was released early for good behavior after serving only three years of his sentence. For a while after his release (and perhaps as a condition of his release), he went around to all the Montana high schools, speaking about the accident and how it had affected so many lives, including his own. Unfortunately, he slipped and fell into drug use again. He was arrested and forced to serve the rest of his sentence. When I spoke with Irene recently, she expressed that she still prays for him and his family and hopes he finds his way to a productive life.

During the summer of 2007, the seed of this story germinated in my mind and I started writing it to honor Dawn. Instead of a biography, I settled on a fictional story similar to the actual one. I changed the main character to a high school student because I wanted to write a story that might appeal to young adults. The story has been a long time in the making, and even sat on the back burner untouched for several years while I weathered more storms of life. In 2010, I left the teaching profession burned out and disillusioned. I enjoyed the students and parents very much, but found the bureaucracy to be more than I could handle. It felt like the death of a dream. I've had several interesting jobs since I left teaching, including a short stint as a legal assistant, and as a deli clerk, cashier, bookkeeper, and front end manager of a nearby Albertsons grocery store. At the time of this writing, I work as a billing director for an amazing physical therapy company. We are never too old to dream, and my new dream is to be able to write full time.

It took me awhile to return to this project. I feared it would never be completed, and then feared it would never be published.

Nevertheless, I held onto the dream that someday I could write a story that would bring honor to the memory of my beautiful friend, Dawn Bowker.

• • •

My dearest Dawn,

Sometimes I feel like you were a dream. Years have passed since you went home. Whether any of us, your beloved friends and family, wanted it to, life went on. I wonder what you would be doing now. At the time of this writing, it is 2020 – incredibly, you would be 39 or 40 now. I think you would be married and have at least three – maybe four – kids. You would undoubtedly still be teaching and finding much success in your career and in life as a whole. The tragedy is that we will never know.

However, *the truth of God is the hope of life eternal with Him. My faith is strong, and I know you still live, just in a different place, one filled with beauty we can't even imagine here on earth, a place where God personally wipes away all tears. For a short time, you were like an angel sent to earth, not just for me, but for every person who knew you.*

Save me a spot, will you?

Love you forever, my special, amazing friend

I hope I have achieved my goal of honoring Dawn's life and keeping her memory alive. I hope you found this story an uplifting and enjoyable read.

May God bless you richly!

Acknowledgements

I would like to thank all of my friends and family for believing in me. I am grateful for having had so many opportunities. I am fortunate to have four children and two stepchildren, all of whom encourage me and bring light into my life. When I started this story, I was still teaching sixth grade, and had mentioned my desire to write a story based on one of their other teachers, my friend Dawn Bowker. The students encouraged me greatly then and many continue to do so now, connected as we all are on social media.

Thanks to my sweet cousin, Kathy, for her editing expertise. (Wish I'd come to you sooner!) Also, thanks to my new friend Toni Kerr for her patience and forbearance as I navigate the choppy waters of publishing for the first time.

I'd like to thank all of the members of the best band on the planet, Daring Greatly, for inspiring me and introducing me to Brené Brown's book *Daring Greatly*, from which they chose their name. Dail, Patrick, Liam, Brayden, Brandon – and Brené – you are the reason I pulled the draft of this story off the cyber shelf, dusted it off, and finished it. This is me, daring greatly.

A special thanks to Angela Townsend, an amazing author of many varied and wonderful stories. Without her help, this little dream of mine might never have become a reality. Like Dawn was, she is one of those special people with a huge, caring heart and a generous spirit. I'm so thankful to call you my friend.

About the Author

Amy Baldwin was the child of an Air Force Officer. She and her family lived in the Philippines when she was very young, and she spent her early adolescence in Germany. She's lived in several states: Wyoming, Colorado, New Mexico, North Carolina, Washington and currently resides in Kalispell, Montana. She feels blessed to have lived in so many places.

In 2003, while studying to become a teacher, she was chosen as the only student representative to travel to Kyrgyzstan (other participants were professors and teachers). This was a Fulbright-Hays sponsored, National Geographic Alliance affiliated trip.

Amy was raised in a family of educators that loved music, and her number one childhood dream was to teach. This dream was fulfilled when she taught sixth grade language arts at Somers Middle School in Montana for five years. She considers herself incredibly fortunate for being able to teach.

Amy's love of music and language sparked her creative talent, and she learned to play guitar at age 12. Her second dream was to be a professional musician, and Amy played guitar every Saturday night at a local pub, The Cottage Inn (in Kila, MT) for two years. She continues to hone her picking ability and to write songs.

Amy lives with her husband, Joe, and their two dogs, Sadie and Stella. Amy's third dream is to write. Her experiences as a mother, grandmother, teacher, singer, and world traveler are her inspiration. *One Small Ripple* is her first novel.